Notary Public Enemy

Notary Public Enemy

By

Tony Iovino

Diversion Press, Inc.

Iovino, Tony, 1958-
Notary Public Enemy

ISBN 978-1-935290-20-9 (alk. paper)

Library of Congress Control Number: 2011930779

Published by Diversion Press, Inc.
Clarksville, Tennessee
www.diversionpress.com

Cover Art from Big Stock Photo
Cover Design by Amy Thompson
Property of Diversion Press, Inc.

To Angela

For, literally, a lifetime of love and devotion

To Amanda & Alison

For filling our lives with joy, and love,

and always, always, laughter

Acknowledgements

The greatest concern when sitting down to thank a lot of people is that you will miss someone who really should be thanked. A good friend of mine, upon receiving an award, thanked just about everyone she had ever met, saw she was running long, and closed her speech abruptly. Only after she reached her seat, to a well-deserved standing ovation, did she realize she forgot to thank her husband.

Oops.

Rest assured that, like my friend, my failure to mention anyone here who should be remembered isn't a reflection on the depth of my gratitude, just my momentary mental lapse. My apologies, in advance.

I want to thank my editor, Amy Thompson, and all of the people at Diversion Press for their faith, understanding and aid.

Thank you to all of my friends and family who read the first draft of this book, for their support and encouragement, especially my brother John. I know you had no choice but to tell me how wonderful the manuscript was—that you all said it with such believable sincerity is a testament to how much you care for me. I appreciate the support very much.

Thank you to my good and great friend Bruce Grossberg, for his honest notes, his humor and his support. Thank you to my longtime partner and friend Joe Bondi for putting up with all the extra-business antics over the years. Thank you to Amy Holman for all her help and productive suggestions. Thank you to John Gorka for his generosity and for hours and hours of listening pleasure.

My unending gratitude for their advice and support goes to Brenda Janowitz, Michael Mulhern, Mary Jane McGrath, Gloria Morano, Jim & Chris Mulvey and, of course, my siblings Jeanine, Jacqueline, Karen & Marco.

Thank you to my children, Amanda and Alison for their ability to keep me grounded, for making their mother and me so very proud, and for not resenting, too much, the time I've spent away from them, either at work or on any one of the obsessions we've lived through!

Thank you to my parents for always being my biggest fans, for setting an example of what it means to be good people and for pounding home the importance of fidelity and family.

Thank you to the clients and colleagues, judges and experts I've had the pleasure to work with over the years. You've allowed me to provide for my family, and, almost as importantly, you've provided me with a lifetime's worth of stories, some tragic, some cautionary, some infuriating, but mostly funny.

And, last, but not least, I can't return to my chair without thanking my wife Angela. Since I developed a crush on her in second grade, there has never been anyone else in my heart. I thank her for her edits, for listening to me drone on and on about the book and all the processes involved. I thank her for not following through on any of the well-deserved threats of serious harm she has issued against me over the years. But most of all, I thank her for walking this path beside me, every day.

Chapter 1

I came back to my office a little before noon on a bright, sunny, August Monday. My mail waited for me on the desk. A couple of bills, a bar association flyer about the annual charity golf tournament, a Staples catalogue. And a police detective's business card with the words *Call me by 2* printed in clean block letters just above the gold shield.

Not good.

Rita, the receptionist, poked her head in and saw me looking at the card. Rita is efficient, Rita is attractive, and Rita is sweet, but Rita is a talker. I tried to derail her before she started. No luck.

"There were two of them, Mr. De Stio. They came in around 10. I told them you were probably in court, but I don't have your calendar, so I couldn't tell them when you'd be back and you don't have a cell phone or a beeper, 'cause they asked me to get a hold of you, but I said I couldn't and they wouldn't tell me what it was about. They weren't very nice about it either. So I asked if they wanted to speak to Mr. Levine, but they said no, they wanted to talk to you, so I told them I could take a message, but the skinny guy just gave me his card and said to give it to you and that's—"

"It's OK Rita, I'm sure it's just about a client. I'll take care of it."

"But the other guy said it wasn't about a case when I asked him—"

"Fine, Rita, I'll take care of it."

"I knew they didn't know you, 'cause they pronounced your name De St-EYE-oh, instead of De Steee-oh, like it's supposed to be, so I told them—"

"Rita, it's OK, really, I got it, thank you, thanks a lot" and I shut my door.

1

Sometimes with Rita a closed door is your only defense.

The Mr. Levine she wanted the cops to talk with was Joel Levine, an old friend from law school and the lead partner in Levine, Johnson, Majors, & Smolinski, the large law firm that owns the building. I've occupied a closet masquerading as an office here for about a year. Joel likes me, even after everything I've put him through. He demanded I take this office and fought with his partners about it. The office is small, but it's all I need. Peter De Stio, Attorney at Law. Former lead litigation attorney for O'Reilly, McManus. Former hot shot rising star. Former husband. Former drunk. My resume of former titles is lengthy.

I sat behind my borrowed wood veneer desk and fingered the card. What on earth would a Nassau County, New York detective want with *me*? He wanted a call back by 2, meaning I had a couple of hours to procrastinate. I held the card in my left hand, flicking at it with the middle finger of my right.

Why? Why me? I put the detective's card in my shirt pocket and glanced at the little $5.00 Radio Shack clock I keep on my desk. It was 12:07. I made my way to the men's room, passing faces that had remained nameless throughout my tenure here. I stood at the urinal for a bit and then washed my hands enough to make a thoracic surgeon proud. The card felt like a brick in my pocket.

Back in my office, I looked at my calendar. I had a 2:00 deposition to do for Joel, questioning a Plaintiff in a car accident case. My Radio Shack clock now said 12:18. That left me almost two hours to eat lunch, call the detective and travel five minutes to the courthouse. What should I do first?

I wanted desperately to go to lunch, to flee the office, to forget about the card. But that wasn't going to help. I needed a drink, I thought. But I knew that *really* wasn't going to help. I stared at the card for a while, trying to divine its hidden code that would let me know why the detective had stopped by, without my actually having to call him. Whatever secrets the card held, it held them fast. I stared at my blank walls. The beige paint offered no aid, either. This was ridiculous. I looked at the card once more, then dialed. It was 12:31. The cop answered on the eighth ring.

"Fisher."

"Detective, this is Peter De Stio. You left your card this morning."

"Counselor, thanks for calling. We need to talk. When can you come in?"

"I have a deposition this afternoon. Mind telling me what this is about?"

"What time will you be done? You know where the 9th Precinct is?"

"Yeah, I know. What's this about?"

"Counselor, what time can you get here? Or would you like me to provide an escort?"

I thought about it for a few seconds. I knew his escort included bracelets. "I'll be there by 5:30."

*****

It was an otherwise beautiful summer day on Long Island. I couldn't sit in my box; I had to get out. I took my brown paper bag, filled up my water bottle at the fountain in the hall, and teetered out of the building. Down the block from my office is the entrance to the Denton Public Botanical Garden. I eat there often. It has become part of my routine during the last year, part of the quiet, low-stress life that I have carved out for myself after rehab. I made my way down the busy street that fronts my building, trying to put the detective out of my mind. I forced myself to think of something else.

I chuckled silently at a sign I had seen on my way to work that morning. A few blocks from the house where I have a second floor apartment is a quaint little white clapboard church. The church has a small, stand-alone white wooden sign on its front lawn. In addition to the service times, the sign always has a little saying, one that changes every week or so. Today's sign said:

Free Trips to Heaven

Details Inside

Whoever did the signs was clever, with a nice sense of humor. I telepathically thanked him or her as I walked to the garden. I am surprised by how few people use it. There's no admission fee, just a donation box at the front gate. I slide a dollar or two in every time I go. It reminds me of the collection plate at church.

I chose my regular path to the left up a slight rise and into a wooded area,

3

passing *Alyssum murale* and columbine, Japanese maples and the children's garden. The rich smell of compost mixed with the light scent from the flowers.

There's a sturdy wooden bench with a nice high back that I like, nestled under a black oak, perched on a shaded hill. The bench sits beside a wandering ribbon of asphalt which carves a path through the entire garden. Shading the bench are tall oaks and maples, pines and some specimen trees.

Each plant or tree has its own little black and white sign announcing its formal Latin name and its regular, common name. *Quercus palustris,* pin oak. *Acer pseudoplatanus*, sycamore maple. Sometimes I think people should have the same naming procedure, a formal Latin name and a regular, common name for everyday use, names that could give insight into a person's family and background. *Attornius divorcium alcohilician,* Peter De Stio.

Maybe not.

Down the hill from my shaded bench, off to the right, there's a small pond with a stream gurgling into it. The garden is home to a few ducks, some robins, lots of sparrows, and an occasional cardinal. Rarely any people, though. Except for the chatter of the squirrels and the song birds, it's quiet.

I found my bench and put my brown bag aside. I settled in and meditated for about ten minutes. I learned in rehab to always start meditating the same way. I try to relax my muscles and concentrate on my breathing, counting my breaths up to ten, then starting over. If my mind wanders, and I lose count, I restart. I can feel everything settling in my mind, like how mud suspended in a pail of water will slowly sink to the bottom, leaving cool, clear water on top. Breathe in, breathe out. Feel the tension leaving with each exhale. Calming. Or as calm as I can be with the detective's voice swirling in my ear and the vision of his card entrenched inside my eyelids. Think of something else, I commanded myself.

That morning I had been in Family Court on an assigned counsel case, appointed by the court to represent a thirteen year old kid charged with shoplifting for the fifth or sixth time. He showed up with his mother and her boyfriend of the week. I met them in the narrow hallway outside the courtroom waiting area. The boyfriend sported a gold tooth and smelled of a combination

4

of liquor and body odor. He was in his thirties, I guessed, standing about 6' 3". He looked mean and he looked like he worked at looking mean. I saw a prison tattoo carved in his forearm. There was a time when I couldn't have identified a prison tattoo from an allergic reaction, but that time was long gone.

I looked at mom. She looked tired and a bit scared. She had been pretty, once. Mom had multiple bruises on her, in various shades, meaning the beatings had been multiple. The two questions in my mind were, who did the beatings, and how could I keep away from Goldtooth without seeming too rude? I got the answer to my first question by asking my client.

"Hey, Jamaal, who slapped your mother around?"

"D'no" was the answer, but his eyes shifted down and towards Goldtooth, who was glaring at us. Bingo. He saw us look at him and came over and told my client to move it. He wanted to talk to me alone. The kid moved away. I concentrated on not getting sick.

I wanted to find a polite way to move the boyfriend along. Goldtooth wanted to confer with me about the *little bastard* as he called him. Thought he should *take a plea, man, maybe go away for a coupla years*. He was *outa control, ol' lady can't handle him anymore, y'know*. I thought about providing Goldtooth with a lecture on the attorney-client relationship, about my ethical responsibilities to the little bastard, about how it wasn't my job to bury the kid just so he could keep banging and beating his mom. I thought about counseling him on the evils of liquor, a subject with which I am well acquainted. I thought about the most reflective, positive way to raise Goldtooth's consciousness.

I'm not some hot-head kid anymore, not at 40 years old. I stood there in the dimly lit, grungy hallway, while wave after wave of Goldtooth's stench blew over me like a nor'easter. I'm 6 foot even and weigh in at about 190, well down from my drinking weight, but still not small. Yet, Goldtooth towered over me, blocking most of the hallway.

I analyzed all the possible peaceful, intelligent alternatives, and carefully chose my course of action. I battled through the stench, leaned in close and whispered "Get the fuck out of this courthouse before I tell that court officer you are drunk and threatening me and my client, you sick fuck. And if you

5

touch either of them again, I will have you arrested, *capisce*?" I'm always pleased with myself when I can use the word *fuck* more than once in a sentence, especially if I use it as different parts of speech. A verb and a noun in that one. Good job.

Goldtooth started to protest, but I turned around quickly and half-yelled down the hall—"Officer, can you help us here?" All heads turned and two court officers, always alert for trouble in this sad building advanced towards us. I turned back to Goldtooth who glared at me, but moved backwards down the hall, away from the court officers toward the back staircase that leads down and out of the building. I waved the officers off with a thankful smile.

The morning ended much like most mornings do in Family Court. Jamaal's case was adjourned for two weeks because probation hadn't finished their report. I gave his mom my card and the number of a shelter where she could get help. I told her to fill out an Order of Protection, right now, down the hall on the right. I saw it in her eyes. She wasn't going down the hall. And she wasn't going to use my card or go to the shelter. She was going home. To Goldtooth. Which probably meant she was going to see the inside of an emergency room at some point.

Or the morgue.

As much as I wanted to sit on that bench for the rest of the day, I knew I couldn't. I swallowed my lunch which sat like a leaden torch somewhere just above my stomach. The question of what Fisher wanted hung over my head and spoiled my lunchtime retreat, a loud, uninvited guest at a quiet dinner party.

Chapter 2

I pulled into the parking lot at the precinct a little before 5:30. I was tempted to park in the first open space, marked *Police Only*, but thought better of it. No need to purposefully piss anybody off.

The lobby of the precinct house was standard issue, with dark wood paneling from the fifties and a black tile floor that was probably clean, but would never look it. It was darker than you might expect a public building to be, as if half of the fluorescent bulbs had been removed. I've been in precinct houses at all times of the day and night. The lobbies were always dim. Maybe the cops were trying to set a mood. I wonder if there is a class in architectural school on the design of police stations.

I stood nice and straight at the high counter. A sergeant with a name tag *Nicoletti* was behind the counter, on the telephone. Hey, a *paisan*. Maybe it was a good sign. Apparently not; he ignored me for close to ten minutes while he finished his conversation. I didn't think his call was about police work, unless there was an impending bust of some wayward sea bass. I hoped Fisher the detective would understand. When Nicoletti was done, I told him who I was and why I was there. Or rather, who I was supposed to see, since I still didn't have a clue why I was there. Nicoletti grunted and then called Fisher, who appeared a few of minutes later from a side door to my left.

"Mr. De Stio? Detective Fisher." He didn't offer his hand. "Thanks for coming down on such short notice."

"No problem."

See, I'm just a nice guy looking to cooperate with the authorities. Fisher led me back down a narrow hallway lined with gray metal filing cabinets. We made a left into a large square room with a wall of windows and eight or so desks paired up, face to face. There were two other plainclothes detectives in the room, one typing with two fingers on an ancient typewriter, the other on the phone. Fisher motioned to the pair of desks in the far corner, by the windows, waving me into a metal chair with a worn padded seat. He sat behind the desk, making a show of adjusting the gun in his hip holster as he did.

I sat. And I waited. Fisher sat. He waited. I had played this game myself with clients and adversaries. Generally the person with the weakest position, or the person most nervous, or the person with something to hide will break first and talk. Back when I enjoyed gamesmanship and torturing people, I would make them carry on a conversation by themselves, using the Tiffany crystal-rhodium mantel clock in my old office to time how long it took for my silence to make them talk. People hate silences and will say anything to fill up the void. When they do, you frequently get the best information.

I looked around the room. Yellowed memos were taped on the wall. A large corkboard had some PBA notices stapled on, as well as a bunch of wanted flyers, tacked up, one on top of the other. I guess once the squad had somebody's particulars memorized they just hung up the next perp-of-the-week over last week's. Or maybe those flyers were about as effective as I assumed.

I fought off the temptation to ask what was going on. Fisher sat. Sometimes he glanced at me. Sometimes he shuffled some papers. I had no papers to shuffle, so I just sat. A vision of the two of us squirming in our seats a few hours later, neither wanting to get up to pee, crossed my mind and the corner of my mouth twitched.

"Something funny, Counselor?" I had given him the opening to start. It wasn't much of one, but I figured he was getting antsy too.

"Nope, detective, nothing funny." I am the king of quick comebacks.

"Do you know Harris Mathews?"

I thought back. "No. Ummm, no. Not that I recall. Who is he?"

"How about Tariq Singh?"

"No, I don't think so, no."

"Do you know Sy Brownstein?"

I did. He was a client of my old law firm, a very wealthy old-school land developer and landlord. He specialized in building and operating large office complexes. I hadn't seen him in years, and back *then* he was an old man. He was tough, a demanding client. Obstinate, with a real mulish streak in him. I had personally handled a boundary dispute he had with a neighbor, and one fairly large case against a contractor. Most of his work had been handled by Gregory Connolly, my old rival in the firm, or our tax counsel. Sy and I weren't close, but we had gotten along. I hadn't screwed up any of his cases. His litigation was over before my drinking had affected my work.

"Sure, I know Sy Brownstein. How is he?"

"When was the last time you saw him?" Fisher was looking at me straight in the face, three feet away. No paper shuffling now. He wanted to read me when I responded.

"How is he?"

"Listen, *counselor*, you can cooperate or not. Which is it?"

Counselor. It might sound nice to those outside the profession, but those of us on the inside know it's a code word. You use it when you want to put an attorney in his or her place. As in *"Counselor*, do you really think you have a case?" or *"Counselor*, why don't we let the witness answer the questions, OK?" Apparently Fisher didn't think much of me. Maybe he had talked to my ex-wife or to my former partners.

I tried again. "Detective, what is this all about?"

"Counselor, I'm just going to ask you one more time. When was the last time you saw Sy Brownstein?"

"Why?" I guess Sy Brownstein wasn't the only one who had mule DNA in him. I wasn't going to answer anything until I had an idea of what was going on.

Fisher pushed away from his desk. "Stay here."

"Am I under arrest, Detective?"

"Just stay here for a second. I'll be right back."

I looked out the window at the parking lot. I should have parked in a restricted space, I thought. Maybe some cop would have come in and asked who the hell had parked that piece of shit Honda in his spot. Then I could have left to move it and sneaked home. Right. I knew I wasn't going anywhere. I'm in the middle of a station house; the man says sit, I sit.

Fisher came back a few minutes later with a short Hispanic woman, in her thirties, a bit heavy, with close cropped dark hair. She was wearing the obligatory blue pin stripe skirt and jacket outfit, white shirt. Sensible shoes that, I assumed, matched. I can never tell. I figure, if the shoes belong to the same pair, they match. I never understood the intricacies of how some shoes match certain outfits or pocketbooks, and some don't. I had a partner who could tell, simply by glancing, whether another woman's shoes were this year's model or last. She tried to explain the importance of that to me once, but I couldn't get it.

Fisher introduced the suited lady as Assistant District Attorney Melendez. She stopped in front of me, hands on her hips. I looked up at her, although I didn't have to look up much. With her standing and me sitting, we were almost eye to eye.

"Peter De Stio?" she asked, as if Fisher might be pulling a fast one on her, maybe having another detective sit in the chair to fool her. My, wouldn't that be funny, her questioning a cop impersonating a very confused, and fairly scared, attorney?

"Yes." Another quick, witty, response. I was on fire.

She turned to Fisher who was easing himself back into his chair. "Read him his rights." Fisher looked surprised. I felt like I was going to throw up.

"Now listen dammit, what is this all about?" I started to get out of the chair, but Melendez just gave me a quick shake of her head. Fisher read me my rights from a card he kept on his desk.

"Do you under*stand* these rights, Mr. De Stio?" Melendez asked me, emphasizing "stand".

"Yes I do. Now what is this about?"

"Do you want a lawyer?"

I breathed in and thought. On the one hand, I *am* a lawyer. On the other hand, I knew full well that I was in no position to properly act as an attorney in this situation. On the other hand, I had already embarrassed my friends in the legal community beyond the point of friendship. I had no clue who I could call. And on the other hand, I was curious as hell to find out what was going on. That was way too many hands. Maybe by answering their questions I could figure it out. Or maybe I'd outsmart myself into major trouble. I was stumped. But I also hadn't done anything wrong, especially not involving Brownstein. I didn't take any escrow funds. I hadn't harmed him. I wasn't even his tenant, so I couldn't owe him any money.

"Well? *Counselor*, we don't have all night." Apparently Melendez had a low opinion of me already, too.

"No, I don't want a lawyer. Yes, I know Sy Brownstein. I did some work for him a few years ago. Last time I saw him was maybe five, six years ago. Now will you please tell me what is going on?"

"Did you see Mr. Brownstein on June 8 of last year?"

I thought. Last June? Last June, fourteen months ago, I was still drinking, heavily. I was already out of the firm about a year by then, though. And out of my house.

"I don't think so. Not professionally."

"Not professionally. Did you socialize with Mr. Brownstein?"

"No, no. What I meant was, I had already left my firm. I wasn't practicing law last summer. Maybe I saw him out somewhere, I don't know. I'm not sure. Don't think so, um, I'm not sure, no. No. Probably not." Wow, what a great witness I was! If I was a client I would be ready to strangle me by now. *Think*, Pete. Answer only the question. Don't volunteer anything. Stop rambling. I was so busy yelling at myself I missed Melendez's next question.

"Excuse me? I didn't hear you."

"Try to stay focused, Counselor. What about on June 10th? See Mr. Brownstein June 10th last year?"

"No. I'm pretty sure no."

"Pretty sure. Are you certain?"

What was going on? "Again, I wasn't practicing last June. I don't think I've seen Sy Brownstein in years."

11

"Did you ever notarize Mr. Brownstein's signature?"

I thought back. In the course of litigation we often have pleadings and affidavits and settlement agreements that clients have to sign. Sometimes I would notarize the signatures, sometimes a secretary would.

"Ever?"

"Last June."

"No. Like I said, I wasn't practicing last June."

"You deny notarizing Sy Brownstein's signature on one or more documents last June?"

"Yes. I deny notarizing his signature. What is this about?"

Melendez leaned over Fisher's shoulder. She pulled a document out of a file and tossed it to me.

"Recognize this, *Counselor*? Does it refresh your recollection?"

I looked at the paper in front of me. It was a standard deed. Dated June 8th of the previous year; it transferred property from Brownstein Realty, Ltd. to Houston Mesquite Holdings, Inc. I looked at the signature on the bottom of the page. Seymour Brownstein.

I flipped the deed over. There was the notary clause printed on the upper left corner. Standard in every way. Nothing to be concerned about except it was stamped with my notary stamp and something that looked very much like my signature was scrawled across the page.

God, I needed a drink.

I stared at the notary. Melendez was asking questions, Fisher was asking questions. I could hear their voices, but only as sounds, like rain hitting the roof while you lie in bed and listen, no pattern, no rhythm. Like a summer shower, just nowhere near as pleasant.

I wracked my brain. *No way* was this my signature, but it looked damn close. I was drunk last summer and was until Bastille Day, July 14th, my first clean and sober day, now 13 months, 2 days ago. Before I stopped drinking, I was a nasty drunk. A fighting drunk. A show-up-at-the-office-massively-hung-over drunk. A never-come-home drunk. A miss-every-family-function, except the ones where I started ugly fights drunk. And towards the end, a not-show-up-in-court-during-a-trial drunk. But rarely a blackout drunk. Unfortunately, most of the time I remembered the appalling things I said and did the night before. But I honestly did not remember notarizing documents for Brownstein.

Fisher was talking now, his voice rising in tone and volume. Asking me if I would just sign my name a few times for handwriting samples. Melendez wanted to know where the money was. Money? What money? Why was Singh killed? What do you know about it? Who the hell was Singh? Killed? Know about it?

I didn't say a word. How long did I sit and essentially ignore them? I don't know. I finally did what I should have done earlier, way earlier, back when I first saw Fisher's card on my desk. I lawyered up.

"I want a lawyer."

Melendez stopped in mid-sentence. "What?" she spit out.

"I'm not answering any more questions. I want a lawyer."

"Counselor, wrong move," Fisher said, shaking his head. "Way wrong move. Cooperate with us, we'll make this go a lot easier, you know that. The company just wants its money back. Just answer a few questions and everything will be fine."

I looked at Melendez. She looked at me, disgusted and angry. I was a traitor in her eyes, an attorney who had crossed the line.

Fisher tried again. "Look, Peter, maybe you got in over your head. You know we found Singh's body and that Mathews has disappeared. You could be next. Help us, and we'll protect you."

I desperately wanted to know what was going on. Singh's body? Who was Singh? What company? What money? How was Sy Brownstein? Who was Harris Mathews? But I knew what I had to do.

"No. I want a lawyer."

Chapter 3

I didn't get a lawyer that night, but then, for reasons they never told me, they didn't arrest me either. They let me sit for about two hours and then they finally let me go home. I guess Melendez wanted to catch *Monday Night Football*. I felt incredibly disoriented and had a terrible lust for vodka. Or bourbon. Or beer. I was spinning, my body was shaking. But when Fisher finally said, "Get the hell out of here," he unknowingly threw me a lifeline. "And, *Counselor*, don't leave town."

I found that funny, very funny. I didn't think anyone actually said things like that. It reminded me of film *noir*, the old black and white movies where the thick-headed cop chases the tough, but misunderstood private eye, while the private eye does the cop's work. It took the edge off, throwing a bit of unreality into a too real situation. It was enough to get me straight home, avoiding bars and liquor stores. I called my AA sponsor and we talked a bit. It was enough. I didn't sleep much, but I spent my time with Dick Van Dyke, instead of with my old buddies, Jack and Bud and Jose.

The next morning found me at my office, tired, but sober. I asked Rita if Joel Levine was in yet. Boiling down her five minute take on where he was, what he was doing, how traffic had been coming in, and how tired I looked, the answer was he wasn't expected back until around lunchtime. I asked her to leave a note asking him to see me and escaped.

I had barely reached my desk when Rita buzzed me on the intercom. I had two clients at reception, should she send them back, my are they a good looking couple, do you want to come get them? I had no appointments for the day and I rarely had clients to the office. I asked Rita to have them wait. I'd be right down. I cleared off the two client chairs that I used mostly for filing and walked down the long hall to the lobby.

"Peter! My favorite attorney!" I heard the voice, loud and brassy and full of energy. Marcia Simpson. But this didn't look like the Marcia Simpson I knew. The Marcia I knew had been in a terrible car accident twelve years earlier. She had been a twenty year old college student, about 50 pounds overweight, a large nose, and the best, most infectious laugh you ever heard. That is until a drunk driver ran a red light and broadsided her car. She spent months in hospitals and in physical therapy while they put her back together. She was one of my all-time favorite clients, helpful, optimistic, and very thankful when I netted her a seven figure verdict after a three week trial. Marcia's trial was a big one for me. It was also before my problem.

The Marcia that stood before me was, well, gorgeous. She was fit and tan and attractive. The guy with her appeared to be in his late twenties, sporting a perma-tan and a tight shirt that showed off a body that screamed thousands of repetitions with heavy weights. She threw her arms around me and kissed me. "Peter, this is Derek Rogers. Derek, this is Peter!" He crushed my hand with a vice grip. In my office, Marcia took control.

"Surprised to see me, huh? I knew we should've called, but we're in a bit of a rush. It took me awhile to find you. Anyway, let me see, I moved to California, did you know that? I just had to get some sun! I'm back here now about three months. Cali was wonderful. I met some great people and a wonderful plastic surgeon. Nice, huh?" she asked, pointing at her nose. "I had these done, too," she said, cupping her now more than ample breasts.

"Derek and I are forming a business partnership. I told him there was only one attorney I trusted and that was you. I didn't know you had left O'Reilly, Mc Manus. They almost didn't want to tell me where you were. But I spoke to Mary and she told me." Mary Robinson had been my secretary. Long-suffering is the term that best applied, I think.

"Yeah, I've been out of there a while now. Marcia, you look great! I don't think I can help you, though. I've really limited my practice these days."

How do I tell this woman who trusted me with her life, that now I only take low-pressure cases, simple plea bargain stuff, nothing that requires a commitment on my part. Nothing complicated. If the law were food establishments, Marcia knew me when I was head chef at *La Cirque*; now I make the fries at McDonald's. Same industry, light years apart.

"I don't care. You have to do this for me. I won't take no for an answer."

I smiled. "OK, tell me about it. No promises, though."

Marcia looked at Derek. "You tell him, Derek."

Derek sat up straight. He had been looking around my office. A bit sparse, I'd agree. Just a desk, my chair, the two client chairs and a filing cabinet. A second-hand, but comfortable, recliner chair behind them. Nothing on the walls. Nothing other than a yellow pad and my $5 Radio Shack clock on my desk. He didn't look impressed. That's OK. I wasn't trying to impress him, or anybody else for that matter. Those days were long gone.

He spoke in a much higher voice than I was expecting. Steroids probably had shriveled his balls. I tried not to laugh.

"I am a certified fitness instructor. I have won three national fitness instructor gold medals, and I was an All-American NCAA gymnast at Notre Dame."

"Oh, Peter, Derek is the best. Totally booked, you can't touch him. He does all the stars when they're in the Hamptons."

"Thank you, Marcia. I'm doing very well, but I would like to take my gift to the next level, really help all those people out there who could use my expertise. The problem is the fitness industry has hit a plateau. Everyone is waiting for the next big thing. We've gone through aerobics and step and spinning and yoga and kick boxing and Pilates and Zumba. Old hat. We need a new program, one that will help our clients attain and maintain fitness, but something that is new and different. Fun. I have found it. And Marcia is insisting on funding it."

"Damn right I insist. This is going to be huge! It combines fitness with the environment. It is amazing! Derek is amazing!"

I tried not to look skeptical. Keeping a straight face has always been one

16

of my strongest assets. Not reacting to the unexpected is an essential tool in my business. I waited for Derek to amaze me.

Derek stopped. "Is this conversation confidential?"

I looked at him. "If you are worried that I'll leak your idea, the answer is don't worry. I won't repeat what I hear today to anyone, without your permission. Attorneys can't divulge confidential information, except to other attorneys or staff that they work with who need to know. And they are bound by the same privilege."

After a brief pause, he continued. "I call it Landsculpting. I have combined proven and accepted physiometric body movements with simple landscaping techniques to effectuate maximum cardio and musco-skeletal benefits. I have synergized these seemingly disconnected disciplines, using cutting edge scientifically adapted methodologies, while incorporating the need to be one with nature, to improve environmental conditions."

I stared at him. "In English. Please."

Marcia came to my rescue. "We are going to outfit a trailer with weight equipment, stationary bikes, that sort of thing, and take it to people's houses. Our clients will come to the site, warm up on the equipment, then do stuff like mow the lawn with a hand mower, trim bushes with hand shears, sweep with a broom. All natural. No power tools. The tools will have weights on them, so we can increase resistance. Not stuck in a smelly old gym. Exercise in the great outdoors! Amazing, huh?"

"And people will *pay* you for this?"

Derek replied, "Our initial market research indicates we can field classes of eight clients at a time, one instructor. $65 per 45 minute session."

"And *they* pay *you*?"

"Yes, of course. It will be an excellent workout, geared specifically for each client." He looked annoyed. "We estimate a gross of $520 per hour. Less the instructor's fee, the depreciation cost of the trailer and equipment, overhead, etcetera, we forecast a profit of $300 per hour. It breaks out to $9,000 per week, per instructor, April through September. I am working on plans for the Fall/Winter season. Perhaps involving firewood."

"They *pay* you?"

Marcia was clutching Derek's arm. "Yes, Peter, didn't I tell you Derek was a genius! This is *amazing*! Landsculpting! Derek's worked out these awesome exercise routines. Sweeping for your arms, pushing the hand mower for your quads and your glutes. It gets you out in the fresh air! It's aerobic and it's green! It will be bigger than Stairmaster. And Derek, tell him the best part."

"No, no, let me guess. The homeowner pays you for doing his yard."

"Yes!! Exactly! See why I *have* to invest! A double-income stream! We will be nationwide by next year! Then public!"

"I see. And what are the terms?"

Marcia practically beamed. "I get 40% of the business. Derek runs everything. All I have to do is put up the seed money."

I looked. And waited.

She half grinned and tilted her head. "$500,000."

"I see. Derek, would you mind waiting outside for a second?"

Derek did mind. "Why?"

"Because I'd like to discuss this *amazing* opportunity with Marcia."

He stood, lifting Marcia from her chair by the hand she had rested on his forearm. "No way. We're partners. Marcia, I told you this was a mistake. Now you know why his old firm threw him out." He gestured around the room. "Some hot-shit lawyer. C'mon, let's go. I know some *real* lawyers we can use." He tugged Marcia out of the office into the hallway.

I guess Derek didn't like me. Seems like there was a lot of that going around. At least he didn't call me *counselor.*

Marcia protested as he half pulled, half cajoled her down the hall. I walked slowly behind them. When they reached the lobby, Marcia pulled away from him and took a couple of steps back towards me. Derek was standing just in front of Rita's desk.

"Rita," I called out. "Meet Derek Rogers. He is a personal trainer to the stars."

Rita just about leaped from her station. "Really! That's incredible! I go to the gym four times a week, and I've used a personal trainer before, but not too often, 'cause you guys are so expensive, not that you aren't worth it! Do you know Angela at Mega Sports Club? She is wonderful, oh, too bad, you'd love her. To the stars? Who? C'mon, you can tell me, I swear I won't tell..."

While Derek tried to free himself from Rita, I whisked Marcia back down the hall and into one of Joel's associates' offices. I locked the door behind us. We spoke in urgent whispers. "This doesn't make me happy, Marcia. How long have you known this guy?'

"Oh, Peter, he's OK, just gets a bit hot-headed sometimes. You were practically calling him a fraud, you know."

"I know I was. I'm concerned. How much have you given him so far?"

"Only $50,000 for the market research. Peter, don't get all lawyery on me. I *want* this investment." She looked fierce.

"Fair enough. How about this?" I tried to rush a bit, as I could hear Derek stomping, and Rita talking, passed the office we were in, heading down to mine. I didn't have much time before body-beautiful found us. Or tore up the office looking for us. "Do *not* sign anything and *don't* give him any more money. Have his attorney draw up some papers for me to review. Meantime, let me look into Derek's background a bit."

"Peter, you are worried about nothing! He is *amazing*! I trust him."

"That's great Marcia. Hopefully you'll make millions. But let me look. Discreetly, OK?"

"OK. I did come to you for advice. We really have to move forward quickly, though. Can you do it right away, and so Derek won't know?"

"Yes and yes. Now get going before somebody around here calls the cops on the Amazing Derek."

*****

With the morning's excitement over, I sat alone and quiet in my office. I had two or three appeals to do, assigned counsel cases for convicts who couldn't afford a lawyer. I didn't mind doing them, especially because there was virtually no client contact and the deadlines were very loose. But today I just didn't feel like working on them. My eyes were burning from tossing and turning all night so I collapsed into the reclining chair opposite my desk, closed my eyes, and thought. I thought about Fisher and Melendez and the notary. I thought about The Amazing Derek. And I thought about my daughter.

I was awake, gazing without focus at the spot on my beige wall where a normal attorney would have hung his diplomas and bar certificates, when Joel knocked on my door and poked in his head.

"Hey, buddy, real busy, huh? Rita said you wanted to see me."

Joel Levine and I knew each other from law school. It was a long, solid friendship that had stood the test of time. Fifteen years ago, when we graduated law school, Joel went to work for an insurance defense firm. He wasn't making any money, was getting abused, and dreaded going to work. Since it was a recession, you took what work you could get. I, on the other hand, got lucky early. I caught a break, moved from a small firm to O'Reilly, McManus, perhaps the premiere firm on Long Island, quickly made partner, and soon commanded formidable power in the firm.

By the time I was the rising star of O'Reilly, McManus, Joel was looking to make a move. Joel wanted to join three other young attorneys in a small insurance defense firm. The problem was that although they were excellent attorneys, there wasn't enough work to support the three of them, let alone a fourth. Still, Joel was respected by them and they felt he could help them make it. The three had started taking in other types of legal work. Joel was worried about making the move, since he had a family and his wife wasn't working.

So I intervened, a bit. I called our corporate department attorneys who represented several insurance companies. I forced them to cut deals so that the insurance companies would send some defense work to Joel. I called clients for whom I had handled large cases; I knew they had smaller, regular work that was under the O'Reilly, McManus radar, but would make for excellent cash flow for a young firm. A few more telephone calls, and evenings out drinking with some key people, and Joel's fledgling firm had more cases than they knew what to do with. Over the years, as my position in the firm grew, I was also able to arrange for cases in which we had a conflict to be referred to Joel. Joel always thought I did it for him, out of our friendship. I never told him I did it as a power play in the office, to yet again jam my will down my partners' throats.

Joel's firm is now well established, representing not only several insurance companies, but also taking in assorted other work. They're a smaller, friendlier version of O'Reilly, McManus. Joel insists that I am the reason the firm is successful. I insist that Joel is the reason I am alive. On balance, I think I owe him.

Joel sat at my desk, toying with my Radio Shack clock. He said he had something to ask me, I told him the same. After trading "you firsts", I told Joel what was going on with me. I told him about the detective and the ADA, and about Marcia, too.

Joel didn't hesitate. "I am going to give you an advance on your fees." As I protested, he vehemently shook his head. "No, I am giving you an advance. Hire Gartner." John Gartner was a classmate of ours who specialized in criminal law. "Use our P.I. for Marcia and for yourself if John thinks you need it. Put it on our tab. Nip this in the bud, Pete. This is bull shit. Pay it back as you can." He named a figure that would more than cover John Gartner's retainer and a fair amount of investigation expense. I tried to say no, but I had no money. Everything I had, I either gave to Lorraine in the divorce or to some bartender during the year-long bender that followed the divorce. Now I was back practicing, but I was purposefully taking no-pressure cases. One of the truths in law is that, by and large, pressure equals money, and vice versa. Few are the jobs, in any walk of life, where the stakes are low and the pay is high. I needed help, and Joel, again, was offering it. In rehab they had stressed being open to receiving help. I swallowed my pride. I accepted the "advance".

"Good. I like you these days, you're much more reasonable."

"You mean I give in to you."

"Exactly!" he said with a smile.

"So what's up? You wanted to talk to me?"

"Um, yeah. I need a favor." He put the clock down.

"Anything, anytime."

"I know, but just listen to what I need first, before you say anything. And feel free to say no." I looked at him. We both knew I would do anything he asked. I just hoped he didn't want me to kill anyone. Or at least anyone I liked a lot.

"We have three new attorneys we just hired. Two are brand new, just out of school. Not even admitted yet. One's got six years experience with the Bronx DA."

"But no civil experience."

"None. We need to train them, get them going. But I'm on trial, should last another month. Got McGowan as judge. We'll be lucky to get done by Halloween. Everybody else is out, too. Traditionally one of us takes the incoming attorneys under our wing."

"Like a pledge class in a fraternity."

"Exactly. But right now we're too short handed to spare anybody's time. I'm afraid if we don't get these guys in the groove soon we'll lose them. Especially Carolyn. She's the DA. Started two weeks ago and already she's a real pain in the ass. Says she only came to us 'cause Mike promised she would be on trial within a month. Personally, I want her out there in the field so she's busting somebody else's balls. Besides, we're paying her well, and all she's doing is indexing deposition transcripts and covering discovery conferences."

For a trial attorney, those two tasks might as well be torture. No wonder she was giving them grief. I didn't recall having seen her, but I knew the two others. They had been wandering around the office together, seemingly joined at the hip, offering to help anyone and everyone. They had even asked me if there was anything I needed.

"So how can I help?"

"Train them for us."

"Yeah, right."

"I'm serious."

"Joel, have you lost your mind? Me?"

"Hey, buddy, there's nobody better. Take them through a civil case, start to finish. Who knows this stuff better than you? Review their work for us, get them ready for depositions. Get the DA ready for trial; she's got one coming up next month. Second chair her if you have to. It'll take you a few hours a week. We'll pay you for your time, not at the per diem rate. A real hourly rate. You'd be doing us a big favor. What do you say?"

What could I say?

*****

After my meeting with Joel, I paced my small carpet. The offer of help was appreciated, and the idea of a new assignment was distracting, but the notary kept torturing me. I needed to move.

A dark suit, white shirt, conservative tie and wing tips were my work uniform. My running uniform also didn't vary much, and I kept it in my car: a gray T-shirt (one of a dozen I had picked up at a flea market), a pair of black nylon shorts (one of a dozen I had picked up at a flea market), a pair of white socks (one of *two* dozen I had picked up at a flea market), and my trusty pair of New Balance running shoes, purchased from an ad in the back of a runner's magazine. I wasn't starting my new position as professor until the following morning. I took the afternoon off to go run. I had mapped out a few different locales for my workouts. Today, I chose the beach.

It was hot, that oppressive dead-air August heat that saps your breath and sponges your strength. I had been running almost every day since I hit rehab. I had lost about 55 pounds, and I was intent on keeping it off. Besides, it helped quell the jolts of desire for alcohol I still felt, every day, at all different times.

I drove down the Meadowbrook Parkway, heading to Jones Beach. The Meadowbrook dissects Nassau County, north and south, heading from about mid-island down to the beach. As it leaves suburbia behind, the Meadowbrook transforms into a series of elegant bridges, gliding from one small, sandy island to the next, until it pours out onto the main barrier island where it becomes Ocean Parkway, four paved lanes of traffic running east-west down the middle of the barrier island like the sand vein in a shrimp.

The barrier island, stretching out for dozens of miles parallel to Long Island's South Shore, is only maybe 300 yards wide at any point. To the south are glistening sandy beaches and crashing ocean waves, bordered by high sand dunes. To the north there's some barrier scrub, then the Great South Bay, calm and flat. It was on this barrier island that Robert Moses envisioned Jones Beach, transforming a barren spit of land which had been donated to the State by the Jones family years before, into the most pure, undeveloped public beach in the world. And it was here that I most liked to run.

I lived at this beach when I was a kid, coming down whenever I could hitch a ride. But as an adult, I rarely made the ten minute trip from my home to the ocean. I don't think I'd ever even brought my daughter here.

It was summer, so the ocean-side parking lots were filled. I parked the car in one of the bay-side lots and walked through one of the pedestrian tunnels which burrow under the roadway, crossing to the ocean beach. I trudged through the thick, deep, soft white sand. The sweat started to gather at my scalp; my breathing thickened. The beach is sectioned off by flags, their staffs driven into the sand by the lifeguards. A section bounded by green flags means that the area of the surf is under the careful eye of the best lifeguards in the country. Areas embanked by the yellow flags mean boogie boards are welcome. Red flags mean no lifeguard, no swimming, no wading. Go in the water beyond the red flags and you'll hear a piercing whistle and see a lifeguard waving at you, scowling beneath impenetrable sunglasses.

Along the shoreline the green and yellow areas are clustered opposite the entrance ways to the several parking lots, but there are long, red-flagged open expanses between the clusters, and beyond the parking lots in either direction. Unlike any other major beach area, Jones Beach can service hundreds of thousands of sunbathers and waders, yet there is space for a quiet reflective walk, or a romantic one.

I sat cross-legged in the sand, feeling the moist grains cling to my legs and hands. I stared out into the ocean horizon, where green water meets blue sky in a hazy, gray line. As I had been taught to do in rehab, I looked for order in my life. I tried to keep to a routine, but not so rigid that I couldn't go with the flow. I started my warm-up the same way each time. I stretched my arms, my neck, my legs, my back, eyes always looking out, ignoring the splashing families safely wading inside the green zone to my left under the watchful eye of the lifeguards. Before me was open water, a red zone, unsupervised surf.

I started my run, the water to my left, the summer crowd now behind me. I ran along, passing only some walkers, some lovers, some beachcombers. The sand crunched away softly beneath my feet, and soon, very soon, the sweat poured from me. I used to imagine that this salty effusion was the liquor being squeezed from my body. After a few months, I thought it was the fat, melted down in a hot running body, escaping my skin like steam through a tea pot lid. I still thought of it as purification, though I couldn't put a direct image to it. Maybe it was my sins.

I ran for about three miles westward, approaching and then passing four more green zones filled with kids playing, greasy from the SPF 40 sun block their moms had slathered on them; and fat middle-aged dads standing around at surf's edge, pretending to watch the kids while they were really sucking on their beers and commenting on the young moms, without shame or irony, that, yeah she's good looking, just needs to lose 10 pounds or so; and teenage boys and girls trying to impress each other without calling too much attention to themselves, a kind of flirting tinged with embarrassment that can only be called awkward. I dodged around these people, much like I had always navigated the people in my life; among them, but not connected with them. Avoiding getting too close to anyone, knowing that, at the pace I was going, any contact would result in injury.

I turned around, making a little loop to my left, close to the lapping waves, but not in the water. I had learned that lesson the hard way. When you run in the surf, the water splashes up on you, especially between your legs. It makes for a beautiful picture for TV commercials, but it also makes for the most horrendous chafing you can imagine. I hobbled around for days after my first "surf run"; it felt like someone had attacked my crotch with sand paper.

I finished my run, toweled off at the car, knocked the sand from my sneakers and drove home barefoot. The hard rubber of the pedals against the soles of my right foot felt almost naughty. A quick shower, a call to John Gartner's answering service with a message that I wanted an appointment as soon as possible, a call to the answering machine of Phil the private investigator, a light dinner of pasta with broccoli in roasted garlic oil, a stop at the Oceanside Public Library to pick up a couple of books, an AA meeting at the Methodist Church of Oceanside, and back home to my one bedroom apartment on the second floor of Mrs. Murphy's house. I read the latest Carl Hiaasen novel until I finally fell asleep around 2 a.m.

A busy day. I only thought about the notary business seven, or eight, hundred times.

Chapter 4

Wednesday morning found me sober and not hung over. A good morning. A great morning. I started the day with a light run, part of the simple routine my counselor and I had set out for me in rehab.

I was to exercise each day and continue to eat healthy. I would either find a new line of work or keep my law-related activities as low-stress as I could, trying to avoid pressure situations or the manic pattern of professional life that contributed to my fall.

I was complying with our plan. I wasn't making much money, but I was paying my bills without losing any sleep. My counselor and I had agreed that it would be best for me to avoid romantic entanglements too early, until I really got my feet under me. I had complied with that as well, fully. Finally, I'd go to meetings and I wouldn't drink. Check.

And so my last year had been spent doing a little minor legal work, a lot of running, a lot of reading, a lot of meditating. Meetings two or three times a day at the beginning, pretty much daily now. I helped Mrs. Murphy with her garden and I had learned to cook. My days and nights were quiet, restful. Even boring. But sober. I needed that boredom. This time of peace was following a lifetime of noisy, hurricane-like activity. It felt like when you come in from the freezing cold, where you are shivering and icy, and somebody wraps a warm quilt around you. You hunker down, wrapping the quilt tightly to you. It takes time for the heat to build up, to take the chill from your body, from your bones. Rehab, and sobriety, had been my quilt. This last fourteen months was the defrosting phase of my life.

Maybe someday I'd feel comfortable enough to take my life out of this holding pattern, but not yet. I wasn't ready to fly free. Right now I needed this structure. To think of life beyond this little cave was too frightening.

It was dark when I started my run, but by the time I finished my three mile route through the residential neighborhood, the sun was starting to rise. I deviated a bit off my regular route, to go past the small white church with the sign. I slowed as I approached; I'm usually in a car, whizzing by unless I'm stopped at the traffic light by the church. A neat, colorful blend of perennials and annuals bordered the church building and in the back I could see a vegetable garden. Somebody had a green thumb or maybe there was some divine intervention at play.

The sign had the pastor's name on it–Reverend Jim Baxter. It was a Presbyterian Church. I must have seen the name without it fully registering. The sign had been changed. Now it read:

Upset By Your Child's Tongue Ring?
Remember, Body Piercing Saved Our Souls

A bit macabre, especially for 5:30 a.m., but alright, a "shout out" for the younger crowd, I guess. I arrived at the office early, around 7. I like getting in before everyone else, always did. When I was a busy, important attorney, I felt it gave me an edge. It was the only chance I had, most days, to get paper work done, to review drafts, to plan and think, to plot, to lay out work for my associates and secretaries, before the rush of the day charged through the office, like the bulls through the streets of Pamplona.

Now, I liked to get in early because it was quiet, and peaceful. I made the first pot of coffee for the office, a task that may have been silently appreciated by the other early arrivers. I still didn't know any of them, except on a nodding basis. I was really a stranger; I had some space here, but I wasn't part of their team. Not even hot coffee could bridge that gap.

This morning I found the current files for my students on my desk. I wanted to review them before "class", but there was something I needed to do first. Quite frankly, I had been too frightened to do it earlier, but after discussing it with others at the AA meeting last night, I knew I had to face my

28

fear.

I made my way to the law library. Joel's firm maintained a very extensive library, even though almost all the attorneys and certainly all the younger ones used the computer service for research. Even though Joel and I graduated just before computer research became widely available, we both were adept at it. His partners weren't, so they wanted the leather bound books on the shelves. I think they also thought that the library showed stability and gravity, as though a major law firm couldn't possibly function without thousands of heavy texts. The truth was most of the books were never touched and the library really was an unnecessary and very expensive token. But it wasn't my money, it wasn't my token and therefore it wasn't my concern. "The power to change the things I can...the wisdom to know the difference..." echoed in my head.

I went to the library to find out what I was facing. I went right to a wall of blue books. *New York Jurisprudence* is a multi-volume encyclopedia covering every topic of New York law. If you have a narrow issue, say, how many days do I get to file an appeal, it's faster and easier to research online. If you are looking for an overview of a topic, there is no better place to go. It's available online, too, but I find it easier and more pleasant to read the texts in hardcover. I like the heft, the smooth blue leather sliding in my hands, the glint of gold leafing proclaiming the importance of its information.

The section on notaries was titled *Acknowledgments, Affidavits, Oaths, Notaries and Commissioners*. I found what I needed to know stated simply and clearly. A notary attests to the world that a particular person signed the document being notarized. That was it. Not that the document was true or that the person was in his or her right mind. Only that sufficient proof had been shown to the notary that the person signing "John Doe" was, in fact, John Doe.

Taking a notary when the person didn't, in fact, sign it in front of you, is improper. If your improper notary caused someone monetary loss, you are responsible. Improperly notarizing a document is a crime. A misdemeanor. Bringing up to one year in prison. And disbarment, if you were an attorney.

*****

Back in my office, I read the files for my class. Two were thin, both negligence defense cases that had just started, both dealing with auto accidents. The third was much thicker, actually four thick redwell folders, each containing several thinner manila folders, stuffed with papers and documents. It was a plaintiff's case, a woman suing a homeowner for a fall involving a ladder. We, meaning Joel, represented the woman who had fallen off the ladder.

The files had a familiar feel in my hands, like when a Hall of Famer picks up a baseball bat at an Old Timers game. I felt the surge of energy I always felt opening a file in preparation for trial. I slashed threw the documents, scanning the pleadings, the correspondence and the expert reports. I tasted the adrenaline in my mouth, coppery. I rocked gently in my seat. Just like the old days. Pavlov's dog. This was how I first started, years before.

During law school I worked for a matrimonial attorney, one of the best on Long Island. Lorraine and I married right out of college. She was working long hours in the City, making good money in advertising. I was free to work as much as I liked, so I did. I learned a lot and was very experienced for a new attorney by the time Joel and I were searching for our first real jobs.

After the bar exam, I got a job with a small general practice firm. For two years I immersed myself in every area of the practice: real estate, wills, the sale and purchase of small businesses, traffic tickets. Anything I could get my hands on. I was a pest, the equivalent of a gym rat in basketball. I got to work before dawn and left long after everyone else was gone. I worked weekends. I soaked it all up.

Of course, that left little time for home. I was present when my daughter Patricia was conceived, but that's about it. I was involved in some trial, or trial prep, or contract negotiation or, well, *something* whenever Lorraine thought I should be at home. To say I wasn't a supportive husband is an understatement.

The partners at the little general practice firm recognized what they had. Quickly all of the litigation was being filtered down to me. The firm didn't keep any major litigation at first; that they farmed out to other counsel, taking back a referral fee. But I got to try lots of small commercial disputes, and a few small personal injury cases.

My entire career, trials seemed to follow me. Some trial attorneys can go

30

months, even years, without taking a case all the way to verdict. Settlements outnumber verdicts, for everybody. But, for some reason, a much lower percentage of my cases settled than was normal. Maybe I pushed my cases closer to the edge, wringing out every dollar. Maybe I subconsciously sabotaged settlements so I could try the cases. Or maybe I was much better prepared than most of my adversaries and was less afraid to proceed when the judge said "Settle, or call your first witness." For whatever reason, I tried cases. A lot of them. Trials take on a life of their own; they demand total commitment, total concentration. When I was on trial, I did nothing else from the time I woke up until I collapsed, often on the couch in my office. My trial prep was legendary, but it took a huge toll on my nerves and the nerves of the people around me.

The last trial I did for the general practice was a small contractor dispute. The contractor was represented by O'Reilly, McManus, one of the top two or three firms on Long Island. The firm had been started in the 40's by Liam O'Reilly. His son, Michael O'Reilly, who was now in his 70's, had taken over the firm forty years ago and had expanded it into the formidable force it now was. O'Reilly, McManus was now eighty-plus attorneys, known mostly for representing large and mid-sized corporations, and for their political clout. O'Reilly, McManus represented companies before state and federal regulators. They handled huge zoning cases and substantial real estate developers. They had a major-league trust and estate department and some of the sharpest tax counsel in the state. They were large and impressive.

I was up against Gregory Connolly, Yale educated, a former Federal Court law clerk, golden boy of the firm. O'Reilly, McManus was involved in this small case only because the client was making them represent him, dangling a massive real estate sub-division before them. The sub-division was worth hundreds of thousands in fees, so the firm agreed to take the case.

Connolly came at me with all guns blasting. That is, Connolly and a team of several associates, clerks, paralegals and prep men. He tried everything. He motioned me to death; he tried to drag discovery out forever; he hired expensive expert witnesses; he deposed anybody who had ever even heard of the job in question. He spent thousands of dollars on computer graphics and trial exhibits. His "team" treated this case like it was a major, federal antitrust case.

My exhibits came from the local copy shop. I had no "team". I had my secretary Mary Robinson in the office; in the courtroom, I just had me. I kicked Connolly's ass. The jury was out for less than an hour before they returned with a verdict for my client that gave us every penny we asked for, plus interest. Connolly about had a heart attack. The contractor and his promised sub-division stormed out of the courtroom. And old man O'Reilly himself, who had stopped in a few times to watch the trial, and who was present at the verdict, approached me in the hallway and offered me a job. I took it.

I brought the same no-holds-barred attitude to O'Reilly, McManus. The difference was the stakes were much higher. The cases much bigger. More money. More demanding clients. A shark tank of partners and associates. Much more pressure.

I was poring through the deposition transcripts when I glanced at the clock. It was ten after ten. I was late.

Chapter 5

I gathered the files together and carried them down the hall, past Rita's desk, to the staircase. They weighed a ton. Rita was busy answering phones, but she gave me a wink and a smile. I returned the smile, but the wink felt too flirty. I just nodded. I climbed the stairs to the second floor and found the conference room that would be my classroom. My students were already waiting.

"Good morning, class, sorry I'm late."

I got back two good mornings, a cheery one from a young woman who was sitting painfully upright, a pad and pen neatly before her, looking every bit like a Catholic-school valedictorian, eager to please and desperate to show she belonged. The other hello was from a thin, anxious looking young man, intense and nervous. Sitting furthest from the door, silently, was my third student. Early thirties. She had to be the former Bronx ADA Joel was concerned about. She sat slightly pushed away from the conference table, leaning back in her chair. A Styrofoam cup of coffee was on the conference table before her and a legal pad, but no pen. She didn't look ready to take notes. Her arms were crossed atop a trim mid-section. She had dark black hair which seemed to shine, perfectly cut, falling in a wave to just about her shoulders. She wore a white blouse, open at the collar, which looked crisp against the tanned skin of her neck. Her eyes were a radiant blue. She was captivating. She was clearly the center of this room and probably any room she entered. She had a look of intelligence and command. And she looked angry.

I sat down at the head of the ten foot long mahogany table. Catholic school girl to my left; nervous guy to my right. Trouble sat across from me. I had the door behind me; from the daggers she was sending my way, I was glad I had an easy escape route.

I started by introducing myself, telling them that Mr. Levine had asked me to pitch in, even though I wasn't a member of the firm. I didn't tell them anything more about me or my experience. I was here to help them, to pay back Joel, and to move on. I wasn't here to impress them, or to prove that I could do this; I was doing it, and was going to keep doing it for reasons unconnected to them.

The tension in the room was palpable; Ms. Former ADA was sending off waves of indignation, like she was a radio transmitter. She was glaring at me; I was trying not to look at her. Catholic school girl was named Mindy Goldberg. Something told me she learned her very proper demeanor somewhere other than at Mary Immaculate Mother of God Grammar School. Mr. Nerves offered his name as Brian Reynolds. His voice wobbled a bit as he spoke. I looked at the end of the table.

"And you are....?"

She exhaled, long and audibly, breaking eye contact while she rolled her head in a small semi-circle to her left, now with her chin tucked close to her chest, looking back at me with those amazing blue eyes. If she had been wearing glasses, she would have been peering over them at me. But without them, it was just a murderous stare. I waited.

"Carolyn. Peterson." She bit off the words. "I *assumed* Levine told you who we were. I thought you were here to *train* us." Sarcastic. Caustic. When she spoke it was like a slap in the face; it had woken me up. I was tired of feeling on the defensive this week. I wasn't going to be intimidated by anybody, least of all her.

"*Mr.* Levine. I asked you your name out of politeness. I *assumed* you came to the firm with basic social skills. I thought I was only here to *train* you in the practice of law." If she didn't like the way she was being treated by the firm, she could leave. Or she could find another attorney to help her, I didn't care.

34

I asked the two younger attorneys to leave the room, go get a cup of coffee. And then I told Carolyn Peterson exactly what I had just thought. She listened, then leaned in, arms crossed still, but now placed firmly on the table.

"This isn't fair. I was trying murder cases, for Christ's sake. Now they have me doing work I wouldn't give to a first year law student. And now this! I have to sit in a "class" with two idiots who couldn't find a courtroom with a map and a seeing eye dog. And I have to listen to an attorney who spends his day reading the paper and defending kids whose biggest offense is cutting too many fucking classes? I don't think so. This is bull shit. And so is this piece of shit case they dumped on me." She gestured with a quick flip of her hand at the files in front of me.

"I had lots of offers. I could have gone anywhere. But I came here because they promised me I would be trying cases, real cases. I shouldn't have to prove myself. This is bull shit."

I didn't know what else to say.

"You're right."

"What?"

"You're right. This *is* bull shit."

"Don't patronize me. Don't *patronize* me. You're Levine's charity case, everybody knows it. Don't pretend to be on my side."

"I'm not on your side. I'm not on anybody's si—"

"Yeah, right."

"Listen *Counselor*, I let you talk, how about giving me a chance, OK?"

"*Fine.*"

We glared at each other. "The firm is caught in a tough place right now. They're impressed with you; I know Joel sees good things in the future. But right now, I'm all they've got to see to the day to day stuff, to make sure you're ready. Civil cases are different from criminal cases. It's not black and white. You don't have a whole police force behind you. When you go into court, you aren't assumed to be the good guy, like you were as an ADA."

"You don't know the Bronx, do you?"

"And this isn't your firm. You screw up a case here, they lose clients, which means people get laid off."

"Yeah, and when I was a DA, if I screwed up, which I never did by the way, some asshole would be back on the street. And people would get hurt. Or killed."

"Fair enough, but you didn't start with murder cases, did you? You started with bull shit. And that's what you're starting with here."

She was still boiling, but it was more of a simmer than a rolling boil.

"Look, why don't we do this. I'm not going to make you sit through Discovery 101 with Hansel & Gretel here. Why don't we meet later and we'll go over this file. Tell me what your plan is, lay out the testimony. We'll go over it like real attorneys. Fair?"

She almost smiled at the Hansel & Gretel reference. Almost. Maybe not. She was still pissed.

"Look, if I can't help, if I've got nothing to offer, all you've done is waste some time. I'll go to Joel and tell him to make other arrangements. Deal?" She didn't say no, so I took that as a reluctant yes.

"Good. Then why don't you go back to your office. I'll see you around four. Tell Bonnie and Clyde to come back in here."

*****

The remainder of my first official Peter De Stio Post-Law School Training class went smoothly. Both of my remaining students had just taken the bar examination and were awaiting the results. In New York, attorneys take the bar in July; they get the results in December. If they fail, they take it again in February. It's a grueling, two-day test, one which nobody wants to have to retake. The months between July and December are long ones.

Since my students had no experience, I went through the basics with them. I discussed how to review an intake file, which forms to fill out, what to look for. How to analyze police reports. Fundamental stuff. I gave them a series of assignments. The class took about two hours, with both of them writing copious notes and, astonishingly, asking intelligent questions. I guess not so astonishingly. Joel's firm hadn't grown in size and reputation by hiring idiots, no matter what Ms. Bronx DA thought. Then again, they did just hire me, even if it was only on a project basis. Chalk it up to a lapse in judgment.

I got back to my office a little past noon. Rita had left my mail and three telephone messages. One call was from my sister, Marie. A small surprise. My family had pretty much written me off. Marie certainly did when I punched out her husband, Lou, at her twins' christening three years back. But there had certainly been some outreach, from both me and my brothers and sisters, during the last year.

The second call was from Gartner. I returned his first, setting up an appointment for 3 the next day, Thursday.

The third call was from Phil the investigator. Phil Ruggierio had been a well-decorated homicide detective for the New York City Police Department. After he retired, he joined a few fellow officers in a small private investigation firm. I had used him at O'Reilly, McManus, especially when I needed a strong presence. I had recommended him to Joel years ago. It had worked out well for both of them.

Phil was in his early sixties. He was pure Brooklyn. Unlike many police officers, he had never moved out to Long Island or Jersey. Avenue P, Bensonhurst, was still his home, a solidly Italian area in a borough that was now the home mostly to new waves of immigrants. I liked Phil. I never knew him to pull punches; his first impression of the witnesses he spoke to for us was invariably dead-on, if a bit cynical. I hadn't spoken to him in quite a while.

I called him. The receptionist put me right through.

"Is this really Peter Freakin' De Stio?"

I smiled. "In the flesh."

"I don't freakin' believe it. Three years you don' call me? What, you don' love me anymore? How the hell are ya?"

"I'm real good, Phil, real good."

"So I hear. Clean and sober?"

"A little over a year."

"Really? How long is that, exactly?"

"Since last July 14th."

"Good. Me, too. Twenty two years, three months." He paused. "Six days."

"Really? You, too, Phil?"

"Fuckin-ay bubba. Went to the farm, twice. It was that, or Gloria was gone with the kids. Best freakin' thing I ever did."

"Yeah, I hear you. I just took care of business a bit too late, I'm afraid."

"Never too late, Petey. Keep it up. Just take it one freakin' day at a time. Ever hear that before?"

We both laughed.

"What can I do for you, Petey? You working with Levine now? Smart boy, you got great guys there, Petey. Not like them scumbags at O'Reilly. Especially that nutless prick Connolly."

"I'm here in the building, helping out, but I'm on my own, Phil."

"No shit? Levine left me a message, said anything you wanted, put on his tab."

"That's great, but I'll take care of you."

"No sweat. Either way. What can I do for you?"

I told him about the Amazing Derek and asked if he could look into him for me.

"Figure he's screwin' her before he screws her outa her money?"

"Not sure. Doesn't really matter. She's an old client. I like her. I'm kind of forcing this on her, so it has to be discreet."

"Discreet is my middle freakin' name, you kiddin'? Serious, Petey, I'll get you what you need to know, no fingerprints. But, you wanna know or you wanna know?" There were legitimate ways of getting a fair amount of information. There were also ways of getting more information, some that, well, crossed some lines. Phil would toe over a few lines if I asked him. He was asking me how much I wanted to know about how he got his information.

"Just do what you have to do. Nothing crazy, be careful. But I leave you to your work."

"That's my Petey. Now tell me what you know about muscle boy."

I told him everything I had, which wasn't much. Phil grunted a bit as I went through it, muttering "to the freakin' stars, my ass" when I told him about Derek's alleged clientele. But he laughed out loud when I got to Notre Dame.

"Jesus Christ, Notre freakin' Dame. No freakin' way. Every asshole ever seen Knute Rockne, or that freakin' Rudy movie, says he went to Notre Dame. Thinks it freakin' impresses anybody, besides some Irish assholes cryin' in their beer. Ten gets you twenty this one's bull shittin', Petey."

"I don't gamble, Phil. No bet."

"Smart boy."

I finished. He told me to give him a few days. And he wished me luck. "Nice to have you back, Petey. You ever need to talk, gimme a call, OK?"

"Thanks, Phil."

"I mean it, Petey, day or night. You call me, you got it?"

"Absolutely. Thanks."

I looked at the message from my sister, but I put it aside. I'll call her later, I thought.

I really wanted to prepare for my meeting with Carolyn. I had read the file before, but now I dove in, like in the old days. My yellow pad quickly filled with notes, questions jotted in the margins. I sketched diagrams, as I tried to visualize the accident. I read the pre-trial deposition transcripts, closing my eyes from time to time, trying to go back to the morning of the accident, putting myself at the scene, on the ladder, on the ground. I poured over the hospital chart, line by line, trying to decipher doctors' and nurses' scribbled notes.

Something didn't make sense. I just couldn't put my finger on it.

Chapter 6

The case wasn't complicated. "Our" client was a sixty three year old widow, named Sophie, who had worked for years as a babysitter for a doctor and his wife. Sophie made virtually nothing watching their three young kids. No benefits, all her pay "off the books". Less than minimum wage. She had needed a repair on her car that she couldn't afford. A big $350. The doctor had paid it. A loan, actually. The fact that without the car she couldn't come to work had played no bearing on his generosity, I'm sure.

She was so thankful, she offered to wash their windows for free, something their regular cleaning woman wouldn't do. I thought that said a lot about Sophie, that she would offer to do manual labor as thanks for receiving a *loan*. I thought it said a lot about the doctor and his wife, too, both that they *lent* the money to the woman who cared for their kids, instead of fixing the damn car for her, and that they accepted her offer to clean the windows for free.

So, early one morning Sophie comes to the house and starts washing the outside windows, on the first floor, in the front of the house. While she's doing this, Doctor Nice-guy goes around the back and sets up an aluminum ladder, 12 feet long. He leans the ladder up against the back of the house, by the garage. Above the open garage doors are two sets of windows. The good doctor puts the feet of the ladder on the nice, level driveway; the top feet of the ladder he puts just under the bottom of the windows, about nine feet up, in the space between the top of the garage door and the bottom ledge of the window.

At the pre-trial examination, the doctor testified he put the ladder up, then called out to Sophie that the ladder was ready. He said she came around, looked at the ladder, then went back around front to get her cleaning tools. Doctor Nice-guy goes in the house. He didn't stay to hold the ladder. I'm loving this guy, already.

Anyway, that much everybody agrees on. No disputes.

Sophie testified at her pre-trial deposition that she was surprised to see the ladder; she wasn't expecting to do the second floor windows. She said that after Doctor Nice-guy went into the house, she climbed the ladder; nobody else was around. She doesn't think she had started to wash the windows when she fell. She doesn't really remember falling, either. The next thing she remembers, she's being carried on a stretcher to an ambulance, and then off to a hospital. Two broken ankles and a fractured skull from a blow to the back of the head. She thinks she remembers the ladder being on the ground as she left, but she's not sure.

The Doctor testified to slightly different facts. He said that *Sophie* had asked *him* to set up the ladder. He acknowledged that he hadn't held it for her, that he had gone back inside the house as soon as she saw the ladder. He testified that about ten minutes after he left her, he looked out an upstairs window and saw Sophie on the ground. According to the doctor, the ladder was still against the wall, right where he left it. The Defendants were taking the position that Sophie fell off the ladder on her own accord.

There were a few sets of photographs of the ladder and the house, together and separately. Probably taken by the homeowner, his insurance company, his attorney and our expert. Some were date-stamped the day of the accident; those pictures showed the ladder positioned up against the wall, just below the window.

I saw Carolyn's notes in the file. She wasn't happy. The attorney who had handled the file for Joel before Carolyn joined the firm had worked up the case. He hired a nationally-recognized expert to examine the ladder. Unfortunately, the expert found nothing wrong. The ladder was in tip-top shape. It met all codes, and had all the proper warning stickers pasted to the side of the ladder. The ground had been level and dry.

Still, her predecessor had sued the doctor and the ladder manufacturer, which meant that a big-time New York City firm was on this case to represent the ladder manufacturer and a local Long Island firm had been hired by the homeowner's insurance firm to represent the doctor. So, Carolyn was facing two very well financed, experienced law firms on her first civil case.

In New York, cases like these are tried in two parts. First, the jury decides whose fault the accident was. They can divvy up the liability, too– say, 20% for one defendant, 30% for another, 50% for the Plaintiff. Whatever. The jury only gets to damages, to money, though, if they first find that somebody, other than the person who fell, was at fault. Unfortunately for Sophie, neither Carolyn nor her predecessor had found any negligence on the part of either the doctor or the ladder manufacturer. Carolyn was looking at her first civil trial in five weeks, with what appeared to be an impossible case. She was looking at a formidable defense. She was looking at a defense verdict. Zero dollars. A total loss. And she knew it.

I reviewed the medical records. Sophie had suffered identical fractures to both ankles, as well as a slight fracture to the back of her skull. She spent a good deal of time in the hospital, then in physical therapy. She made a pretty good recovery, considering, but she would need a cane at the very least, maybe even a walker.

I put the file aside. I had a little while before my meeting with Carolyn. I could feel the adrenaline rush again. I could taste it and I thought about a glass of scotch, the ice cubes clinking against cut crystal, the way the—I stopped myself. This was what I had spent the last year avoiding. I had to calm down; this wasn't my case. So I escaped to the Garden. I had to move.

I always drank, since I was 15 or so I guess. I played all different kinds of sports in school. I was pretty good at most. A bad loser, though. I got tossed out of a college softball game once, an intramural tournament. I kept yapping at the ump from the parking lot; he called security and got me thrown out of the park. Nobody had ever seen anyone thrown out of the *park* before. We thought that was hysterical later, drunk at the frat house.

My counselor said it was part of a pattern with me: whatever insecurity fueled my uncontrolled passion to win also fueled my need to drink. Whether or not he was right, my drinking certainly ramped up after I joined O'Reilly, McManus. The litigation department at O'Reilly, McManus wasn't very large when I joined the firm. It wasn't a profit center, but more of a convenience the corporate attorneys could offer their clients. Within a few years, though, the litigation grew from 5 attorneys and a small support staff, to over twenty attorneys and an entire floor of the largest office building on Long Island. And every single one of those people reported to me.

I rolled from one trial to the next, representing our clients throughout the country. I earned enough frequent flier miles to travel to Neptune and back, with a three-day layover on Mars. I worked seven days a week. I was quickly made a full partner. I became O'Reilly's fair haired boy, and I was making the firm a huge amount of money. Those two things bought me a lot of clout within the firm, and I wasn't afraid to use it. I protected my turf. I spent hours playing internal firm politics. I demanded, and received, huge bonuses, not because I wanted the money, but because I liked forcing my partners to give it to me.

Greg Connolly, my adversary in the contractor case, and I fought at every turn for old man O'Reilly's affection. Greg didn't stand a chance. My work was exciting; my work was daring. I marched through the office with my arms held high bellowing "I am Spartacus" after a victory (and a five cocktail celebratory lunch).

I took Connolly's key associates. I undermined him with his biggest clients, some of whom switched their allegiance to me. I even eventually took his corner office. The other partners, for the most part, wanted to keep me pleased. I knew it; they knew I knew it. I was feared and I was obnoxious. I took great pleasure in aggressively attacking my fellow partners (except old man O'Reilly, of course) at our partners' meetings. None of their failures or mistakes went unnoticed or unremarked upon by me. I was living and working full-throttle. I pushed and shoved and elbowed and bit and clawed for every dollar, every perk, every advantage, in every case, with every client, with every attorney in and out of my office. I cut corners, I walked lines, I pushed envelopes, I pushed people. I broke rules. I simply didn't care about anything, except winning whatever game was before me.

Connolly's efforts to derail me failed. He tried to point out that my behavior was deteriorating, that I was jeopardizing the firm's reputation. He tried to regain his influence with some of the older partners, especially with those I abused. It didn't work.

I treated my partners like serfs, and they took it because of one simple fact: I was making them a fortune.

They went home to their spouses and families with more money than they had ever earned before, more than they could have imagined. Me? I lived at the office. I never went home.

Actually, that's not entirely true. I was at home often, at the beginning. But as soon as I walked in the door, I would have a drink. Then another. Then another. Benjamin Franklin said that the man takes the first drink, the first drink takes the second drink, and the second drink takes the man. It was true in my case. When I got home, my goal was to unwind, fast. I "unwound" myself each night until I passed out. Mission accomplished.

Lorraine protested, of course. She complained, with increasing bitterness, that I was missing our daughter's childhood. That I wasn't a good father. That I was a worse husband. She wasn't wrong, and I guess I always knew it. But who wants to hear that? So I started going out more, doing more of my drinking in bars, crashing many nights at the Garden City Hotel. And not always alone.

Back in the Garden, I did some walking meditation along the asphalt path, just concentrating on my feet touching the ground, heel to toe, feeling the pressure shift under my feet, feeling my foot lifting off, striding slowly in mid-air. Trying to step gently on the earth. Trying to feel its peace, its massiveness, its calm. Trying to keep the notary and the detective and even Sophie's case from my mind.

I had just finished my second lap, when it hit me.

Bingo.

I knew what was bothering me. There was one fact that Sophie and the doctor disagreed on that was key.

Somebody was lying in the ladder case. And I knew who.

Chapter 7

Carolyn came to my office exactly at four armed with a legal pad and a scowl. I knew the legal pad was a permanent fixture; lawyers cannot think without one. It appeared the scowl was permanent, too.

I asked for her take on the case.

"It's a piece of shit. There's no liability. Nothing. A nice old lady lost her balance and fell. Too bad for the old lady. Next."

I waited. I had to decide how to handle this.

"You more worried about the old lady or your career?"

"Fuck you. Don't play psychologist with me. Save it for your own shrink."

I breathed in and out, slowly. Twice. "Fair enough. Anything you don't understand about this file?"

"Like *you* could clear it up for me? Huh? I tell you what I don't understand. I don't understand why this piece of shit is even in suit. Can you explain that? And I don't understand why a supposedly *major* firm like this needs someone like *you* to train its new attorneys. This is fucking ridiculous."

Now I just waited. I'd let her vent enough. Now she had to decide if she was going to continue to act like a two year old or if she was going to be a professional. I said nothing; I just waited.

I could see the muscles in her jaw flexing. "Alright. I have one question, Mr. Family Court. Why didn't the ladder manufacturer move for summary judgment, get out of the case early? There's no evidence against them at all."

I ignored the dig. "Good question. See who represents them? Mike

Baylor. Baylor is the biggest whore in the business. Well, maybe not the biggest, but he's up there. Guaranteed he told the manufacturer they're in deep trouble. He'll run this bill up big time, take it all the way through verdict. Lots of hours prepping the case for trial. Lots of trial time. Lots of fees. He doesn't want out. He wants a defense verdict, so when the client bitches about the fee, or when they have another case in New York, he can say, hey, I won the last one for you, saved you hundreds of thousand of dollars. Why didn't they move for summary judgment? Fees. That's why."

"That's bull shit. How do you know that?"

I didn't say anything.

"Alright, so what do I do?"

"Dismiss the case against the manufacturer. Get them out of there. Concentrate on the doctor."

"But everybody tells me to keep them in. Maybe they'll toss a few dollars into the pot to settle this before trial."

"It's not worth it. And they won't. Keep your eye on the ball. It's the doctor. Only the doctor."

"You're wrong. My best bet is to get both defendants to cough up some nuisance money before jury selection and get out of this goddamn thing."

"Do that, and you're walking away from hundreds of thousands of dollars."

"No fucking way. You're crazy. Is that the way you handle juvenile delinquent cases at Family Court?"

I stayed calm. "Carolyn, how well did you do in geometry in high school?"

"What? What does that have to do with it?"

"Humor me. How well?"

"I don't know. Well enough to get into Cornell. Why?"

I smiled. I had her attention.

I picked up the phone and dialed a number I had looked up earlier. I put the phone on speaker.

"Engineering. Arthur Klein speaking." The voice was deep, melodious, statesmanlike.

"Dr. Klein. Good afternoon. It's Peter De Stio."

"Peter! It is so good to hear from you! How have you been?"

"Very well, professor. How is everything at the University?"

"Marvelous, Peter. Say, are you back with O'Reilly, McManus?"

"No, doc. I'm working with an associate at Joel Levine's office, Carolyn Peterson. I have her here. You're on speaker phone."

"Wonderful. Nice to meet you, Ms. Peterson."

"Nice to meet you, sir." Ah, she had social skills after all.

"Professor, we'd like to retain you on a case. Do you have a few moments?"

He did. I laid out the facts for him. He let me talk, interrupting me occasionally for clarification.

"Alright, Peter. I think I have the facts. I don't understand something, though. If you already had International Engineering look at the ladder, and it passed muster, why call me? They are very good. If the ladder wasn't defective, what is your theory"

I looked at Carolyn. She had replaced the scowl with a skeptical frown.

"It's not my theory, Professor. It's Pythagoras'."

"Come again?"

"Doc, I've used ladders in the past. I'm looking at a photo of this one, lying on its side. There's a yellow sticker, with a black angle drawn on it. Am I correct that there is a proper angle for ladders to be placed up against a wall?"

"Most certainly. A standard, unanchored ladder such as the one you've described is best placed at a 75 degree angle. This way the weight can be evenly distributed between the wall and the ground. Anything more than an a 5 or 10 degree deviation, either way, would be unsafe."

Carolyn leaned forward. "Why is that?"

Klein shifted into the tone he had used for a dozen juries for me. He was a great witness, authoritative without being condescending, willing to give up points he couldn't defend, with credentials that could not be attacked.

"Well, Ms. Peterson, imagine that you placed the feet of a ladder against the base of a wall, so that the ladder was straight up and down. In that case, if you tried to climb the ladder, your weight would shift the center of gravity of the ladder. It would pull away from the wall and you, and it, would fall backwards. On the other hand, if you laid the ladder flat on the ground, then placed one end a few inches up the wall, as you started to walk on the ladder, it would immediately slip off the wall back to the floor, correct?"

I could see Carolyn trying to imagine an almost flat ladder. I slid a pen to her so she could draw a diagram. She did and she nodded. "I get it."

"Now those are obvious exaggerations. But there reaches a point where a ladder can be placed either at too steep an angle, or too flat an angle, for safe operation. The exact angle depends on many factors, including the person's weight, the composition of the ground surface. Many factors. But, still, the angles can be calculated with a high degree of accuracy and confidence. Peter, you seem to have worked this out already. Please give me the numbers again."

"OK, doc. The ladder was 12 feet long. There was only about a foot between the top of the garage door, which was open, and the bottom of the window. The ladder had to be placed in the area between the garage door and the window. Below that area was air because the garage doors were open. Above the area was the glass window. So I figure it was put at its highest point, just below the window. That's 9 feet."

Carolyn interrupted. "Why the highest point?"

The professor answered. "If one were to desire to wash windows, and reach the top, one would naturally put the ladder up as high as it would go. Do we have measurements on the height and width of the windows?" We did, and Carolyn gave them to him.

"Hmm. Actually, I'm not sure she could have reached the top of the window, anyway. Very well. Peter, your theory?"

"Well, if I remember it correctly from high school, to find one side of a right triangle, when you know the two other sides, you use the Pythagorean theory: the old a^2 plus b^2 equals c^2. If we know the height, 9 feet, squared that's 81. That's a. We know the length of the cross piece, what is that called, again?"

Carolyn jumped in. "The hypotenuse!"

"Yeah, that's it. If the hypotenuse, the ladder, is 12 feet, squared, that's 144. That's *c*. We move *a* over to the other side of the equation. 144 minus 81 leaves 63. Taking the square root, I figure that's around 8 feet."

"Correct, Peter. Continue."

"Well, that means that to place a 12 foot ladder so that the top is 9 feet off the ground, the legs would have to be out about 8 feet from the wall. I measured out 8 feet, and I'm thinking, that's *way* too far out."

"I did the calculations while you spoke, Peter. You are 100% correct. To be properly situated, the ladder could not be more than approximately four feet from the base of the wall. This ladder was placed too far out. It created an *extremely* unsafe angle. As your client climbed up, the center of gravity shifted. At some point, and I will calculate it for you, the friction of the ladder's feet against the driveway would be overcome by the downward force of your client. The feet of the ladder would slip out, and the ladder, and your client would fall."

"Straight down, correct?"

"Absolutely, Peter. Straight down."

"Where she would break both ankles upon impact, and fall backwards, hitting her head and losing consciousness."

"Yes, very likely. Quite probably, as a matter of fact. And since the defendant-doctor put the ladder up, he bears culpability. In other words, it was mostly, if not all, his fault."

I thanked the professor. I told him Carolyn would be sending him copies of the documents and photos he would need to write his report. And his retainer check.

After we had hung up, I looked at Carolyn. She had a puzzled look.

"I suggest you discontinue against the manufacturer. I suggest you get Dr. Klein's report as soon as possible and serve it on your adversary. I suggest you set your sights on an appropriate settlement figure." I named a number in the hundreds of thousands. Carolyn looked shocked.

"Stick to your guns. Don't sell this short. From a review of these transcripts, the jury is going to love Sophie. The Doctor and his wife, not so much."

"How did you come up with this?"

"Something was bothering me. If she fell off the ladder to the side, how did she get two identical ankle fractures? I mean, if she fell off the side, I could see breaking one or the other. But both?"

I looked at her. "The stories were almost identical, except for one key point: was the ladder still standing after Sophie fell? I just thought through the fall. If the ladder stayed up, the injuries don't make sense, unless Sophie jumped backwards off the ladder, which I think we can rule out. Otherwise, she wouldn't have hit both ankles on the ground at the same time. If she just slipped, one of her legs would have hit the ladder coming down, maybe she would have landed on her side. But she didn't. So the ladder had to come down too."

"We were both led down the wrong path by your predecessor. He was looking for a defect in the ladder, when the problem was how it was put up. That's the lesson here: look at each case through fresh eyes. Put yourself on the ladder, or in the car, or walking down the sidewalk. Act it out, if you have to. You would have found this as you went on, I'm sure, you just needed to calm down a bit."

"It comes down to this: somebody was lying. It was the doctor. That ladder came down. Check with the EMS workers, see if they remember anything. Either way, this makes more sense than any other version. So have fun with it. And go get Sophie some money."

Chapter 8

I took in an AA meeting that night. I just felt I needed it; the afternoon with Sophie's case had set me on edge. I chose a closed meeting, which is where only alcoholics are supposed to attend, not their families. I didn't mind open meetings, most nights. But this notary thing had also shaken me up; I needed this meeting to stay focused. I wound up sitting in the basement of the church having coffee with a couple of other guys until pretty late. They were newer to the program; I found it incredible that I was becoming an informal sponsor; I still didn't feel like my own feet were firmly planted in the soil of sobriety. How could I be of any real help to others?

Speaking of advising others, I had agreed to meet Batman and Robyn early Thursday morning. I was covering a deposition for a negligence-mill attorney named Barnaby at 10, then I had my meeting with John Gartner scheduled for the afternoon. Barnaby couldn't stand me, and the feeling was more than mutual. I had gone out of my way to screw him once on what he thought was a sizable case. After testimony started on our case, I arranged for a client with offices in Paris to hire Barnaby's key expert witness as a "consultant", conveniently making the expert unavailable to testify. Since the trial had started already it was too late for Barnaby to hire a new expert, and since the judge was an old friend of O'Reilly's, Barnaby's requests for an adjournment, and then a mistrial, fell on deaf ears. Barnaby settled for peanuts, saving my client much more than the two week Parisian vacation had cost.

So there was a good deal of mistrust and bitterness on Barnaby's part towards me. Why did he hire me to do some of his depositions? Maybe he liked the idea of the hot-shot De Stio working for him. Maybe he believed in second chances. More likely he liked the fact I was charging about ½ the going rate. Whatever. It was easy work, no pressure, and it paid a couple of bills.

I got in the office at 7; Ralph and Alice were waiting for me. Eager little beavers.

We went over their assignments. I reviewed their case files with them. I gave them new assignments. It should have been quick. But I was finding that there was a bit more to these two; there was a spark, a drive.

I don't know how, but they got me talking about old cases, war stories we call them in the profession. I told them of some successes, and some failures. I tried to stress the moral of each story, give them something to watch out for.

They asked me questions, lots of questions. How to deal with clients, with other attorneys. With the partners. We talked for two and half hours. I was becoming more and more impressed with my students. I ran late to my deposition, but I felt like I was a village elder, passing down the tribal secrets. It felt good.

The deposition was standard stuff, a simple trip and fall. Very simple. I represented the Defendant store owner in the case. I don't think the Plaintiff's attorney was expecting anything other than a new, inexperienced, unprepared attorney. He was wrong. He hadn't prepared his client well enough. She made mistakes, some pretty bad ones. The attorney and I looked at each other a few times during the deposition. I felt bad. We both knew he had just lost his case. All that was left was some motion practice and then he would have to explain the bad news to his client. All I had to do was write a report, and my responsibilities on the case were over. Some first year associate would make a motion for summary judgment and, boom, the case would be dismissed. We started the deposition at 9:30; we finished by noon.

I drove back to the office, composing my report in my mind. I would type it up myself, then deliver it and the file at Barnaby's on my way to Gartner's.

Rita gave me a funny look as I walked through the lobby, no hello, no wink, no wave. I made my way down to my office, tossed the file on one of the client chairs, and turned on the computer. On my desk were a couple of phone messages, and my mail.

I looked at the top of the small pile of mail. And my heart stopped. Rita had signed for a certified letter from the 10th Judicial District, Appellate Division, Grievance Committee. That's the "bar association" everybody threatens lawyers with, the guys who suspend, and revoke licenses. No wonder Rita had acted so strangely.

I picked the envelope up, and put it down, three times. I couldn't open it. My hands were shaking. I tried to stand, but I couldn't. My mouth got dry, except under my tongue, where saliva, metal tasting, was pouring out. I thought I was going to be sick. I finally pushed away from the desk and staggered to the bathroom. I stood for a long time, my hands on the counter, my head poised over the sink. I tried to concentrate on breathing, tried to calm down. I felt my heart, pounding and racing, finally, finally, start to slow. I washed my face, wiped it off with brown paper towels from the dispenser, the kind that don't soak up any liquid, and slowly went back to my office. If there was a 25 foot poisonous snake coiled on my desk, I couldn't have approached that letter any more slowly, or with any less trepidation.

I steeled myself, and opened the envelope.

The cover letter was from the counsel for the Grievance Committee, ordering me to appear for a hearing to determine if my license should be suspended pending completion of the Committee's investigation. I looked at the date of the hearing. I had until the Friday before Labor Day weekend; just 15 days.

The complaint was in the form of a letter from the President of the New Amsterdam Title Insurance Company. It complained that a "massive fraud" had been perpetrated. It alleged that I had notarized forged signatures on deeds. It alleged New Amsterdam had relied on those notaries, and, as a result, had insured title on a mortgage, covering the two properties, for a total of $13,400,000.00.

$13,400,000.

$13,400,000.

The letter went on to state that notaries of forgeries occurred only through negligence or fraud. "Since Mr. De Stio personally had worked for the purported signatory, that is Seymour Brownstein, and therefore knew him, he cannot claim that an imposter appeared before him with false credentials. Therefore, either Mr. De Stio notarized the signatures without witnessing same, or he had knowledge that the signatures were forgeries and was an accessory to this massive fraud."

The letter stated further that I had represented Houston Mesquite in the loan transaction with Island Savings Bank. Therefore, I had to have either conducted this massive fraud alone (he kept using the word "massive", as if a fraud involving $13,400,000 needed a qualifier), or as an accessory. Either way, they wanted the Committee to know about it. And now the Committee wanted a response. The letter went on to detail the fraud:

A)   A deed was forged from Brownstein Realty to Houston Mesquite last June 8th. The deed was filed with the Nassau County Clerk on June 9th;

B)   A second deed was forged from Brownstein Realty to Houston Mesquite, on another property, last June 10th, and was filed the same day;

C)   On June 24th of last year, Houston Mesquite borrowed $13,400,000 from Island Savings Bank, using the two properties as collateral for the loan.

The letter stated that the fraud was only discovered recently, about a year after the loan was made, because payments were made on the loan until February. It wasn't until foreclosure proceedings were started that the bank found out that the properties had been re-deeded to Brownstein Realty on June 25th of last year, just a few weeks after the original deeds, and that the earlier deeds were forged.

I re-read the letter twice. If I had it straight, somebody had fraudulently transferred properties from Brownstein Realty, borrowed money on the properties, and then put the properties back in Brownstein Realty's name right after the closing. Then they made payments on the loan for about a year. Why? Why didn't they sell the properties after forging the deeds? Why did they make payments on the mortgages? Why get a bank to give you a fake loan, and then pay some of it back?

Why had they gotten me involved?

Attached to the complaint letter were copies of the deeds, both from Brownstein Realty to Houston Mesquite, and from Houston Mesquite back to Brownstein Realty. I could barely make them out, but with effort I was able to read the County Clerk's stamps on them. It would make finding the recorded documents at the Clerk's office easier. The deeds from Brownstein were "signed" by Sy Brownstein. The deeds returning the properties were signed by a Harris Mathews. Detective Fisher had mentioned Mathews. Now I knew why.

But the worst part was this: all of the signatures had been notarized by....me. I didn't understand it. I couldn't think, and I couldn't get air into my lungs. I had to get out. I needed a drink, no I just needed some air. Call my sponsor, no, just get out. Out. I tossed the papers on my desk and strode out of the building. I was afraid I was going to throw up.

Outside it was cloudy and muggy. I pounded down to the Garden, but I didn't feel like going in. I stopped. I started back to the office, and then turned again. I don't know how many times I did it, but I must have looked like one of those ducks in a carnival that switches direction back and forth when you shoot it.

I put my hands on my knees and bent over, my shirt clinging with sweat. Get control. Get control.

I took breaths in by the gulpful. Slowly the nausea subsided. I had to prepare that deposition report for Barnaby and then get over to Gartner's. Get back to your routine. Talk to Gartner about it. One step at a time.

I headed back to the office. Rita just half glanced at me as I came in the door. She'd been around a while; she knew what letters like the one I received meant.

I headed down the hall to my office. The door was open. Carolyn was inside. It was clear from the papers in her hand, and the aghast look on her face, that she had just read the grievance letter.

"What do you think you're doing? Are you reading my mail?!?"

"It was on top of the file. I thought it was something I had missed." She pointed to Sophie's file, which was still on my desk. "I, I needed the file to send the pleadings to Klein. I didn't mean to...."

We just stared at each other. I could feel the heat in my ears. I was blushing with embarrassment. I brushed past her, taking the complaint from her hand. I put it in the top drawer of my desk as I sat down. She remained standing.

"Look," I finally said. "This has nothing to do with you. Since you read it, though, let me tell you. I didn't do it. Somebody forged my signature, too."

"What about the stamp?"

"I don't know how they got it, I don't even know if it's mine. You can get them at any office supply. But I wasn't even practicing law when these documents were signed."

"What were you doing?"

"It's really none of your business. What do you want?"

She looked at me, and sat down.

"Did this happen while you were drinking?"

"Yes, but, no, I mean, yes I was drinking, but I didn't notarize those documents. I didn't represent that Houston company. I couldn't have."

"Why not?"

"Because when this all went down, I was drinking myself into a coma every night and passing out! Every single day. I wasn't doing any legal work, none. What, was somebody going to come up to me on the floor of some beach house and say, here, notarize this? It's not like I was at an office, or anything. If the closing wasn't at a bar, I wasn't there."

"Where were you?"

"You really want to know this? Some hot gossip for the office? Fine. Where was I last June? Pick a place. I left my old firm two years ago, April. I spent over a year getting sloppy drunk. Everyday." I stood, pacing the small area next to my desk. "I mostly stayed out in the Hamptons. I was sleeping on floors, in doorways, on the beach. Old friends would rent a beach house, I'd crash until they threw me out. Emergency rooms. Shelters. I was a fall down drunk. I almost died a few times. I got picked up for disorderly conduct a couple of times. Spent a few nights in Yaphank, in a holding cell. I didn't stop drinking until last July. Bastille Day, July 14th. Independence Day for me and

60 million Frenchmen. There. You know the whole story. Satisfied?"

"Joel Levine put you in rehab."

I sat again. "What makes you think that?"

"There isn't much that's secret around here. Rita hears a lot. Before yesterday afternoon, all I knew was that you had been a drunk and that Levine was watching out for you. Everybody here thinks you're just a burnt-out drunk that Levine's taken pity on."

"I am. They're right."

"No, they're not. After yesterday's performance, I checked you out. You weren't just some hack. You were great. More than one trial attorney told me you were the best lawyer he had ever seen. And I found out that you helped get this firm on its feet."

"I don't know where you got your information from, but you're wrong. I'm just an old friend of Joel's. You had it right yesterday. I work assigned counsel cases. I'm just Joel's charity case."

She winced. "I'm really sorry about that remark. It wasn't right. Even if it was true, and it clearly isn't, it wasn't a nice thing to say. I apologize."

I just nodded.

"Can I help?"

"Thanks anyway, but I'm going to see a criminal attorney this afternoon."

"John Gartner."

"How in the hell do you know that?"

"Peter, the phone message is right here on the desk. I know John. We tried a rape case last year. He's good. Let me come with you."

"Thanks, but no. Not your problem."

"Listen, I can help. I can give you the DA's perspective. John is a very good defense attorney, but he's been out of the DA's office a long time. God knows I have time to kill here. Let me come. Please. I feel terrible about yesterday. Let me make it up to you."

I thought about it. In rehab they had pounded into us "Get help, accept help." So I accepted.

Chapter 9

John remembered Carolyn immediately. His smile got bigger, his voice more mellow. He looked a bit smitten with her, although he told me later she was tenacious and fought like a tigress over every issue. "Bitch" was one of the words he used. But, his guy had been convicted, something John hadn't volunteered when he told me about Carolyn's abilities, so I chalked it up to John being a bit of a sore loser. That's OK. I wanted a criminal attorney who minded losing.

They chit-chatted a bit, Carolyn smiling for the first time since I had met her. It was a 20,000 watt, melt-your-heart smile. John seemed very pleased Carolyn had come along.

But he wasn't happy when she said she was staying for our interview. They haggled back and forth about the intricacies of the attorney-client privilege, until I took out two one dollar bills and handed them each one. "Now you are both retained. Can we get started?"

John Gartner, Joel and I all went to the same law school, St. John's in Queens New York. John had gone to work for the Nassau County District Attorney's office. He stayed there about seven years, and then moved on to his own practice. He handled only criminal cases, and he was recognized as one of the best. Both Joel and I referred all of our criminal work to him. He had made a lot of money from us. So when I started the conversation with an offer to write him a retainer check, he got angry.

"Go to hell, don't insult me. You get indicted and I got to do some work, I'll charge you. Right now, put your checkbook up your ass and tell me what's going on."

I told them both everything that had happened so far. They peppered me with questions about Sy Brownstein, about my year long drinking binge. About my finances. I wasn't happy talking about all this, but it was necessary.

"How much money do you have?"

I told them about the advance from Joel. "Other than that, a few hundred dollars."

They looked at each other. "Debt?"

"None. Except what I owe Joel now."

John cleared his throat. "Pete. What happened to your money? You must have made a ton at O'Reilly's."

I really didn't see where this was relevant. It was beyond this problem, as far as I could see. I told them that.

"Wrong, my friend. The cops are going to look for this money. They are going to want to know if you've gone overseas lately, if you've called overseas, if you've made any large purchases, or paid off large debt. They are looking for a trail, and it's always best to follow the money, honey."

Carolyn nodded her agreement.

So I told them. "When my drinking got completely out of control, Lorraine threw me out. Around the same time Connolly and some of the others were convincing O'Reilly that I had to go. I saw what was happening. So I hired Sol Goodman to represent me in the divorce action. I gave Lorraine everything."

John looked at me. "Everything?"

"Yeah, he thought I was crazy, too. About made me take a Breathalyzer the morning I signed the papers. He even took a video of him telling me I was making a huge mistake. But I knew what was happening. Lorraine just couldn't take it anymore. I knew I was on my way out at O'Reilly, McManus. I knew my drinking was way out of control. I just couldn't stop. Honestly, I didn't think I was going to live much longer. I couldn't promise to pay maintenance and child support. I knew it was all collapsing. So I gave her everything. The house, which was paid for. The vacation house on the Cape that I had never been to. The stocks, the 401(k). I signed over my partnership interest in O'Reilly, McManus, too. When I left, they paid my share to Lorraine. Actually, I kept about 20 grand. I drank it up."

They looked at me. "Listen, I wasn't being a nice guy here. I just didn't care."

"Sol insisted that the Agreement state that I didn't have to pay any ongoing support, that my giving up my half of the assets covered my support obligation. I think he felt he had to get me *something*. It was still a great deal for Lorraine, though I think she still thinks I screwed her. I made her life, and Patricia's, a living hell. So she got my half of the assets in exchange for support she probably wasn't ever going to get from an unemployed drunk. I figured, what the hell, it's only money. Either I was going to get better, in which case I could make it back. Or I wasn't going to get better, in which case, screw it, I'd just drink it away until I died. I'm back working, sort of, so, I cut a check to Lorraine once a month. The law says 17% for one child. So I send it. I don't have to, according to our agreement. But I need to, if you know what I mean. I caused all this. But you know, Lorraine hasn't cashed a single check yet."

"If you don't mind me asking, how much were all the assets worth?" John asked.

I added it up in my head. I told them. John said, "Jesus Christ. No wonder Sol thought you were crazy."

"We had a lot, because Lorraine was good with money, and I never spent any. Never had the time. She even bought my suits for me. I never took a vacation, and I never did coke. And I never gambled. Booze only costs so much. When I crashed in hotels, I expensed it to the firm. So you take away leisure time, drugs and gambling, and you add to the equation the money I was making, it piles up pretty fast."

I had been looking at the floor while I spoke of my divorce settlement. But now I looked them in the eye. "They can look all they want. I live very simply. I don't travel. I don't call long distance. I don't spend big money. I have no debt. I live on what I earn. I didn't steal any money. I had no reason to, and no desire to."

John and Carolyn talked like I wasn't in the room. They decided I needed an attorney specializing in grievances. They tossed around a couple of names, then landed on a retired judge they both knew who was doing this kind of work. I told them, thanks, but I wasn't sure I was going to contest the grievance charges.

"What?!? Are you crazy?" John and Carolyn spit out simultaneously. "Why not?"

I had been thinking about it, especially since I saw my reaction to Sophie's case. Maybe this was the wrong profession for me entirely. So much of it is centered on people's misery, and on conflict. Maybe I couldn't be an attorney and stay sober.

Besides, I was tired. What did I need this for? Just turn in the license and walk away. They were waiting for an answer. I didn't know how to articulate it.

"Forget it, you're right," I told them. "I'll give him a call, set something up before the hearing." Carolyn looked suspicious, but they moved on.

They decided I needed to have my handwriting analyzed and compared against the forgeries, immediately. We also needed to have the notary stamp analyzed, to see if it was, in fact, mine. They each had their favorites, and their voices raised as they disagreed. The person Carolyn felt strongest about, John never heard of. John's first choice was dismissed by Carolyn as "a fucking whack job" that no DA would believe. Since we all agreed we would rather pre-empt criminal charges than defend them, John reluctantly backed off his first choice.

They settled on a former New York City detective with an office in Manhattan. John called while I sat there and set up an appointment for the next day, Friday.

John and Carolyn then debated the usefulness of a lie detector test. John was dead set against it, but Carolyn felt that if we used the right person it might persuade the DA, and maybe it could be used in the grievance procedure. They argued for a while, until I ended the debate by saying, yes, I would take the test. We agreed to do it without first telling the DA, which would diminish its effect a bit, but would protect me if I somehow failed it. But we would use a woman

John had used before one who was most likely acceptable to the DA. John set that up as well.

John called ADA Melendez. They chatted for a few minutes, and then John said he was representing me. He was silent for a bit, listening to Melendez, scratching some notes as he went along. "Uh huh, uh huh, uh huh. OK. Next Wednesday at 11. I'll be there."

"Well?"

"She's not a big Peter De Stio fan, my friend."

"So I gathered. Are they pursuing this?"

"Yep. First the bad news. Seems they've compared the notary stamp on the forged documents with other documents with your stamp. It's a match, no question. Something about a letter that was partially worn down, made your stamp unique. That hurts, but it's not conclusive. Assuming it was your stamp, it doesn't mean that you were the one who used it."

"Right. Anything else?"

"Yep. They're waiting for their own handwriting analysis. Guess who they are using?" He half-smiled at Carolyn and gave her the name of the "fucking whack job" she had just said no DA would believe.

"Doesn't make her any saner. Just means that Melendez might be crazy, too."

"Where did they get my stamp and my signature to compare to the forgeries?"

They both looked at me as if I was an idiot. John: "How about from any of the four million documents you've filed with the Courts since we were in law school, moron?"

Oh, yeah. Those.

I asked if the forged deeds could be fingerprinted. They didn't know. Score one for me. Carolyn said she would make a call or two to see if it could be done.

Finally, we talked about the one thing that troubled Carolyn. And John. And me.

How did my notary stamp get on the documents?

Chapter 10

Friday morning found me in the office earlier than usual, about 6. I found on my desk another message from my sister Marie, which I had forgotten to return; a message from Marcia, telling me she was going to have the proposed agreement faxed to me, so please look it over right away; the faxed agreement, which had come over the afternoon before, just a few minutes after Marcia had called to say it would be coming; the assignments I had given Siegfried and Roy yesterday, duly completed; and an envelope from Joel containing the check he had offered.

It was quiet in the office at that hour. I set the alarm on my $5 Radio Shack clock for 20 minutes. I sat down and meditated until it buzzed.

I reviewed Marcia's agreement. It was pretty standard. It gave complete control to the Amazing Derek, including the right to give himself a salary. She would get 40% of the stock and the profits. If he was legitimate, and if the idea didn't sound so crazy, it was a simple deal and the agreement was largely acceptable. *If* he was legitimate. That would await Phil's report. And, *if* the idea wasn't so crazy. I didn't think there was anything I could do about that, but I'd keep thinking. I typed a few notes, including some suggestions that would help them both, in the event this bizarre project actually took off.

In the midst of all of this activity, an idea crossed my mind. I would have to wait for Rita to come in, though. I jotted a note, telling her what I needed, and left it on her desk.

I had to be in Manhattan at the handwriting analyst's office by 11. I still had some work to do.

I reviewed the Bobsey twin's work, marking the pages up with a red Flair pen, making suggestions, adding, deleting. I wrote on one of Nervous Brian's affidavits that "Lawyer's don't end sentences in prepositions." At least not on legal documents. I would bet the check Joel had left for me that this kid had no idea what a preposition was. Or rather, I would bet the check that Joel had left for me that this kid had no idea of what constitutes a preposition.

Double or nothing he asks a secretary. If she's over 55, she'll know; under 55, it's anybody's guess, such is the condition of American education today.

I finished reviewing their work and gave them each new assignments. In addition to their first drafts, they had given me lists of their assigned cases, and left a few of the files on my chair. I left them each enough work to do for the entire day, although I hoped to be back later.

Rita came in at 8:30 and found the note I had left for her. She came in to see me holding some paper.

"You OK?" she asked quietly.

"I'm fine, Rita. Thanks for asking. I have a question. When I came here last year, you ordered my stationery and supplies, right?"

"Yes, I did. You're not missing anything are you? Do you want me to order more, 'cause remember I told you that Mr. Levine said that whatever you need, to order it through the firm, 'cause we have a company that delivers everything, they're like a warehouse, so it's one-stop shopping—"

"Yes, I know. I remember coming here and finding a box of supplies."

"Well, yeah, we have a checklist of supplies we order for all new attorneys and Mr. Levine said to just order it. You know, about two weeks before you came. When I saw your note, I pulled the purchase order from the records."

I held up my notary stamp. It was about an inch and half wide, maybe three inches long. It was a self-inker. As you pressed down, the rubber part with the letters rotated down and touched the paper. When you lifted the stamp off the paper, it rolled back up and pressed against the ink pad.

"Did you order this for me?"

"Let's see...it looks like the kind we order, but then there are only so many kinds....um, no." Rita looked at the checklist. "No notary stamp. Why, don't you like this one? Is there a problem? Do you want me to order you a new one?"

"No, no. Thanks a lot, I appreciate it. Big plans for the weekend?"

"You bet! My friends and I are going to the City on Saturday, then on Sunday I'm probably going to the beach, but I'm hoping....uh, yeah, I've got some nice plans thanks!" She left me alone.

I had been shuffling the papers around as she spoke. I guess she got the hint I had more work to do.

I got ready to go. Rita's news wasn't helpful. I guess I had brought the stamp with me. I just didn't remember. I don't think I brought anything with me. Notary stamps are designed so you order them once, then forget about them. The stamp contains your name, your County, your assigned number, and the expiration date. But since the number stays the same when you renew, it's standard to leave the year blank; so mine read "Commission expires February 15, ____." I just add in the year as I sign.

I used the stamp on a blank piece of paper, then pulled out the copies of the forged deeds from the envelope the grievance letter came in. The stamps were different. Different lettering. Different size.

If this was my old stamp, if I had brought it with me from O'Reilly, McManus, then there was no way the stamp used on the deeds had been mine.

Except.

Except I knew I hadn't brought anything with me from my old days. I had walked out of O'Reilly's without cleaning out my office, without ever returning. I had come here literally with the clothes on my back.

Rita had to be wrong. She must have ordered the stamp I held in my hand for me, regardless what her inventory checklist said.

I made a mental note to call my sister Marie, and I filled out a deposit slip. I would stop at the bank on my way to the train. Carolyn knocked on my door and informed me she would be coming, too. My protests went nowhere.

As we were leaving, Rita stopped me. "I found another receipt. Clara in bookkeeping found it right away, cause I told her it was important, I mean I don't really know if it is, but you never ask me for anything, so I figured it must be something unusual, anyway. OK, I know you have to go. See the thing is, when I got to the notary stamp on the checklist, I didn't know your number. So I asked one of the interns to find out what it was the next time she went to the County Clerk's office. And that's when we found out your notary had expired *years* ago. And the clerk told her that since yours had expired *so* long ago, you couldn't just renew, you needed a whole new application. So I had the clerk pick up the new application and I filled it out for you. You signed it when you first got here, but we had you sign so many papers, you probably forgot. I mean, I forgot, too. You didn't get that new stamp until you had been here, oh, I guess one or two months. Does that help?"

"Thank you, Rita, it most certainly does!"

I raced back to my office, Carolyn following closely. "We're going to miss our train. Where are you going?"

The stamp used to forge the deeds wasn't my current stamp. It was an old one. It meant that while I still had no idea who forged Brownstein's and my signatures, I knew one thing more than did ten minutes ago– the person or persons who did this to me worked, or had worked, at O'Reilly, McManus. The person who did this to me had to have had access to my old office. And that lowered the potential suspects from the six billion people living in the world to the few hundred who might have had access to my stamp. Much better odds.

*****

I learned a bit more about Carolyn on the trip into the City. We had missed our train, so the only way to make it on time was by car. Assuming, of course, the traffic was only horrendous, its normal state. If it was worse, we'd be late.

Carolyn drove. Actually, she maneuvered the car like some stock car racer from hell, weaving and tailgating, with a mouth that made me glad the windows were up, so nobody else could hear her. Made me wish I had a window between us, too.

They say that anybody who drives faster than you is a maniac; anybody slower, an idiot. Other than Carolyn, there were no maniacs on the Long Island

Expressway. Just really big trucks, the backs of which flew at the windshield like we were in a video game. I had wanted to pretend to sleep so I wouldn't have to talk to her. It didn't work. A narcoleptic on barbiturates couldn't have slept in that car.

We made the appointment with the handwriting expert with time to spare. Which was a good thing, seeing as how I needed time for my hands to unclench from the ride.

On the way, Carolyn asked how old my daughter was, her name, what school she went to. I just grunted. I may have told her the Patricia was now 14 and went to Massapequa High School. But I made it clear I wasn't in a talking mood. Maybe it was because I've always been pretty private, and yesterday's discussion about money and my divorce still left me uncomfortable. Maybe it was because I really didn't want to talk about the fact that my daughter wouldn't talk to me, or see me, or have anything to do with me. Or maybe it was because I honestly thought death was at hand with every lane change and I didn't want to distract the driver.

Carolyn, on the other hand, obviously felt more comfortable, because she didn't shut up. I found out: she was divorced two years now from her doctor husband who had, by the way, cheated on her with his nurse, how's that for a fucking cliche, no pun intended; her four year old son Kyle was beautiful, the smartest four year old who ever existed; she had a wonderful live-in nanny named Luz, which is Spanish for light; Carolyn's mother also watches Kyle a lot, which is a mixed blessing because she criticizes Carolyn about everything and really hated it when Carolyn worked in the Bronx; her former mother-in-law helps out too, because although she was a real pain in the ass while they were married, she hates the new wife and loves Kyle, so she's been much better with Carolyn.

I think that's it. It's all I remember, anyway. I think I might have mumbled a few "yes, dears" in there by force of habit. I could see by her intensity why Joel had hired her. She was focused, almost manically so. She was passionate about whatever she was talking about. She had an excitement, a force about her that screamed *life*.

In contrast to the drive in, which felt like an amusement park ride designed by Satan, the visit with the handwriting analyst was tranquil. Alan Reid was the expert Carolyn and John had agreed upon. His office was on the 12th floor of a building on West 32nd Street. Unassuming, I guess was the word. Alan was part of an investigation firm, which, from their brochure in their small waiting room, specialized in pre-employment screening. We didn't wait long. The door between the waiting area and the offices opened, but no light came in through the doorway. Alan Reid was in it.

Alan was huge, an imposing, hulk, standing about 6' 5", at least 350 pounds. It looked mostly like muscle, though. About a 22" neck, at least, with a hand so huge, I wondered how he could handle small scraps of paper and delicate equipment. He was in his mid-forties. He led us to his cubicle, positioned away from the window in an open area filled with cubicles. His desk and walls had the artifacts of fatherhood; photos of the kids, handwritten crayon posters saying I Love You Daddy. There was a large photograph of a man with a Van Dyke beard; it looked like it was from the 1800's. He waved us into our seats.

"I already spoke with John. He's getting me the best samples he can. I prefer to use originals, but they aren't available, I understand."

"Why do you need originals?" I asked.

"I use them to measure the strength of stroke, to see where somebody presses down more. For instance, you might emphasize the tops of your letters, or the turns. A forger might use even, unbroken glides. You can't see that as well on photocopies. By the way, do you know where the originals are?"

I thought about it. In Nassau County, the original deeds are sent to the County Clerk for filing. There they used to be filmed onto microfiche; now, their images are scanned into the computer. Either way, the original is returned; it's not kept by the Clerk. There is a box on the backside of the document that the preparer fills in, telling the Clerk to where it should be returned. I didn't notice that on the copies we had, which, I now realized, I had left in the office!

"Damn it! I forgot to bring the copies of the documents with me."

"No problem, Peter. John is sending me a fresh set. Besides, if you thought I was going to give you my opinion right now, you were wrong."

He then explained to me the procedure he would use, and the equipment that would be applied. "I'm going to scan all the samples into the computer, and enhance them so I can overlay them, and compare them side to side. I'll use a double-windowed microscope, too, so I can magnify the writings." Carolyn asked him what he was going to look for when he did the comparisons.

"I'm going to look at the size of the letters, and their shape. Spacing is important, too. So are the curves of the letters, and the loops in letters like 'e' and 'y'. I'm going to check out the upstrokes and the downstrokes. People often start letters with a downstroke, while a forger might make the same shape, but start the letter with an upstroke. I'll look for stops and starts, for retracing, things like that. We have a whole protocol we use."

He said he would rush the job, but it would still take a few days.

Then he had me sign my name. Fifty times, 5 times each on 10 pages. I asked him why.

"You can mask your handwriting if you are only signing a few times, but not when you do this many. And by using multiple pages, you can't use a prior signature as a guide. Helps prevent you from defrauding me. I also told John I want samples of your handwriting from over the past few years. He said he'll have it for me by tomorrow."

I continued signing.

"The problem with just analyzing a signature is that it's easier to forge a signature than anything else."

"Why?"

"If it was a letter, or even a sentence, the variables in the letters, how they attach and connect, would be much greater, giving us more points of comparison. Look here. You have three E's in your name. One follows a P, one follows a T, and one follows a D. E is the most common letter in English. In a regular, 10 word sentence, E can appear 10, 20 times, following the same letter more than once. With a signature, the person is merely *copying*; with a sentence or more, he is *forging*, forcing his handwriting to *become* yours. It requires much more fine muscle coordination, much more skill and practice. A signature is much easier. It can even be traced, although I have equipment here that can help detect that."

I hadn't thought of that. Neither had Carolyn. We both looked a bit more worried.

"The real problem with signatures, though, is that people sign their own name a little differently each time. That's why I want so many of your signatures. I'm going to compare them all."

I looked at the signatures I had finished so far. They looked pretty much the same to me, but I could see a few differences. I continued signing, my hand cramping up nicely.

While I did, I nodded at the old photograph. "Is that your grandfather?"

Reid looked over at the photo. "No, that's Albert Osborn. He's the father of the whole science involving questioned documents."

Carolyn interjected, "You mean handwriting analysis?"

Reid stiffened. "This is not handwriting analysis. Handwriting analysis is a parlor game, like reading tarot cards. This," he said with a sweep of his arm, "is the scientific analysis of documents." He pointed to a piece of equipment that looked like a camera on a stand. "That, Ms. Peterson, is a Video Spectral Comparator. We use it identify inks, and to examine documents that contain erasures. Does it look like a Ouija board to you?"

Carolyn and I spent the next few minutes calming Reid down, convincing him that we obviously took him and his science very seriously, or we wouldn't be here. As penance, we listened to Reid's story about his hero Albert Osborn, and his one man fight to have this science accepted in the courts of America.

I finished signing my name. I thanked Reid for his time, wrote him a check, and asked him to hold it a couple of days. We left. *I* drove back to the office.

Chapter 11

We got back to the office intact. Carolyn and I were both restrained on the return trip. I guess she needed the adrenalin rush she got from pretending her BMW was an assault vehicle to fuel her conversation.

Waiting for me on my desk was my mail, a second message from Marcia, a third message from my sister Marie, a message from Phil the investigator, and a message from the calendar clerk at Barnaby's. I called Phil back first, but he wasn't in. I left a message, including my home number in case he wanted to reach me over the weekend.

I called the clerk at Barnaby's next. I had a deposition Monday morning, but, yes, I could handle a short Court conference for them Monday afternoon.

I called Marcia. I told her I had received the agreement, but that I needed until Monday or Tuesday to review it. I didn't tell her I had already looked at it. I was buying time for Phil, but I didn't tell her that, either. She asked if I could make it Monday, rather than Tuesday. I told her I'd try.

Finally, I called my sister.

"There you are. What's the matter, you don't want to talk to me?"

"I'm sorry. Some things just came up."

"I thought you were done with that nonsense. Thought you were taking it easy."

"Yeah, well..."

"Are you OK?" My sister didn't believe in beating around the bush.

"Yeah, yeah. I'm fine. No problems, um, just lots of stuff, you know."

"OK. Have you talked to Patricia?"

"No, why, is something wrong?" I could feel myself jump at the mention of my daughter's name.

"No. I'm just asking."

"Nah. I keeping writing, but she's not interested."

"This is stupid. I'm going to talk to that girl. This isn't right, I don't care what an ass you were, everybody's–"

"Please, Marie. We've been over this. Please don't."

"Alright." She snapped out "alright" but it didn't sound like it was alright with her, not at all. I knew we would have this discussion again. And again.

"What's up?" I asked.

"I need a favor. Lou and I are invited to a wedding tomorrow. Remember Matt and Paula? Matt's sister. The whole family and all of our friends are invited. Well, everybody except you. My mother-in-law is going to watch the kids tomorrow, but she can't be here until 2. I have to leave here by 10 to make the wedding."

A cold knot started forming in my stomach.

"I need you to watch Jeffrey and Michael tomorrow. 10 to 2."

Oh, shit.

"Me? *Me?*"

"Yes you, *you*. I've got nobody else. My babysitters are both busy, and everybody else is going to the wedding. You're it."

"Marie, are you crazy? You want *me* to watch the twins?"

"I need you. You keep saying you want to make amends, be part of the family again."

"Yeah, but I meant like come to Sunday dinner. Maybe paint your house or something."

"I don't need my house painted. I need my boys watched. Four hours. Tomorrow."

"Marie, I've never changed a diaper. Are they housebroken?"

"Peter. Your nephews are almost four years old."

"And that means, what?"

"It means if you want me to continue talking with you, you'll tell me you'll be here tomorrow and will take care of your nephews properly for me for *four* hours."

My sister was the matriarch of the family, even though she was the youngest of us five. My parents had three boys and two girls. Marie was the toughest, we all agreed. She remembered everything, all the little details of family life. And she kept everybody in line. She had a sharp tongue but a big, warm heart. She was the last to write me off, and the first to open the door again. I couldn't say no.

"Sure. I'll do it."

"Good. Try to be here a little early, I'll go over the list with you."

"OK. Um, is Lou OK with this?"

"No, he's not. But I am." Her voice made it clear that Lou had as much luck trying to derail my sister's harebrained plan as I did.

"OK. I'll be there around 9:30, tomorrow morning. Just one question."

"Yes?"

"Seriously, are they house broken?"

"Peter Anthony! Yes, they are potty trained. For goodness sakes."

"And they have all their shots?"

She hung up on me. That was gallows humor on my part. I sat behind my desk, petrified. What was I going to do with two three year old boys? I'd only met the kids a couple of times. I had never even had my own daughter alone, much. When I did, and she'd go in the diaper, I used to wait until Lorraine would come home, and swear up and down that the kid must have *just* gone. I wasn't left alone with her much.

This was terrible. What a week.

*****

As withered as I felt, I had to get to work on the appeals I had been assigned by the Court. I had finished reviewing the transcripts on one, the *People* v. *Simmons*, and had outlined my notes. It was time to write.

Ben Simmons had tried to burglarize a sporting goods store. My guess is Ben wasn't much of a camper, so he was probably more interested in the guns and ammunition than he was in the imitation deer musk scent, or the all-weather sleeping ponchos. In any event, late one night Ben climbed on the roof of the shop, and promptly stepped through a dilapidated ancient skylight, falling 12 feet. Luckily for him, he landed on a display of battery-heated hunting socks the proprietor had just set up.

Problem was, Ben couldn't climb back out of the roof; it was too high up, and there was no ladder available. The doors were dead bolted, with the locks on the outside, so he couldn't get out through the doors, front or back. And the store front window, the only window in the entire store, was covered by an iron roll-gate, which, again, was locked from the outside.

Ben couldn't get to the guns, or even the hatchets, because his tools were still on the roof. He could have stayed there all weekend, eating Power Bars and dehydrated soups, except that when he landed, he set off the motion detector alarm.

When the first officer arrived, he found Ben staring out at him from inside the store. The officer drew his weapon, and told Ben to come on out of there. Which Ben couldn't do, as he told the officer.

So the cop asked him, "Then how the hell'd you get in there?"

And Ben told him.

Ben's trial counsel had argued that since the police officer knew Ben was, at least, a suspect, he had the responsibility to read him his rights before questioning him. And, therefore, she argued, he should have read Ben his rights before asking him "Then how the hell'd you get in there?" The defense wanted Ben's statements, and everything the cops found after the statement, including his rooftop burglary tools, suppressed. That is, not used during the trial.

The judge denied her motion. The transcript doesn't say whether the attorney kept a straight face while she made the motion, nor whether the judge was laughing when he denied it. Either way, Ben was convicted at trial. I was writing up the brief to the Appellate Division, as best I could, seeing as how visions of the horror that awaited me with the twins kept flashing in my head, when Carolyn came in.

"I talked with the EMS dispatcher on Sophie's case. The guys that responded were volunteers. They're going to contact me when they get in."

I just looked at her. I guess my panic was evident.

"What's the matter?" There was real concern in her face. "Do you feel OK? Is something wrong? Did you hear from Gartner?"

"Um, no, no. It's nothing. Nothing to do with this stuff."

"What is it? Tell me."

"Seriously, it's not your concern. It's a family thing."

"Your daughter? Is something the matter with your daughter?"

"No, no, nothing like that. It's silly. It's just that, well, oh *shit*." I exhaled. "My sister is making me watch my twin nephews tomorrow morning. For *four* hours."

Carolyn laughed. Another first. Out loud. You might even call it a guffaw.

"Oh, my God! What I wouldn't give to see that! You should see your face– it's like you're facing the electric chair!!"

"Yeah, yeah. Laugh it up. What the hell am I going to do with two little kids tomorrow, huh? Any ideas?"

Carolyn wiped her eyes. "Sure! Why don't you come with Kyle and me tomorrow? I have a great outing planned– it would be perfect."

"No, thanks. I couldn't impose. Besides, don't kids need car seats and things?"

"Well, how old are the twins?"

"I'm not sure. They're short. About this high." I stretched out my arm, low.

"You're ridiculous. C'mon, how old are they?"

"Almost four, I think."

"Then they need car seats. Ask your sister. You may be better off just taking her car for the day. The twins will get along fine with Kyle, and I'll get to watch you play uncle. This will be great!" Yeah, great, I thought.

Carolyn told me her plans, insisting that I agree to meet her and Kyle. I had as much luck arguing with Carolyn as I had with my sister. She gave me directions where to meet her at around 11 the next morning. That should give me plenty of time to get acquainted with the boys. Right.

I made one more phone call before I went back to the Ben Simmons brief.

I had been dreading it, but it had to be made.

If I was going to find out what happened to my notary stamp, and who might have been involved, I needed someone on the inside at O'Reilly, McManus. Somebody I could trust.

Chapter 12

In the old days, my meeting place of preference was an imitation Irish pub in Garden City, a stone's throw from the Supreme Courthouse. O'Malley's. There was no O'Malley, and probably never had been. But the beer was cold, the bourbon smooth, the waitresses pretty and the bartenders friendly. Who could ask for anything more?

I had preferred that bar for a number of reasons, not the least of which was that it had a private room, of sorts, up a narrow set of stairs. It really wasn't more than an oversized loft. It had quiet booths along the walls, a few small tables in the middle, and very dim lights. The privacy I enjoyed as much as anything. I used the upstairs room to meet clients, prospective clients, and adversaries. And I used it, late at night, when I was drinking heavily and wanted to be alone, and unseen. Or if I was with someone not my wife.

I needed to meet with my O'Reilly, McManus mole. Prospective mole, actually– I didn't know if she would do it, yet. I needed some place secluded, but I had no interest in returning to O'Malley's. Instead, I chose one of the many Starbucks coffee houses that have sprung up on Long Island like dandelions on an untended lawn. I know they aren't dark, and I know most areas are wide-opened, but I didn't want to set myself up for failure, as the counselors say, by revisiting one of my old haunts in a pressure-filled situation. I also figured my O'Reilly mole wouldn't appreciate meeting me in a bar. So I chose the Starbucks on Old Country Road, near the Family Court, but far from the offices of O'Reilly, McManus. Its biggest advantage was that it had a large seating area, part of which wrapped around a wall, and therefore was partially hidden from the door and the counter. It also had, I thought, very nice decor.

My prospective mole was unimpressed by the decor, by the locale, or even by Starbucks in general. Mary Robinson was my former secretary, the one who had passed on my location to Marcia. Mary, who had been my secretary with the old general practice; Mary, who I had brought with me to O'Reilly, McManus. Mary, who had covered for me so often, and so well, and for so long, that the professionals would call her an "enabler". Mary, who considered herself, as I did, a loyal assistant, and a friend. Mary, who I hoped, desperately, would be my mole within the hallowed halls of O'Reilly, McManus.

I had met Mary on my first day of work as a newly admitted attorney with the small general practice. It was her second day, so she reminded me, from time to time, that she had more seniority than I did.

Mary was a tall woman, in her late 40's when I first met her, dark hair, brown eyes, and skin the color of coffee with just a drop or two of cream. She was married when I met her; she still was the Friday evening we met at Starbucks. Her husband, Henry, had been her high school sweetheart. Henry Robinson worked for the telephone company, up on the poles early in his career. Later he would be a foreman, then a supervisor. They had three kids, all of whom used the gentle discipline and no-nonsense prodding of these fine people to springboard themselves through college and on to promising careers and lives.

I'd met Henry dozens of times. We shared laughs about Mary's habits, imitating some of her favorite sayings. But neither Henry nor I was brave enough to tease Mary about her church-going, as Henry called it. Mary was serious, dead serious, about her religion. The kids, in their youth, were regulars at her church; Henry made enough appearances to keep her grumbling about his soul to an acceptable minimum.

Mary had been a stay-at-home mom for most of her adult life. She had taken a secretarial position to help put the kids through college. She attended a year-long secretarial-business school to prepare herself; indeed, by a stroke of fate her graduation and my swearing in ceremony as an attorney took place on the same day. Lorraine and I had celebrated by taking the Number 2 subway from downtown Brooklyn, where I had been sworn in, to lower Manhattan. We ate lunch at the Windows on the World, high atop the ill-fated World Trade Center. Mary and Henry had celebrated, with the kids, family and friends, in a backyard barbeque.

Mary's skills grew as she and I learned the job together. I protected her from her initial screw-ups; she did the same for me. Mary may have needed to learn how to correctly collate a motion, but nobody ever had to teach her how to get along with people, how to make each client seem like they were not only the most important person we represented, but really feel like they were the *only* person I was representing. People loved her for the way she made them feel; they put up with me because I won their cases.

I knew how important she was, so when old man O'Reilly asked me to come over, I told him I would, but only if Mary could come, too. When O'Reilly and I negotiated my salary, right there in the court hallway, I negotiated Mary's, as well. We both enjoyed a substantial raise. Henry was so happy, he started talking about retirement.

When we initially came to O'Reilly, Mary and I attacked our workload. She put in a lot of overtime, Saturday's, too, but never Sundays. We were a team, and since we came in together, and since we were stirring the waters a bit, to say the least, at old O'Reilly, McManus, there was a bit of stand-offishness from the existing staff. Especially because Connolly was still ripping mad about losing to me, our welcome wasn't exactly with open arms. As my successes and ego grew, as I threw some elbows in the intra-firm skirmishes, as I made partner far more quickly than anyone else had ever done, I became more feared, more of an outsider than one of the guys. It didn't bother me, but it did initially affect Mary. Combined with a subtle underlying racial prejudice by some of the staff, Mary's start at O'Reilly, McManus was slow, socially. But as people came to know Mary, the person, instead of Mary, Peter De Stio's secretary, those barriers came down.

As my situation deteriorated at O'Reilly, McManus, Mary tried to protect me as best she could. It's just that it's hard to make excuses when the boss shows up drunk, wearing the same clothes for the third day. Or, when the boss fails to show up for the second day of a trial, because he's passed out in some hotel room.

My termination/resignation from the firm took place during a short, ugly loud conversation over the telephone. I didn't come into the office; I didn't talk to Mary, or anyone else other than O'Reilly. I couldn't bear to say goodbye. Then I went off for a year-long bender. In rehab, Mary was one of the people to whom I directed an apology letter. I just couldn't get myself to see her, or talk to her, directly. So, until Mary walked into that Starbucks, I hadn't seen her or talked to her in over two years.

I arrived before she did. I am always intimidated by the ordering process at Starbucks. I can never seem to get it out, without stumbling. I ordered a large coffee. I got back a *venti*. Was that what I had ordered? I didn't care. I took it, tried not to burn myself carrying the paper cup to the preparation area, poured some skim milk into the cup, and found a seat in the farthest corner I could.

Mary showed up a few minutes after I scalded my tongue on my first sip of the *venti*. She came with Henry. I half stood, half waved.

Mary marched to the table and stood over me with her arms crossed. Henry stood slightly behind her, a half smile dancing on his lips. He knew what was coming; she must have practiced in the car on the way over.

"Peter De Stio. You better start apologizing now, because I do not expect to live much more than thirty or forty years, and I do *not* think that will be enough time for you to finish apologizing to me. My goodness, you left like a thief in the night, not even a goodbye note. And then, after all I've done for you, bless my soul, I go for two *years* without so much as one of your dumb how-you-doin's? Don't even start, yes, I got your pitiful apology letter, but you come home and you don't come to see me? Me, who worried about you more than anybody on this earth except your mother, may her soul rest in peace? Well, what do you have to say for yourself young man? Hmmmm?"

"I'm sorry?"

"That's all? Two years and all you can come up with is 'I'm sorry'? My gracious goodness, you are a pitiful man, Peter De Stio, simply pitiful. Have you found Jesus, yet? Have you?"

"Henry? Some help?"

"Oh, no my friend," he said with a broad smile. "You are on your own!"

Mary gave me more than a piece of her mind, standing with her arms crossed, her head sliding side to side in an angry shake. Henry just chuckled. I kept my head down, looking up to her once in a while, trading off between "I'm sorry's", "Yes, ma'ams", and "no, ma'ams". She finally tired out after about five minutes and sat down.

"Peter, Peter, Peter. Alright, I never could stay mad at you. Henry, sit down and stop grinning like a fool. And, you, Peter De Stio can go buy me one of those fancy latte things. The most expensive one they have."

"Yes, ma'am," I said with a half-smile. "Henry?"

"Just a coffee. Decaf, please. Doctor's orders."

I got on line and ordered. While I waited, I watched them at the table. They were talking low, leaning into each other. I saw Mary touch a tissue to her eyes a couple of times; Henry held her hand, putting his other one on her back, comforting her. I had caused that woman a lot of pain. My chest felt heavy. I had a catch in my throat. I felt like I wanted to cry, myself.

I came back to the table and sat down. Mary straightened up as I sat.

"I am so sorry I didn't call before now, or stop by. I just didn't know what to say, or how to say it. I am so sorry. So sorry."

Mary looked at me with moist eyes. "Alright, that's enough. You are forgiven. It is not my place, Lord knows, to judge you." Her eyes narrowed. "Just do *not* let this happen again, is that clear?"

"Perfectly."

I looked at Henry. He was still smiling. I guess he had figured out how this was going to end even before it started. Henry looked a bit older, a bit thinner than when I last saw him. He was wearing a collared golf shirt. On the front, where the left pocket would be, was written:

I am a loyal employee of:
~~AT&T~~
~~New York Telephone~~
~~NYNEX~~
~~Bell Atlantic~~
~~Verizon~~
Aw, hell, I'm retired

"Nice shirt, Henry. How you feeling, these days."

"Just great, Pete. I'm retired and feelin' fine."

"No, you are not feeling fine, you old liar." Mary turned to me after slapping his arm. "Henry just had a double bypass two months ago. I thought I was going to lose him, and him not right with the Lord yet." I guess Henry was overdue for church.

Henry wanted to change the subject, "Enough about me. Pete, what's up?"

I took another sip of my *venti*. It had cooled a bit; now it just tasted burnt. I told them both everything I knew so far; I held nothing back. They both looked concerned, especially when I told them that the notary stamp had to have been taken, or used, by someone at O'Reilly, McManus.

"I just cannot believe it. Do you really think so?"

"Mary, I can't figure it out. But I didn't take anything with me when I left, did I?"

"No, you most certainly did not. First thing that Mr. Connolly did was have your office boxed up, lock, stock and barrel. I have never seen anything like it. You would have thought you had the plague. They all but sprayed the carpet."

"Any idea what they did with the stuff?"

"I believe they left it in the storage closet on the fifteenth floor, you know the one right by the small conference room? Then after a while I think they sent your boxes to storage."

"Any idea when?"

"Not really. I guess when you didn't come back, didn't even *call* anybody, not that I'm bringing that subject up again, mind you, they probably just shipped your things over when they did a file closeout. I don't think they threw anything out. I think I remember Mr. O'Reilly talking with Mr. Connolly about

82

that, now that I think about it. Mr. O'Reilly said, make sure the boxes are secure. I think he hoped you'd get help, and then come back. I think he still does."

Every so often, the attorneys at O'Reilly would review their files and designate which ones could go to the storage facility. Normally a few junior associates were put in charge of preparing the files for closing. Some firms used clerks, but O'Reilly thought the work required a bit more expertise. The associates had to make sure original documents were secure, that extraneous material was shredded, that any of the client's personal documents were sent to back to the client. Then the associates were responsible to make sure the files were properly coded, boxed and delivered to storage.

O'Reilly, McManus rented a number of rooms at a self-storage facility a few towns away from the offices. Island Self-Storage offered security, 24- hour access, and amenities that came in handy, such as a shredder, a photocopier, and spare rooms where files could be reviewed in case an attorney didn't want the whole file brought over. If an attorney needed a closed file, all she had to do was look in the computer for the room number and the number of the box the file was in; an O'Reilly, McManus clerk would go retrieve it.

O'Reilly, McManus started using Island Storage because Island had to pay off a very large fee they owed from two cases I had won for them. I had saved Island Storage's business, but at the end of the day they owed us a fortune. I arranged for them to provide free rental to O'Reilly, McManus for a few years, until they worked off the fee. After the fee had been paid off, O'Reilly, McManus had stayed on, and was now one of Island's largest customers. Apparently my things, including my old notary stamp, had been shipped there.

I told Mary what I needed. I wanted a list of the names and last known addresses of everyone who had been employed at O'Reilly, McManus from about a year before I left, until now. I wanted to know who was with the firm still, and who had left, and when. I also wanted to know where the box of my things had been stored, the room and aisle number, if she could find out.

Mary looked upset. She could get me the information; she could access it

83

through her computer. But it would mean entering areas she didn't regularly enter. It would mean revealing her employer's confidential information to an outsider. And, it could mean her job.

I told her if she was at all uncomfortable that I would absolutely understand. I didn't want her doing anything she didn't want to do. She sat silently.

Henry reached over, held her hand, and looked at me.

"You are asking a lot of Mary, Peter."

"I know."

"She could lose her job."

"I know that, too."

We sat silently. Mary looked at Henry. They seemed to be conversing through their eyes. Finally, he nodded to her.

Mary looked at me and said softly, "If it wasn't for you, I never would have been at O'Reilly, McManus. I never would have made the salary I make, let alone the bonuses. And the 401(k). We couldn't have sent our children to the schools they wanted to go to. And Henry would still be working, heart condition and all."

"I'll do it." She sat up straight, put her shoulders back. Her voice got louder and stronger as she said: "Under *one* condition."

Henry got a broad grin on his face.

"Anything. What is it?"

"You are coming with me one Sunday to church services. With all this law breakin' I'm going to be doing for you, the least you can do is come pray for my soul. Deal?"

"Deal."

"Good. You can sit with this heathen while I sing with the choir."

Now it was my turn to smile at Henry.

Chapter 13

I spent the rest of Friday night alone in my apartment. I could hear Mrs. Murphy downstairs; some of her friends were over. They played cards, canasta I think. It was the same group she took the bus with to Atlantic City. She told me her grandson called them "Grandma's posse". They liked that.

I made myself dinner; I needed some comfort food. I never cooked a thing in my life, not even toast, until I went to rehab. There I had to help out in the preparation of the day's meals. I found I enjoyed it immensely. I found the prep work, the chopping and dicing, very relaxing. I had read a lot about cooking after I got out of rehab; the Food Channel probably had my favorite shows on TV. I had experimented a lot. When she was home, I often brought plates of food down to Mrs. Murphy, especially if I thought it came out OK. She seemed to enjoy the thought, if not the food itself, and as far as I knew, I hadn't given her food poisoning. Yet.

Since rehab I had tried to cook healthy, but tonight I wanted something that would stick to my ribs. I made a frosia. Frosia was a family recipe which my mother had always pronounced "froy-sha". I never found it any Italian dictionary, or in any cookbook, but it was one of my favorite quick and hearty meals. I never made it with her while she was alive, but I engineered it from memory after rehab.

I started with three egg whites. God, was I healthy now! I scrambled them up in a bowl with some milk. Then I cubed a handful or so of leftover ham. I shredded some reduced-fat cheddar and chopped up some leftover broccoli. I dumped it all in the bowl. Then I stirred in, slowly, some seasoned bread crumbs, until I had a loose paste. I poured this mixture into a medium-hot frying pan, a little olive oil sizzling on the bottom. I let the bottom cook golden and crisp, then flipped it over. Once it was cooked through, I plated it, a sprinkle of salt, and viola! Instant comfort.

I collapsed onto the couch, satisfied and lazy, but with a stomach still jumpy and nerves that kept sending jolts of energy through my system. I lay with my arm dangling off the couch, the remote gripped tight in my hand, my fingers working the buttons ceaselessly. I surfed through all 89 channels, not stopping for longer than a minute on any program. One hour, two, three, four. The TV flashing blurs before me, nothing registering. I finally fell asleep around 2, the channels still flashing, flashing, flashing.

I woke up Saturday around 7, groggy and stiff from the night on the couch. I had some time before I had to head to Marie's. I thought about going for a run. Would I use up energy I would need later, chasing the twins? Or, did I need to loosen up, limber up, for the big day? I decided to run.

My apartment was really the second floor of Mrs. Murphy's private home. It had been built as an apartment for one of her sons, before he moved away. I had a fairly large bedroom, a living room, an extra room that was depressingly empty, a small but well-equipped kitchen and a bathroom with a full tub. Double-sliding glass doors led from my kitchen to a raised deck in the back of the house; wooden stairs led down to the backyard. There was an interior set of stairs, leading from my living room to the front door. When Mrs. Murphy was home, I only used the rear entrance; I felt like I was invading Mrs. Murphy's privacy if I used the front door, even though the staircase was sealed off from the first floor.

I stood out on the deck, breathed in deeply, and stretched. The air was already thick and hot. The sky was clear and bright blue, but the humidity felt like a precursor to thunderstorms. Probably around sunset. Shouldn't affect my day with the boys, though I briefly hoped for a sudden hurricane to cancel the wedding Marie was going to.

I came down the stairs to find Mrs. Murphy busy in her garden. She was an avid gardener, both flowers and vegetables. She had a built-in pool, a beautiful patio and a lovely screened-in porch attached to the house. She encouraged me to use them, but I rarely did, and never when she was home. Most of the rest of her backyard was dug up in beds. I know; I had dug a good deal of them.

The day I got out of rehab, Joel Levine came to pick me up at the Center. We got in his car after we finished hugging. As we drove, he laid out his plan for me. He told me about the spare office he was renting to me, at a ridiculously low rent. And he handed me an envelope. In it were the keys to the apartment, a check, and some cash. An investment, he said. A loan, I insisted. I paid it back quickly.

Mrs. Murphy, a widow, had lived in this house for over forty years. She had raised three children here, none of whom lived on Long Island anymore. Her daughter and grandchildren lived in Florida. Mrs. Murphy had a condo in the same town; she spent Thanksgiving through April there. One of her sons lived on Martha's Vineyard; Mrs. Murphy spent part of the summer there. Her other son worked for the State Department; he was currently stationed in Japan. His "stateside" home was in L.A.

Mrs. Murphy didn't need the money from a tenant. She like having one, though, because the house was empty so often. She didn't even need the house, but I guess she liked the idea of a home base. I had met her Martha's Vineyard son and his life partner; they picked her up and dropped her off for her summer stays with them. Nice guys. I hadn't met the other two kids, yet, though I had seen lots of photos and had heard all their stories over tea.

I never did learn how Joel found out about the apartment, or why Mrs. Murphy had agreed to let me come into her home, sight unseen. I was grateful, though, and wanted to pitch in. I simply incorporated the chores she needed done around the yard into my work-out routine, as I lost weight and tried to rebuild my health. Maybe the Amazing Derek *was* onto something.

In the fall, I raked leaves and cleaned beds, shoveling hundreds of pounds of compost onto the barren garden, a natural quilt for the winter. In spring, I dug and hauled and turned the ground, rehabilitating old beds and creating new ones. Mrs. Murphy offered to pay me, or to take something off the rent. I refused; it was the least I could do, and besides, it filled the time. In return, though, I got an education in flowers, learning how to tell the difference between annuals and perennials; how to split them; how to transplant them. Me, who could barely tell the difference between a rose and a tulip, now I could identify Rudbeckia, and columbine, and Shasta daisies. Me, who thought flowers were only something you ordered to try to get out of the doghouse with your wife. Mrs. Murphy was a patient teacher, and I supplemented her actual experience with dozens of books and magazine articles from the Oceanside Library. I found I enjoyed the feeling of working with living things, and with the soil. It felt...healthy.

The only problem I had was that with Mrs. Murphy in Florida, the house had been very lonely the past winter. I had been very lonely. Oceanside seemed to be a nice neighborhood, it's just that I didn't know anyone, and from November to April the house was quiet, very quiet. The holidays had been torture. I wasn't looking forward to another round of them. I had spent a lot of time at AA meetings. I knew it would be another test of my sobriety. Of course, there was absolutely nothing I could do about it. If you can't control it, accept it. One day at a time. One freakin' day, as my friend Phil so eloquently put it.

Mrs. Murphy and I chatted a bit. I picked up the pile of weeds she had pulled as we spoke. She was a sweet lady; Joel had chosen well.

I started my run. A light jog at first; my feet felt like lead, every muscle stiff despite the stretching. After about a mile I could feel the beads of sweat forming at my hairline, my body warming to hot, almost uncomfortable, then the sweat started pouring out. Funny, regardless of whether it was the dead of winter, or oppressively hot and muggy, like today, I burst into sweat around the mile mark. That first mile is always the toughest for me.

I coursed my way through the neighborhood. There were others running, and walking, starting early to beat the heat, no doubt. I recognized a few faces, they recognized me. We exchanged little waves, or nods of the head as we passed. I turned onto Foxhurst Road, a busy two lane street, one of the first cut through this town, existing before the Revolutionary War. About a half mile up I came to the little Presbyterian Church. The sign had been changed. Gone was the bit about body piercing; usually the signs stayed up at least a week, so I guess there had been flack from the parishioners, or whoever was in a position to give flack. The new sign read:

Stop, Drop, and Roll
Will Not Work in Hell

Pretty fitting, what with the firehouse half a block down, on the right.

In the backyard of the Church, I saw a large man, on his hands and knees, pulling weeds from the vegetable garden. His back was to me as I passed. I wondered if he was in charge of the signs, if he was a handyman or if he was the Reverend Baxter whose name was on the sign. Either way, I again silently thanked the sign person and continued on my way.

I was feeling loose now, and full of energy. I was almost bouncing as I ran. I left my regular route, and started exploring a new neighborhood. Oceanside is an interesting town, one of the oldest on Long Island. Especially on the north end of town, far from the water, on any block you'll find tiny boxes of houses sandwiched in between large, beautiful homes. Most, big and small, are well-maintained, but every once in a while you hit a house that's about to fall down. The south end is newer, with more areas that were built as developments, so the houses, although very nice, have more of a suburban cookie-cutter feel. The south end may be more pleasant to live in; the north end is infinitely more interesting to run, or walk, through.

I finished my run with a three block sprint. I pulled up short of the house, and walked the last hundred feet or so, turning slowly up the driveway which extended up the left side of the house to the back, ending near my stairs. Mrs. Murphy had already called it a day; I could hear her air conditioning humming. I stretched some more, having learned that the post-run stretch is more important than the pre-run stretch; it kept me from being sore all day.

I showered and dressed and drove to Massapequa, the South Shore town I grew up in, where my ex and Patricia lived, and where most of my brothers and sister still lived. I had called Marie a bit earlier and told her about my plans. She said she would prepare what the boys would need, and that, yes, I should use her minivan. I stopped for a bagel and coffee on the way; I ate in the car as

I drove. I pulled up and parked at the curb at around 9:30. I waited a bit, breathing slowly, counting my breaths, trying to calm down. The trip from Oceanside is only about 15 minutes, but as often happens when you dread your destination, the time seemed to fly quickly.

Marie and Lou had a magnificent home, right on the canal that led to the Great South Bay. The back of their house, both floors, was all glass; the view was spectacular, especially from the second floor. I walked up the driveway, which lead to an attached two car garage. The doors were open; there was a mini-van and an SUV parked inside. The SUV barely fit. I continued to the front door and rang the bell. After a few seconds the inside wooden door slowly opened. Nobody was there. Then I looked down. Staring up at me was a pint-sized human being. I assumed it was one of the twins. He didn't say anything; he just turned and ran. I just stood there for a while, then figured, what the hell. I opened the screen door and called out as I stepped inside "Marie! It's Peter! I'm here!"

I heard "just a minute" from the second floor. I waited by the door, looking around. I had last been in the house at the boys' christening party, when I had punched Lou out. I don't remember why.

The front door opened into a spacious living room. In the back of the house there was a country kitchen that opened into a huge family room, complete with a fireplace and large screen TV. They basically lived back there, taking advantage of the water view.

I stepped into the front living room, much more formal than the family room out back. It was the kind of room that Italian-Americans of a certain age would have filled with plastic-coated furniture. Marie's taste in all things was expensive, and exquisite. I'm not good at these things, but I would have guessed this front room contained a fair amount of antiques. The room's decor was so impressive that it wasn't diminished at all by the sprawl of a Toys-R-Us warehouse worth of trucks, cars, books, games, balls and God knows what else that covered the floor, the furniture, and every surface imaginable. It was as if some giant creature had swallowed Santa's workshop and then had thrown up on the room. Marie came down the stairs, putting an earring in. She smiled when she saw me, but then she saw the room.

"LOUIS! JEFFREY! MICHAEL! Get *in* here, NOW! Louis, I thought you were watching them! Look at this place! LOU*IS*!!!"

Lou came barreling up the stairs from the basement. "What is it-- Jesus Christ!! *Boys*, get in here! Marie, I swear, I left them alone for just one second, I had to get something downstairs." He just looked at me. No hello.

"Hi , Lou." Not even a nod. He just started picking up the toys; I reached down to help, too. The boys, meanwhile, were nowhere to be found.

Marie found one of them a couple of minutes later. He apparently was trying to see if the toilet bowl would hold an entire roll of unraveled toilet paper. I heard yelling, and then some tears. The other guy was found in the play room, coloring quietly, the picture of a little angel, except, of course, he was coloring on the walls. Marie plopped them both down in front of the TV, and put on a DVD of some sort. It seemed to satisfy them.

Lou and I finished cleaning the front room, while Marie finished her makeup. He made it clear I was there over his protest. I knew Lou for almost fifteen years. He didn't win too many arguments with my sister. Then again, neither did I.

Marie called me into the kitchen. On the table she had a large bag with handles and straps and zippers and pockets. She narrated as she held each object up, before placing it in the bag.

"This is their lunch. Jeffrey likes peanut butter and jelly, Michael likes cheese. The sandwiches are cut in fours. Don't give it to them all at once, they'll just throw it at each other. In here are carrot sticks and some slices of apple. Don't give it to them until they eat their sandwiches, or they won't eat. These are juice boxes, you know how they work, right? I'm giving you two each. Jeffrey doesn't like the apple juice. If you give it to him, he'll just squirt Michael with it, so be careful. In here are some pretzels and some c-o-o-k-i-e-s for you to bribe them with. Michael wolfs his food down, so be careful with the pretzels, in case he chokes. In the side pocket of the bag, here, are wipes and hand towels. Wipe their hands before *and* after they eat. Tissues are in here, Michael has had a bit of a cold, so watch him. I'm giving you a change of clothes for both, but I don't think you'll need it."

Stuff was flying into the bag. How much could it hold? Or was it a magic bag?

"Here is Jeffrey's medicine. He has to take one of these at noon. Slip it in his sandwich if you have to. There are CD's in the car to keep the boys occupied, but I'm giving you some coloring books and crayons, too. If you let them color, watch Michael, he likes to put the red crayons in his ears. Just the red ones. I don't know why. Jeffrey still uses his binky, but only when it's time for a nap. I'm putting it in here, 'cause he'll never sleep without it."

She stopped. She looked directly in my eyes. "Peter, do *not* lose this bag, whatever you do."

Back to the bag. "They should get tired around one, so they may sleep in the car for you. If they fall asleep, just put the car in the garage, windows down, engine off, of course. Do *not* wake them up. I'm giving you my camera, just in case they do something cute. I'm also giving you a couple of bottles of water. I made you a couple of sandwiches, too, turkey with mustard, OK?"

I must have looked panicked. "You'll be fine. Here's a list with everything I just said. I put my cell phone number on there, and Lou's. We'll be at St. Bridget's for the ceremony, I don't have the number, but then the reception is at Russo's On the Bay, the number is right here. The pediatrician is on vacation, but here's the on-call's number. When in doubt, head to the emergency room, Lord knows we've been there enough times already. There's some Neosporin and band-aids in this pocket, in case they get cut. Jeffrey likes the ones with characters on them, but don't use those with Michael. He rips them off. Use the plain ones, here. If one gets cut, the other one will want a band-aid, too, don't worry about it."

She stopped again. She looked at me again. I was catching on; when she was going to say something *really* important, she made sure she had eye contact. Probably worked with three year olds. Let's hope it worked with me.

"Don't let them go to the bathroom together. They like to have pee fights. Take them one at a time."

Back to the bag. "If you are going to be out in the sun at all, sun block them. Jeffrey uses this blue one, with Elmo on it. Michael uses this yellow one, with the rocket ships. It's the same SPF, they'll just give you too hard a time otherwise. Put it on every hour or so. Put the tubes back in this plastic bag, or I'll have sun block all over everything. Jeffrey likes to wear a beach hat, so here it is. I'm giving you one for Michael, too, but he'll just take it off and hit Jeffrey with it, so don't bother."

Eye contact again. "Don't let them out of your sight. Here's the keys to the van and to the house. Jeffrey always sits behind the driver. Keep Michael away from rocks, he likes to throw things. My mother-in-law will be here by 2 to relieve you. If you come back early, just play the movie that's in the DVD, it'll keep them quiet. Again, do *not* lose this bag, got it? Any questions?"

"Uh, nope." I was too scared for questions.

She brought me over next to the TV and re-introduced me to the boys. They never stopped looking at the screen. I looked down at them. They looked identical. They were dressed identically. No name tags. Oh, boy.

Marie shut off the TV and told the boys it was time to go with Uncle Peter. The one I was pretty sure was Jeffrey looked at me with a cheerful smile, a jovial little glint on his sweet little face. He took my hand as we walked out of the house.

The other guy, the one I thought was Michael, was a different story. He looked up at me with a guarded expression. His eyes were slightly narrowed. At age three, he looked like a miniature hit man, with cold, hard eyes. His stare gave me the willies. He refused my hand. He just walked ahead.

Lou helped me put the kids in their car seats. He was still unhappy. Marie came out of the house. She was all dressed, and she looked great. She was carrying the bag on her shoulder.

"Peter. Listen to me. You never, *ever*, go anywhere without this bag. Clear?"

"Clear."

I took the bag and put it on the front passenger seat of the van. The boys sat in their seats, duly strapped and buckled in.

Lou finally spoke. "Do you have a license?"

"Yeah, Lou, I do."

"No DWI's or anything?"

"Nope. Clean. Listen, Lou, I'm really sorry. I don't know what else to say."

Marie took Lou's arm in hers. "It's OK, Peter. Forgive and forget, right, Lou?"

"Yeah. Forgive and forget." He didn't sound convincing.

I got in the van and backed out slowly. As I pulled away, I looked in the rearview mirror to check on the boys. The one right behind me was smiling and happy. Chuckles. I glanced to other one. He was staring at me in the mirror. A dead stare, dark and unblinking. Like a shark. The Assassin. There was a CD in the player, so I turned it on. Some kind of sing-song kid's music. Chuckles started singing along. As soon as I turned my attention back to the road, though, The Assassin threw a book at my head.

This was going to be four hours of heaven.

Chapter 14

I pulled into the parking lot of the Cold Spring Harbor Fish Hatchery and Aquarium a bit past 11:00. The trip up had been interesting. At the first red traffic light, I reached around by his seat and removed anything that could be used as ammunition by The Assassin. In addition to the first book he had thrown at me, I had been pelted with another book, a toy horse, an empty plastic cup, the lid to the empty plastic cup, and a sneaker. I took a rubber duck out of his hand, and a metal car from the seat next to him. I took off his other sneaker, and I felt around for anything else that might be a potential missile.

I patted him down.

He was clean.

Chuckles, on the other hand, just kept singing along, happy as a clam. Except he made me play the same insipid song fifteen times. Oh, and I found out he had a great facility for imitation.

Massapequa is on the South Shore of Long Island. Cold Spring Harbor is on the North. There are only a few direct routes, and they are always jammed with traffic, even on the weekends. The one exception is the Seaford-Oyster Bay Expressway, known as the S.O.B. to Long Islanders. This child of the sixties was supposed to run from Jones Beach on the south to Oyster Bay, the home of Teddy Roosevelt, perched on the northernmost shore. Unfortunately the road designers didn't count on local opposition. The environmentalists killed the portion of the roadway that would have extended south to the beach; the wealthy and powerful residents on the Gold Coast on the North Shore killed the northern extension. So this six-lane expressway was named for two destinations neither of which it reached. It was the most under-used road on Long Island, as far as I could tell. I had traveled on that road all my life and had never encountered a traffic jam.

Until that Saturday morning.

I got on the S.O.B. heading north. The whole trip from Massapequa to Cold Spring Harbor should have taken me about 30, maybe 40 minutes. It took me over an hour. Halfway up the expressway, traffic came to an abrupt halt.

"Shit," I said, under my breath. Or so I thought.

Chuckles immediately substituted every word in the song we were listening to for the tenth time to "shit", his little voice sing-songing, "shit, shit, shi-iiit, shit, shit shit shiiiiit" in time with the music.

When I turned off the CD, he started crying.

"Hey listen, I'll turn it back on, but you can't be cursing, alright? Your mother is going to kill me if I take you home talking like that. Let's sing the song the right way, OK?"

"Shit. Shit. Shit."

And so it went.

I got off the S.O.B. and made my way further north, through the back roads, up to Northern Boulevard, a two lane road that meanders through quaint little towns, near the Gold Coast mansions of Long Island's North Shore. I headed eastbound until I saw the sign for the Cold Spring Harbor Fish Hatchery and Aquarium. It's across the street from the Cold Spring Harbor Research Institute. I told the boys that the Institute was where they mapped the human genome, paving the way for the future of man. They weren't impressed.

I pulled into the unpaved driveway and parked in a small parking lot, the gravel crunching under the wheels of the van. I looked around. There were three or four other cars in the lot, but no Carolyn. I relaxed; I had been afraid I was going to be late.

I extracted the boys from their car seats. Chuckles thought it was funny to pull at my hair while I bent down to figure out the buckle. The other guy didn't say a word, move a muscle, or make any facial expression. I guess he was pissed because I had disarmed him.

I took out the bag, and felt around until I found the sun block. As I started to coat Jeffrey with the gunk from the tube with the rocket ships on it, he screamed like I was applying liquid fire. What? What?!? I frantically checked his skin, the bottle, my hands. Then it hit me. Duh. Jeffrey, blue Elmo; Michael, yellow rocket ships. I apologized, wiped the stuff off as best I could, and danced the blue Elmo tube in front of his face. Jeffrey calmed down. Michael didn't utter a sound.

As I greased the kids, I looked at the facility. Towards the back, away from Northern Boulevard was an open green area with a couple of wooden tables and some shade trees, perfect for a picnic. Near the entrance, to my left, was a long, low building, with a sign identifying it as the aquarium. Next to the aquarium was a long cement tank, with netting over it. Across the parking lot was a small booth next to an open gate. The gate led to an area, maybe 200 feet by 200 feet, enclosed by a 6 foot high chain link fence. It had several in ground cement ponds, some circular, some rectangular, each with a cement retaining wall about a foot high. There was a pimply faced kid in the booth, thumbing a magazine.

I had just finished slathering the boys with their requisite sun block, when I heard gravel spitting near the entrance. The car, a familiar looking BMW, must have been flying down Northern Boulevard before cornering into the driveway, perhaps on two tires. It slowed to a crawl through the parking lot, though, and eased into the spot next to Marie's van. Out popped Carolyn. I glanced in the back of the car to see if Kyle's face was pulled back, like the astronauts' faces are when they sit in the centrifugal force machine that tests their ability to handle high gravity forces. If he was affected by his mother's driving, he didn't show it. He seemed happy enough.

I threw the sun block in the plastic bag, and tossed the plastic bag into the big bag. I left it open, in case I needed anything, like the camera. In case the kids did something cute. I slung the bag over my shoulder and grabbed the boys' hands in a death grip. Parking lots make me nervous. One of the problems with being a lawyer, besides putting up with all the jokes, is that you hear the most horrendous horror stories of how small miscalculations in everyday life can cause tragedy. The slip in the tub. The roof that suddenly collapses. The driver who reaches for a tissue and hops a curb. The train gate that fails to operate. The boy who sticks his penis in a vacuum cleaner with an unguarded fan. It can make you paranoid.

As we crossed the parking lot to the little booth, I sized up the terrain. The area we were going into was sealed off by the fence, except for this wide open gate to the parking lot. I figured that I would stand in the opening and let the boys roam. If I saw either one climbing the fence, I'd stop him. But other than that, since there were two of them and only one of me, I couldn't play them man-to-man. So I planned to stay put at the gate, playing a sort of zone. Should be easy.

At the booth, I paid for the admissions for all of us, over Carolyn's objection. I also bought three buckets of fish food, little hard pellets. The buckets reminded me of the plastic pails kids use at the beach to make sand castles, and holes for unsuspecting joggers. We gave each kid his own pail, which seemed to me to be too heavy for them, but they managed. We all walked to the first circular cement pond, which was in the middle of the open area, a bit off to the left. In it were dozens of brown trout, each about a foot long, swimming in water about two feet deep, at most. The water was crystal clear. The pond looked like a miniature in-ground swimming pool, about fifteen feet in diameter, with cement walls and floor. The walls stuck up only about a foot above the ground, like a ledge, so the kids had no problem seeing the fish.

Carolyn showed the kids how to feed the trout. She took one of the pellets and tossed it in. As it hit the water, the fish went into a frenzy. It was as if she had turned a blender on in the water. At least ten of the fish struck at the pellet, churning the water, and splashing us with drops of water. I had to admit, it was pretty cool. Kyle and Chuckles squealed with delight. The Assassin only stared at the water, both hands holding the handle of the heavy pail in front of him.

We all stayed at the pond for a few minutes, each taking a chance at tossing a pellet in and watching the water come alive. Carolyn then took Chuckles and Kyle to see the giant turtle. I stayed. I put the bag down, and kneeled next to The Assassin. He and I took turns tossing the pellets, though,

98

truth be told, he was firing the pellets at the water with the same intensity he had earlier put into hurling objects at the back of my head. All was calm, elsewhere. There were only a few other groups of people in the place, though more seemed to be arriving.

I looked across the grounds, and made the first mistake of the inexperienced babysitter. I lost my concentration.

Carolyn had taken the boys to our right, near the fence line. Apparently there was a giant turtle sleeping in his own area, just on the other side of the fence. Kyle decided to go to the cement pond a few yards away, and Carolyn went with him. Chuckles stayed looking at the turtle. My mistake was in watching Carolyn. She was dressed in a bright red cotton blouse, with white shorts and sandals. Her legs were tanned and shapely. She had firm, almost muscular, arms, and long fingers. Her hair was pulled back, with sunglasses perched on her head. She had caught the eye of the bored kid in the booth, and, I noticed, the dads who were with their own kids. She was enjoying herself, laughing lightly with Kyle, clearly comfortable and relaxed and, well, happy. Happy. It was an emotion I personally hadn't felt in a long time, so I wasn't sure if that's what it was, but it looked like it. I watched her move, walk, kneel down next to Kyle. She looked over her shoulder, caught me looking at her, and smiled. I felt my ears turn red.

I looked away... to Chuckles, who was trying to dump his entire pail of food into the turtle cage. I leaped up and ran towards him, saying "No, no, no" loudly, but not yelling. He looked at me, smiled broadly, and while still looking straight at me, dumped the pail. I reached him just as the last pellet fell. I've always lived by the 5 second rule. That is, if you pick food up off the floor within 5 seconds, it's still OK to eat. I didn't know whether the 5 second rule applied to fish food, but I quickly started scooping the food back into the pail, just in case. That's when I heard a splash behind me. I looked back to the pond from which I had just come. Standing at the edge of the cement pond, perfectly dry, was The Assassin. He was watching something floating in the middle of the pond.

The bag.

The little bastard had tossed the bag into the pond.

The top was still open. It was floating upright, but it was starting to list to one side. I only had a few seconds before it did its Titanic imitation and sunk, carrying with it the lunches, the medicine, the change of clothes, the camera and the rest of the paraphernalia my sister had so carefully packed.

I raced back to the pond, and without a moment's hesitation, hurdled the short wall, landing perfectly in the knee high water. Three strides later I had, without pausing, saved the bag, crossed the pond and cleared the other side. As my first foot hit the water, I had hoped trout weren't related to piranha. Frankly, I didn't care. I would rather have had my legs gnawed off below the knees than face my sister with a ruined bag.

I pirouetted triumphantly on the other side of the pond, holding the bag high. I turned to Carolyn, expecting, perhaps, applause, when I saw she was pointing behind me. At the open gate. And at The Assassin who was using this opportunity to sprint for the parking lot.

The pond was now between me and the gate. I had only one option if I wanted to stop this prison break. I took off back across the pond.

I cleared the wall fine. But as my foot hit the bottom of the pond, I slipped. Trout droppings, in case you were wondering, are *very* slippery. I felt myself falling to my left, full body heading for the water. Many thoughts crossed my mind as gravity yanked me downward. Can I save the bag, which was still clutched in my formerly triumphant arms? Was I far enough away from the cement edge so that I didn't crack my skull and sleep forever with these fish? Can I save the bag? Are these fish going to attack me? Can I save the bag? Can I stop the kid before he gets crushed by an SUV in the parking lot? Oh, yeah, and can I save the bag?

As I fell, I twisted, throwing my arms skyward, holding the bag aloft like an offering to the Sun God. In midair, I yelled "Motherfu–", but I was cut short when my head went underwater. I hit the water, body fully extended. Water, and fish, flew everywhere in a tidal wave explosion.

I lay on the bottom of the pond, eyes open, staring at a somewhat surprised brown trout, for maybe a second. I leaped up, holding high the damp, but not soaked, bag as I struggled to my feet. I had saved the bag. Everything after that happened in slow motion. Me, slogging through the water, droplets flying all over. The shocked faces of the young parents, mouths open, staring, like photographs taken at a horrible accident scene. The little kids, starting to laugh, throwing back their entire little bodies. The pimply faced kid, his face clenched in rage, charging towards me, no doubt furious that I decided to go for a swim.

But my eyes were only on The Assassin. He had reached the open gate, and was just starting to turn the corner, when an arm reached out from behind the fence and snagged him. It was a white-haired gentleman, just entering the facility with his grandchildren. He told me he saw the rascal running, and he figured he'd intervene. I thanked him profusely, trying not to drip on his white pull-on sneakers. I held The Assassin's hand, tightly. Carolyn brought Chuckles and Kyle over. She was crying, she was laughing so hard. I was sopped, and smelled like, well, I smelled like trout shit. Kyle and Chuckles couldn't stop laughing, either. Carolyn gasped, when she could catch her breath a bit, that maybe it was time for a little lunch. I agreed.

Carolyn took control. She calmed the pimply faced kid. I knew she had him when she lightly touched his arm. The next thing I knew he was showing me into the employee's locker room. I first dripped my way into the gift shop and bought a Fish Hatchery T-shirt. I washed off as best I could, but my sneakers, underwear, shorts, wallet and keys were soaked.

I found Carolyn at one of the picnic tables. The boys were all coloring, munching happily on some carrot sticks. I tried to remember something Marie had said about crayons and carrots, but I couldn't. Carolyn smiled as I approached, and softly shook her head.

"That was classic, Uncle Peter. Classic."

"Classic, my ass. That bag goes under, I'm a dead man. D-E-A-D. Did it get very wet?"

"No, not bad at all."

I looked at the twins. "Do you think they orchestrated that move?"

"Which move? Diverting you, or having you do a swan dive in the trout pool?" she asked sweetly.

We fed the kids. I offered Carolyn one of my sandwiches, but she said she preferred yogurt to trout-smelling turkey. While I fed Chuckles the third piece of his sandwich, Carolyn slid a couple of the fish food pellets across to me. "In case you're still hungry."

The rest of my babysitting time was spent on the picnic area. After we finished eating, the boys started chasing a soccer ball Carolyn threw out on the grass. She and I sat down on a picnic blanket she dug out of the trunk of her car. We talked about Sophie, and the office, and the colleges we had gone to. Favorite movies. Favorite food. We purposefully avoided the entire notary mess, but we both knew it was sitting with us on the blanket. We just ignored it. We watched the boys play. The ball rolled near us. As I reached out to grab it, I was attacked.

First Chuckles, I think, then The Assassin, then even Kyle leaped on me. We wound up rolling in the grass, with the boys diving on me, one at a time, sometimes two, sometimes all at once. They jumped on my legs, and my back and my head. I'd grab one and toss him off, or I'd reach out as one was getting ready to attack and gently shove him back on his tush. I tickled them; they punched me. We all were laughing. Even The Assassin.

After a bit, the boys took off to play some more. Carolyn and I cleaned up, and got ready to go. As we did, she asked me what my plans were for the rest of the weekend. Maybe I thought she was asking out of something more than politeness. Maybe I was starting to feel something I hadn't, not for a long time. Or maybe I was just in a vulnerable state, and was foolishly hoping. In any case, I told her I was pretty open. "And you?" I asked. Which was when she told me she was going to a concert at the Jones Beach Theater with the guy she had been seeing for a few months. Name was Steve. A financial analyst. She told me more about him. I pretended to listen. I may have even pretended that I didn't feel somehow disappointed.

We loaded up the cars, and said goodbye across the cars with a wave. I watched her drive away, and felt like I had just been turned down for something, even though I hadn't asked for anything. I shook off the empty feeling I had felt the instant Steve's name had come up. I told myself I was being silly. Carolyn had just done me a great favor as repayment for the help with Sophie's case. Any thought of anything more was just...crazy. Why would she be interested in an old wreck like me?

I put the boys in their car seats, roughhousing with them a bit as I did. I checked out The Assassin for weapons, and mentally noted that I had to watch my language on the way home. I talked with the boys, asking them what their favorite colors were, getting them to count for me. We sang a couple of songs. It was fun.

The ride home went quickly. I pulled into Marie's driveway to find the SUV in the open garage. Marie was standing at the front door, in regular clothes. She rushed out to meet us.

"What's the matter? Why are you here?" I asked.

"Peter, I should have given you my cell phone. I had no way of getting in touch with you. As soon as you left, Lou got sick. I think he has the flu. So we didn't go to the wedding. You didn't have to babysit after all."

"It was no problem. We had fun."

"What *smells*?"

As I took the boys out of their car seats, I told Marie part of what happened. I left out the mad dash to the gate by The Assassin. I just told her I had to fish out the bag, so to speak, and fell. She checked out the bag; it must have been OK, she didn't say anything.

Both boys ran to their mother. She held them, and I think, checked them out, too. OK again, I guess. I told Marie I was going to head out. She thanked me again. I gave her a kiss and started to walk away.

"Boys, give your Uncle Peter a kiss goodbye. Go on."

Chuckles clung to his mother's leg, looking around at me. He smiled and blew me a kiss.

The Assassin, though, ran to me, grabbing my leg. I picked him up, and looked him in the eye. He leaned forward, kissed me on the cheek, and then clutched my neck with his thin little arms.

"Don't go. Stay wid me."

"Jeez, you must rate. He doesn't even give me a kiss half the time," Marie said.

"Stay. Peez?" he whispered in my ear as he squeezed tight. He buried his head in my shoulder. I could feel his heart beat. My throat clutched. I swallowed, hard.

"I'll be back. I promise." I held him close. "I'll be back... Michael."

Chapter 15

The rest of the weekend passed less eventfully. I stopped at the video store on my way home and rented a few of the newest releases, and a couple of my old stand-bys. *Die Hard. Hoosiers*. Can't see those enough.

I also stopped at the vegetable market near my house. They had the freshest produce I'd found yet in town and a small butcher shop. It was run by a Korean family. Mother at the register; father behind the meat counter; uncle stocking the fruit and vegetables; daughter around to translate. I smiled and nodded hello. I stocked up on fruit, all kinds. I never used to eat the stuff, but since rehab, I couldn't get enough. I picked up some vegetables, too, some red peppers, mushrooms, onions, and a big head of garlic. I grabbed a container of bean sprouts, and ladled out two cakes of tofu from the barrel they were floating in. I nodded to the father and had him package up a couple of pounds of chicken cutlets.

I spent the evening alone. I was tempted to go to a meeting at the church, but I got involved making a stir fry for myself. While I chopped, sliced and seasoned the chicken, peppers, onions and mushrooms, I was moved by a memory of Patricia and me, in our old kitchen. She must have been about six or seven years old. I remembered Lorraine had to go away for a weekend somewhere—I couldn't recall where or why. I did remember having to watch Patricia for the weekend, all on my own. I guess no relative or babysitter was available. I remembered being angry with Lorraine, probably because I couldn't go into work if I was watching the kid , or maybe because I really had no idea what to do with her.

As I heated the oil for my dinner, I remembered Patricia in a little pink apron. We made cupcakes from a box mix. I remembered being amazed that she could measure out the ingredients, even cracked the eggs herself. I remembered laughing. I even remembered I didn't drink that entire weekend. It was glimpses of moments like that, messing around in the kitchen with her, that pained me with the realization of what I had thrown away. It made me wish even more I could somehow reconnect with Patricia, and maybe not miss all the days yet to come.

I finished preparing the stir fry, laid it over some brown rice and tasted it. Not bad. And there was enough to have for lunch tomorrow, too. Always a plus.

I called my sponsor. We spoke for about an hour. I filled him in on everything. We spoke at length about Carolyn. I told him I didn't know if I was ready for the relationship game. I told him also that I thought maybe the law wasn't the right profession for me. It felt strange hearing the words out loud. The talk helped calm me down.

I plopped on the couch, fed and a bit less anxious. A Robin Williams' comedy played in the background as I nodded off.

Sunday came and went without much fuss. I woke up early; the day was going to be beautiful and I wanted some air. I made myself a big salad. I took the leftover stir fry and mixed it, cold, with some arugula. The stir fry was already seasoned, and wet, so I didn't need any dressing.

I didn't want to be stuck in the apartment. I headed down to the beach with my headphones, some Jimmy Buffett, the latest murder mystery by Hallie Ephron, the Sunday Times, and a soft cooler filled with ice, bottles of water, fruit and my salad. I spent the day there. I ran. I walked. I slept in the sun. I thought a lot about the notary. A lot about my daughter. A lot about Carolyn. I came home, showered again, then took in an AA meeting. It was a full day.

*****

I set my alarm for early Monday morning, very early. It was going to be a long day. I started off by unsuccessfully meditating on the deck; the notary kept pounding and stirring, leaving me more anxious when I stood up than I had been when I sat down. I burned through a 3 mile run, at way too fast a pace. I felt like running more, but I had things to do.

I got to the office well before 7. I made the coffee and then settled in to work. I finished up the appellate brief for Ben Simmons and mailed copies off to the Court and the D.A. Even though I didn't have to, I sent a copy, with a personal letter, to Simmons. I told him I didn't hold out much hope, but I wished him luck in any event.

I had a deposition to do in the morning for Joel, then a Court conference at 2 for Barnaby. I had arranged for Ike and Tina to come in early, so we could go over their work, and plan out their next assignments. They arrived at a quarter to 8. As they came into my office, my telephone rang. I waved them into the seats across from me, and I picked up the phone. It was Phil.

"I figured you'd be in, you always was the early bird, Petey."

"Morning, Phil. How's it going?"

"Pretty good for me. Not so good for your lady client."

"What'd you find?" My students made motions to leave; I nodded them back down into their chairs.

"Well, first, no Derek Rogers ever graduated from Notre Dame. That's a fact. I'm ninety percent sure he never went there, just like I predicted. He ain't listed on any gymnastics team for the last twenty years, either. So, the All-American bull shit was just bull shit, if you know what I mean."

"Derek Rogers isn't listed with any of the national fitness organizations. I called around to some guys I know. Connected deep in Hollywood. They ain't never heard of him, and if these guys ain't never heard of him, he just ain't been around. Period."

"Anything else?"

"Yeah. He's got no driver's license. No listed phone. And unless he's the only freakin' guy in the free world that ain't got a credit card, or a car loan, or something, his name ain't Derek Rogers, 'cause no Derek Rogers matching his age and description has a credit history. Not bad credit. Not good credit. None. Nada. As in nada freakin' thing."

"So, what do you figure?"

"Seriously, Petey? Sounds like a scam. This guy's got a history he's hidin'. Your client a nice kid?"

"Yeah, she is."

"Then tell her to stay clear. This can only be bad."

"Thanks, Phil. Send a bill. If I need anything more, I'll let you know."

"Anytime, Petey. You need anything, you call. You needa talk, you call me, 24/7, *capisce*?"

"Thanks, Phil. I will. Thanks for everything."

I filled my students in on what had just happened, how Phil found the things he did, why I wanted it done. We went through their work, and talked, until I had to leave at 9:30.

As I was walking to my car, Carolyn came running out of the building. "Wait!"

I turned. "What's up?"

"Listen, I got some news Sunday from the EMS workers on Sophie's case. I wanted to call you, but I didn't have your number. And you're not listed, either, how come?"

"Um, Joel got the phone. He ordered it unlisted; I just never changed it. What did the EMS guys say?"

She was beaming. "They remembered where the ladder was. When they got there, Sophie was laying on the ground next to the ladder. As they were leaving, they saw the doctor putting it back up. One of them remembers saying that they were probably going to have to come back later to scrape up the doctor when the ladder fell again! You were right! Thank you!" And she hugged me.

I kept my hands at my sides. I didn't know what to do.

She stepped away. "I didn't tell you before, but I met with Sophie when I first got the case. She is *such* a dear. She reminds me of my grandmother. I wanted so much to help her, I was just so frustrated. You saved the day. Thank you *so* much."

"Not a problem. You would have found it anyway."

"No, I wouldn't have. And thanks for Saturday, too. Kyle never gets to horse around with a guy like that. His father isn't.... well, Kyle had a great time. Thank you."

"Well, I had a good time, too, all things considered. I've got to go. I'll talk to you about Sophie later." I gave her my home telephone number, just in case, I told her. She didn't offer me hers. I guess that was a sign. I'm sure the financial analyst had it. She just walked away, half-turning at one point to call out "Anyway, we had fun Saturday. Thanks again, Jacques Cousteau. Happy swimming!"

*****

The morning deposition ran late, uneventful, but late. I went straight to the Court conference without going back to my office, so by the time I got back, around 4 o'clock, Henry Robinson had been sitting there a while. Rita had been fluttering over him, but Henry didn't seem to have minded the wait.

Back in my office, Henry declined a chair. I apologized for keeping him waiting; I didn't know he was coming.

"No problem. I just sat out there, read some magazines. Watched the comings and goings. Lots of young people here, reminds me a lot of Mary's office, in the old days, anyway. This package is for you. Mary made it clear I had to personally deliver it."

"Want a receipt?" I asked with a half-smile.

"Probably should get one, but that's OK." Henry smiled back. "Mary said everything you asked for is there. She said don't worry, she didn't have any problem getting it. She said she added a couple of things that might help you, too."

"Thanks so much, Henry. And thank Mary for me, too."

"You can thank her yourself, at church, thank you very much."

After Henry left, I put the large manila envelope he had given me aside. I checked my mail; there was a check from Barnaby's. The rest was junk. The telephone messages included a call from my sister; a call from Marcia requesting the status; and a call from Gartner confirming our appointment the next day for the polygraph, although he was discreet enough to just say "appointment" without the description.

I was just about to open the manila envelope when Rita came over the intercom. She sounded concerned. There was a man with papers here to see me. I came out to the lobby and accepted service of the law suit the title insurance company had started against me, among others. So now I was being sued, too. I skipped to the end, even though I know it doesn't mean anything; yep, I was being sued for $13,400,000. Plus punitive damages. I thanked the process server. After all, it's just his job. And I have certainly sent my fair share of process servers out to spoil people's days. I winked at Rita; she didn't react at all. I folded the papers and returned to my office.

I reviewed the civil complaint. It pretty much mirrored the Grievance complaint, except it had one extra nugget of information– they were alleging that I represented the borrower, Houston Mesquite Holdings, Inc., at the actual closing of the loan. Which means they have witnesses who would claim I was physically present when the loan papers were signed.

Of all the guns being pointed at my head, this civil suit bothered me least. I was most distressed by the cops, obviously. I was concerned about the Grievance Committee, but not really as much as I thought I would be. The thought of simply turning in my license still seemed appealing.

As upset as I was opening the letter and complaint, the truth is, I was barely using my license now. There were a lot of other things I could do, besides being a lawyer, given what I was currently earning. I could, for instance, fold towels at Target. I wasn't concerned about the public or professional embarrassment disbarment would cause; other than Joel and my three students, few attorneys knew I was still alive, and I had already embarrassed myself beyond redemption with everyone else.

I wasn't concerned about the law suit, at all. Even if they got a judgment against me, what could they collect? I had nothing left. Freedom's just another word for nothing left to lose, as the song goes. As far as the civil suit was concerned, I was a free man.

I called my sister, Marie. She thanked me again. Apparently the boys had a great time; they couldn't stop talking about it. Would I come to dinner this Sunday? I said I would be happy to.

I called Marcia, and asked her to come in to see me. She wouldn't. She wanted to move on this, *now*. I always hate to tell clients bad news over the phone. I think it's too impersonal and I have found that people are much more likely to be belligerent and argumentative on the phone. Something about being face-to-face seems to calm most people. But Marcia wouldn't let go. So I filled her in on Phil's report. I gave it to her straight. There was silence for quite a bit, then a clearly choked-up Marcia said thank you, please send me a bill. I would, but it wouldn't be one I'd send with glee.

It was just about 5 o'clock. I left a message on Gartner's machine that I'd meet him in the morning, at 11.

Once again, I started to look at Mary's envelope when I was interrupted, this time by a knock on the door. The knock was followed by the entrance of Joel, Carolyn and Mickey and Minnie. They knew my office; they brought extra chairs with them so they could all sit.

"I hope you kids won't be disappointed, but I'm not buying Girl Scout cookies this year."

They smiled; maybe you would call it forced.

They all looked at Joel. He looked at me.

"Listen buddy, we've been talking. Wait until I finish before you say anything, OK?"

"OK."

"First of all, I can't tell you how pleased we are with the work you've been doing with these three. It's been a huge help. We're very happy."

I waited. I know when I'm being conned. I had only worked with these guys a few days, way too early for enough results to make anyone happy. Joel was softening me up for something.

"We know you've got this thing going on. I know Carolyn went with you to the handwriting analyst. I know you've got the polygraph tomorrow. I know you just got served, I assume with a civil suit. And I know you have the grievance going, too. That's a lot for anyone's plate. So here's what we're going to do. Carolyn, Mindy and Brian are now assigned to you. Use them to draft pleadings, do research, whatever. I don't want any arguments on this. I saw Henry Robinson sitting outside. Unless Mary's finally decided to divorce him, I figure he's running information for you. Use these three, and Phil. Do what you have to do."

He looked me dead in the eye. "I want you coming out of the other side of this whole and healthy. Understand?"

I started to protest, but it was useless. I tried to remember the last argument I had won with *anyone*. We finally agreed that everybody would keep time records so that I could reimburse the firm. This way I salvaged some respect. Joel understood, and agreed. And then he left me to my team.

I asked them to assemble in Conference Room C. I wanted to review Mary's material before I went any further. They had just left, and I had just opened the envelope, when there was another knock on the door. Maybe the envelope was magic, and called people to me whenever I opened the flap.

This time it was Phil Ruggierio.

"Petey, glad you're still here. I had to see a coupla guys here about a trial they got next week. Figured I'd stick my head in and give you this, y'know, two birds with one stone kinda thing." He gave me his written report on The Amazing Derek.

"You got a bill for me in here?" I asked, waving the envelope with the report.

"Nah, Levine said add it to the monthly. You guys settle up, I ain't getting involved." He smiled, and then he dropped his voice and put on his tough guy face. "Unless I don't get paid, in which case I will get very freakin' involved."

I smiled. A thought crossed my mind.

"Phil, you got a minute? Can you sit in on a meeting with me in Conference C– it's about something that's going on with me."

"Absolutely. You want me to wait in there?"

"Yeah. There's a couple of Joel's new attorneys in there, they'll be working with me. I'll be in in five."

"Take your time. I'll regale them with my success stories. Never forget, the new attorney today is the freakin' partner tomorrow, *capisce*?"

Phil left, and I finally got to look at what Henry had brought me. The first thing I pulled out was a computer generated report. It had on it the names of every employee of O'Reilly, McManus for the last 10 years. The list was alphabetical. In the columns next to each employee's name was the date of hiring; the date of termination; a code to indicate whether the person was an attorney, paralegal, clerk, secretary or other; and the person's date of birth.

I did a fast estimate; there were over five hundred names on the list.

Mary had also enclosed a photocopy of the firm's collection of newspaper clippings featuring the firm and its clients, and copies of the firm's "face books" for the last four or five years. O'Reilly, McManus printed a firm brochure. It described the firm, its history, significant cases and deals, that sort of thing. It also had a photograph and brief biography on each attorney. The brochure was edited and reprinted occasionally, to keep it current. Mary had accumulated a dozen or so. It wasn't a complete set, but there was probably a lot of repetition, anyway. I opened a brochure from four years ago; there was my smiling face, and a list of recent accomplishments. My biography sounded impressive. I looked at the most recent brochure. I wasn't in it. No surprise.

Lastly, Mary had written, in her neat, clear style, the location at Island Storage of the two boxes containing the remnants of my O'Reilly, McManus office.

I took the packet Mary had sent, along with the Grievance material, and the new law suit, and brought it down to the conference room. Carolyn already knew a lot about what was going on, but Phil and the Captain and Tenille didn't. So I started off with a monologue to bring them current. Except for a couple of "Oh, my's" from Mindy and couple of "You're freakin' kiddin' me's" from Phil, my story wasn't interrupted.

"So. Since Joel has assigned you as my team, what do you think? What should we do next?"

Phil spoke first. "Ya gotta lay out the story, like on a blackboard. ID everybody that was involved. Ya know ya got the guy who forged Brownstein's signatures, the guy who forged you, this guy Harris Mathews, if he even freakin' exists, pardon my French." He ticked these off on his fingers; I saw Mindy taking down notes.

"Ya got the guy who impersonated you at the closin', which has got to be one freakin' ugly guy, by the way. This ficacta Houston Mesquite, who's behind it? When was it formed, where, all that shit, pardon my French. They could all be one guy, but ya gotta look."

Carolyn spoke up. "Why did they pick on Brownstein? Where did they get the information on the properties?"

"Who handled the loan application? Who represented the bank at the closing? Was there a loan officer? Who'd they speak to or meet with?" This came from Brian. He appeared embarrassed at having spoken out loud. He shrugged. "I was mortgage broker before law school. Somebody had to appraise these properties. Did they do an on-sight? If they did, they probably met with somebody."

"And who had access to your stamp?" This was from Mindy.

"And where did all that freakin' money go, pardon my French?"

Carolyn looked intense. "I understand why they would forge the first deed. But why forge two?"

Brian answered. "They may have found that they didn't have enough collateral for the loan they wanted. To secure 13 million, they would have needed properties totaling at least $20 million. Maybe the first one wasn't valuable enough."

"OK then," Carolyn continued. "They deed the properties to themselves. Why mortgage them? Why not sell them?"

Brian again. "Mortgaging is faster, especially if you have all your paper work in line, and the buildings appraise out."

I chimed in. "Besides, there's something else going on here. This isn't a simple scam and run. According to the civil suit, payments were made on the loan for almost a year."

Phil laughed. "That's like somebody stealin' your freakin' car and makin' the payments for you!"

I laughed, too. "Carolyn, you see a lot of those kinds of thieves in the Bronx?"

She wasn't amused. "I still don't get it. Why did they deed the properties back to Brownstein?"

We all sat silent for a while.

Mindy asked, "Would the deed back to Brownstein cut the mortgage out? I mean, would a new owner have to pay the mortgage off if Brownstein sold?"

Brian answered, "No, the mortgage wouldn't be cut off. It would stay with the land. It would still be valid against any new owner, if it was a legitimate mortgage."

A thought crossed my head. "Brian, if somebody owns property with no mortgage on it, where do the tax bills go?"

Brian didn't hesitate. "Directly to the owner."

"And when are the taxes due?"

"Four times a year. The Town and County are due July 1 and January 1. The school taxes are due the first day of October and April. The bills go out a month or so before, if I remember correctly."

"Makes sense. So since the properties were transferred mid-June, if they weren't deeded back to Sy, the first he would have known something was wrong, would have been around September when he didn't get a tax bill, right?"

Mindy jumped in. "So, because the property was deeded back to Brownstein, the tax bills would keep going to Brownstein, without interruption."

I nodded. "If Houston Mesquite had kept up the payments, nobody would have known about this fraud, until Sy went to sell or mortgage one of his properties, something he didn't do, ever."

"Even if Houston Mesquite missed a payment or two, Brownstein wouldn't have known about it," said Brian. "The default letters would have gone to Houston Mesquite, not Brownstein."

"So the first Brownstein would have known something was wrong was when his tenants got served with their copies of the foreclosure action," I said.

We came to a consensus that the reason for the deeding back, and the payments, was to delay the discovery of the fraud. But why? And if it was so important that nobody discover the fraud, why did Houston Mesquite stop paying? As Brian pointed out, once Houston Mesquite stopped paying, the bank must have sent them default notices, and then turned the loan over to their attorneys, who sent more default notices. Sooner or later, though, it was inevitable that the lawyers would start the foreclosure suit, which required a full search of the title, which would immediately show that Brownstein owned the property, and the fraud would be discovered.

We were pretty sure we now knew what had happened. Now we needed to know who did it, and why.

We made a list of our investigation targets. Brian and Mindy took Mary's list. They figured somebody had to know something about deeds and real estate to pull this off so they were going to start with the attorneys, see who was around, who was practicing where. If they had no luck, they were going to move to the paralegals, then the secretaries.

Carolyn was going to come with me to the polygraph, and help me make contact with the title company's attorneys. Eventually, through discovery in the civil case, they would have to answer a lot of questions; maybe we could get them to answer a few now. She was also going to research Houston Mesquite.

Phil was going to start to nose around about the money and Brownstein and Harris Mathews, see what he could find. I said I was going to make a few calls, too.

Whoever did this had to know something about me and the way Sy Brownstein worked. I slipped a note to Phil. "Check out Greg Connolly." Phil looked at me and nodded.

Then Phil said he'd reach out about the dead guy, Tariq Singh, see what he could find out from the cops and "other sources". The reference to death got the room quiet. Phil cleared his throat, and said "Petey, I want to be very clear about somethin'. You've gotten yourself dragged into a freakin' mess here. I know you want to fight your way out of it, but remember somethin'. We're talkin' big bucks, and at least one dead body. You-- and you guys, too-- gotta understand– this could be dangerous. I mean it. If somethin' different happens, if you think your bein' followed, if somebody says somethin' to you that's off, don't be a hero. Call 911, call me. Just be careful. All of you."

I thanked him and told the other three that I didn't want them doing anything that would endanger them. My suggestion that they could withdraw was met with brisk "no ways" from all three.

We broke for the day. Despite Phil's warning, or maybe because of it, my team seemed excited. I felt better. I always liked playing offense better than playing defense. I felt like we were finally on the attack.

Chapter 16

Tuesday morning brought with it a monsoon. The rain was so heavy, the clouds so thick, I thought it was still night as I drove to the office. I had canceled my early morning run; I don't mind running in the rain, in fact, I think it's kind of fun. But this was scary outside, thunder and lightning and pounding, driving rain. I figured I'd skip the run and grab a salad; that should balance it out.

Brian and Mindy had been busy, late into the night. The way they seized onto their assignment reminded me of someone. They were a bit bleary eyed as we went over their real work. I could tell they were both itching to get back to Mary's list. I reminded them that even though they had Joel's blessing, they had to keep up with their regular work. The firm had several partners. It made no sense pissing off a majority of them by neglecting work, especially work assigned by their actual bosses.

I put an hour or so into another appeal. It was straightforward stuff; the only basis for the appeal was a weak argument centering around whether the defendant's counsel did a competent job; it was called the "ineffective counsel" appeal. It virtually always fails. It would fail here. The attorney hadn't been Clarence Darrow, but he hadn't fallen asleep at the defense table, either. The law doesn't expect every attorney to be perfect in every case. Like every other profession, the law has its share of great, good, fair and poor practitioners, probably in equal proportions. The one who had tried this case was likely fair, though he might have been a good one having a fair week. The prosecution's case was strong. It would have taken a great trial attorney, having a great week, combined with some serious bribery to win this one. I would do my best, but I was more hopeful about Ben Simmons' appeal, and I was highly doubtful with that one.

Before I left, I put a couple of calls out to old acquaintances in the real estate business. I wanted a handle on how Sy Brownstein was doing, if there were any rumors, things like that. I left detailed messages on a half a dozen voice mails. I guess the monsoon was keeping people at home today. I wasn't sure if any of them were still talking to me, but I figured I had nothing to lose by calling. I seemed to recall peeing in one guy's pool during his annual backyard luau. That is, peeing into the pool from the second story balcony. A call back from him might be a long shot, but hey, you never know.

Carolyn joined me on the drive to meet John Gartner and the polygrapher. We exchanged pleasantries, but not much more. She seemed tense. I was tempted to ask her how the concert with Steve had been, but I really didn't want to open up that door. I had to work on squelching whatever feelings I had, or thought I was having. What if she said she had a great time? Would that depress me? What if she had a lousy time? Would that get me unreasonably excited? I had spent the last year keeping my life simple, avoiding all ties, emotionally, socially, professionally, waiting until I could handle them. Especially now, it made no sense to open myself up for disappointment, or worse. I had enough on my plate.

The polygrapher was named Judith Drummond. She was a professor at the State University at Farmingdale, with a doctorate and credentials that were as long as the list of people I had pissed off. John Gartner was already there; he introduced us.

Judith Drummond was, like so many people in these ancillary fields of law, a former police officer. She had been trained as a polygrapher by the police department; she stayed on the force until she got her masters, and this teaching job. The doctorate in criminal science wasn't necessary for her side business as an expert polygrapher, but it didn't hurt, obviously. Her career on both sides of the fence, and a reputation as a straight shooter, gave her credence with both defense attorneys and the DA's. Her credibility was her golden ticket;

she was going to call it as she saw it, and she let me know that up-front. It was OK with me. Carolyn looked a bit more nervous. Something was wrong, but I didn't have the time right now to inquire. Maybe on the ride back to the office.

Dr. Drummond asked me how much I knew about polygraphing. I knew a bit; OK, I knew a lot. But I told her, not much. I wanted to see if her spiel and my information jived. My own lie detector, of sorts.

Drummond launched into an explanation of the machine and the process. It probably was the same one she gave to juries.

"Polygraphing is often called lie detecting. Of course, that's not accurate. Let me tell you right away, the polygraph is not perfect. However, used correctly, it is a very accurate tool. But the test has to be performed correctly."

She walked us over to a small, dimly lit room. In it was a small table, and two comfortable-looking desk chairs. On the table was the lie detector.

"This is the polygraph machine. It is not a lie detector." Did she read minds, too?

"A polygraph is actually made up of a few separate instruments, which are set to simultaneously record their findings. This machine measures changes in your blood pressure, your pulse, and your respiration, in response to very specific questions. Most polygraphs do these tests. This particular model also tests changes in your skin's electroconductivity, which are caused by sweating. Increased sweating is often a response to fear. The more you sweat, the more it interferes with the current running along your skin's surface. In fact, all of the body functions measured by the polygraph are related to the built-in "fight or flight" response humans feel when faced with an attack. When you are posed a question to which you have to lie, your body will automatically sense this internal crisis, and will, in most people, trigger changes in blood pressure, breathing, pulse, etcetera."

Carolyn interrupted. "Can't some people beat the machine?"

"Well, we don't like that phrase, but yes, the machine has some difficulty with certain people. That would be people who react very unusually to emotional distress, or who are in considerable physical discomfort or pain, or people who are pathological liars." She smiled. "Despite what you may have heard in the popular media, these populations are extremely small, almost statistically insignificant."

"So why aren't the results accepted in Court?" Carolyn asked.

"Because the tests have some built in variables. The polygrapher must be well trained, and the test administered under stringent conditions. It is a sensitive test."

Carolyn kept playing student. "What kind of conditions?"

"Well, there are several. The room should be quiet and comfortable. It should be plain, without much stimulation. The subject should be somewhat at ease. The questions must be written in advance and be without any ambiguity. The questions must not confuse the subject, in fact, the subject should know the questions in advance. Too much pre-test questioning, however, can be harmful. People tend to over think the questions, setting up ambiguities in their own minds which clouds their responses."

"What exactly is all this stuff? I've sent people for lie detect- um, polygraphs, but I've never actually seen one performed." Carolyn pointed towards the jumble of wires, boxes and the apparatus on the table.

Dr. Drummond moved fully into the room; we all followed. I looked around. The walls were painted a pale blue, with white trim. Nothing on the walls. No other furniture. There was a mirror on the back wall. I figured it was a two-way, to let people observe. I didn't bring it up.

Dr. Drummond held up each piece of equipment as she spoke. "This is called the pneumograph tube. It is fitted around the chest, to help measure breathing, or respiration. This is a simple blood-pressure cuff. It obviously measure changes in blood pressure and pulse rate. These wires, here, attach, painlessly I assure you, to the subject's fingers and hands. They measure electroconductivity. All of these instruments measure changes simultaneously and in minute detail. They transmit their measurements to this unit, which records the responses on this moving graph paper. I will mark directly on the paper the number of each question I ask. I will then interpret the responses."

"True or false?" Carolyn asked.

"It's a little more complicated. Essentially I will conclude either that the subject's responses were significant for truth, significant for falsity, or inconclusive."

"I always wondered about that. How do you get an inconclusive finding? I had a few in the Bronx."

"Sometimes it's because the questions aren't tailored tightly enough. Sometimes it's because there are hidden factors at play. For instance, let's say a subject presents himself for questioning about a robbery at a liquor store. He may not, in fact, have robbed that liquor store on the day in question. But, suppose, he had *planned* to rob it. Or suppose he robbed a different store around the same time. If we don't pull out those facts, and ask those questions separately, the subject may lump all of that in his response. It would show that he wasn't necessarily lying, but he wasn't necessarily telling the truth."

Drummond turned to me. "That's why before your attorney and I complete the questionnaire, he must know everything. Do not hide anything from him. Do not tell me; I am not protected by the attorney-client privilege. But if you tell Mr. Gartner, we can make sure the questions are crisp and clear. Understood?" Understood.

John, Carolyn and I went over the facts again. Other than my concern that I may have notarized Sy's signature at some time in the past, I couldn't see any other conflicts. John and Carolyn met with Drummond for a while. They shuttled back and forth to me. Drummond wanted to keep the questioning short; John and Carolyn wanted to make sure the DA would be satisfied that nothing was left out. When they were ready, Drummond led me alone into the room. I assumed John and Carolyn were going to watch from the two-way mirror. The room was probably miked for sound, too, so they could hear us.

Drummond went over the questions with me, with the machine off. She asked me a number of questions about my health, what I had eaten that day, drugs, alcohol, that sort of thing. She had me initial the responses, and sign some release forms. Then she attached me to the polygraph, talking me through it the whole time while putting the tube around my chest, the cuff on my left arm, the electrodes on my hands. I felt myself perspiring a bit. I tried to control my breathing. I was nervous, no question about it.

She gave me some final instructions and then told me she was turning on the machine. She started.

"Is your name Peter De Stio?"

"Yes."

"Are you on any medication or under the influence of any drug or alcohol this morning?"

"No."

"Are you female?"

"Yes."

"Are you a licensed attorney?"

"Yes." For now.

"Have you ever met anyone calling himself Harris Mathews?"

"No."

"Are you sitting in a chair?"

"Yes."

"Did you represent anyone in a loan transaction involving Island Savings Bank last June?"

"No."

"Are you forty years old?"

"Yes"

"Did you notarize a signature purporting to be Sy Brownstein's last June?"

"No."

"Did you participate, in any way, in a transaction last June in which properties were deeded and a mortgage obtained in the sum of $13,400,000?"

"No."

"Do you know anyone who did participate in that transaction?"

"No."

"Is my shirt blue?"

"Yes"

"Did you receive any money from a loan obtained last June by Houston Mesquite Holdings, Ltd. from Island Savings?"

"No."

She ended the questioning and shut the machine off.

She asked me to wait outside. I exited the room in time to see Carolyn and John coming around from the two-way mirror perch.

"Female, huh?" John asked me with a smile.

"I was directed to lie on that one, you know that. She wanted a read on how I responded when I lied."

"Sure, she did. I didn't hear those directions, did you, Carolyn?"

Carolyn didn't respond. She wasn't paying attention. She leaned against the wall and was staring out the window. Her right shoe dangled from her toes as she wiggled her foot back and forth.

We waited. It was probably only a few minutes, but it seemed a lifetime. Finally Dr. Drummond emerged.

"As far as I can see, within a reasonable degree of certainty, you, sir, are telling the truth."

With that, Carolyn rushed from the room.

*****

The ride back to the office was quiet, and, since I was driving, not one other driver gave us the finger. Carolyn was subdued. She had come back to the room to say goodbye to Professor Drummond, but had said little since, other than that she didn't want to talk about it.

As we approached the office, I lowered the music. All you could hear was the beat of the windshield wipers, and the pelting of the rain on the tin of the car, and the swoosh of the water beneath the tires.

I broke the human silence. "Back there, I felt like I was waiting for a jury to come back with a verdict. Same butterflies, you know?"

She didn't respond.

"There were some cases I thought I was going to throw up, right at the table, waiting for the verdict to be read." I glanced over.

Nothing.

I tried again. "How about you?"

We drove in silence for a while. We reached the office parking lot. I found a spot pulled in, and shut the car off. The rain seemed louder. I turned to her.

"Hey. Listen. Tell me what's going on, please? Did I say something wrong? Did I not say something I was supposed to? What?"

She looked at her lap. "I've tried murder cases. I've tried rape cases. I tried a guy for molesting his own son. I don't know. I don't know why. But I was never as nervous as I was waiting for Drummond to give the results."

She looked out the window. "I think the thing that upset me the most was that until she came out, I really wasn't sure if you were guilty or not. I think I'm ...relieved. I think I'm feeling guilty, too, for not believing you, totally."

We sat a bit. Finally, I opened my door. I turned to her as I was climbing out.

"That's OK. I wasn't so sure about myself, at the beginning. Let's go see what Popeye and Olive Oil have found for us."

What they had found was very interesting. My two eager beavers had used the New York State Court system website, the lawyer's telephone diary, telephone calls to firms, and assorted other sources on the Internet to locate the lawyers on Mary's list.

They handed me a series of lists. The first list was of attorneys still with O'Reilly, McManus. The second list was of attorneys who had died before the forgeries. The third list was of attorneys who were now with other firms, or who had retired, or who were out on their own.

The fourth list intrigued me the most. It had three names on it. The three attorneys they couldn't find, anywhere, yet. Charles Johnson, Vincent Helms and Andrea Schneider.

We talked it out.

We all agreed the two dead guys probably didn't reach out from the grave to use my stamp. My team wanted to rule out anyone still with O'Reilly, McManus, on the grounds that no one would be so stupid as to participate in a multi-million dollar fraud and use a notary stamp that could be traced back to the firm. I wasn't so sure. I had treated a lot of the people there pretty badly. Revenge is a powerful force. I agreed, though, that the list of attorneys who had gone elsewhere seemed more promising, especially any of the attorneys who had spent time in the real estate division. But the most curious, to all of us, was the list of three missing attorneys. Johnson, Helms and Schneider. Where were they?

We each grabbed an O'Reilly, McManus firm brochure and started looking for their bios. Brian started tapping on his laptop.

We found Johnson's information first. He had been in the real estate division, something that immediately sent up flares. Carolyn read out his bio. Harvard, Yale Law. Blue blood all the way. I remembered him well. He had been with the firm when I joined and was there when I left.

The good news, as far as our search went, was that he didn't like me. I made a drunken pass at his daughter at a company function. When she tried to push past me, I lost my balance and drenched his wife with my martini. So we had a possible motive for him wanting to hurt me.

The bad news was he was about 80 years old when I joined the firm and not only did he come from money, his first wife (deceased) was not-so-distantly related to old railroad money, and his second wife, she of the ruined Versace, was a trust fund baby in her own right. I signaled for the group to move on– I told them that Phil would probably find Johnson fairly easily, and that he'd either be at a villa in Tuscany or deceased.

Carolyn suggested we rule out Andrea Schneider. The handwriting didn't seem to be female, and, besides, whoever had forged the notaries had also passed themselves off as me at the mortgage closing. I agreed, trying to lighten up the mood of the room: "That would have to be one ugly young lady right there." We all agreed, though Mindy said she'd keep trying to track her down.

That left Vincent Helms. Mary's list had him joining the firm three years before I left; he terminated with the firm last June. The same month as the forgeries.

I called Phil. I left a message asking him to see what he could find on Vincent Helms, Charles Johnson and Andrea Schneider. I gave him the dates of birth from Mary's list, and a quick sketch of what we knew about each of them.

As I left the message, my team found Helm's picture in one of the firm brochures. I vaguely remembered him. Little guy, blond, thin. Narrow head, almost like a bird. He wasn't a litigator, and I didn't remember working with him, at all. I culled through the brochures until I found the first brochure he appeared in. He must have just joined the firm when it was printed. Like many attorneys new to the firm, his bio was short.

VINCENT HELMS: Vincent joins the mergers and acquisitions department after a successful stint at Kremer, Ludley and Finch. He is a graduate of the University of Wisconsin, where he received his B.A. in mathematics, and the Harvard University School of Law. Vincent is single, and enjoys all kinds of sports.

The later brochures added the names of clients he had represented, and his deals. All corporate work, the buying and selling of businesses. Nothing about lending institutions, or real estate. Seemed like he might not have had the expertise to pull this off.

We started going through the names on the list of the attorneys who had left the firm, highlighting those who had worked in the real estate department. I wasn't sure. Something bothered me.

I took the laptop from Brian and started searching. While the others were talking among themselves, I found the website I was looking for. I scrolled through one screen, then another.

Bingo.

Kremer, Ludley and Finch, attorneys-at-law specialized in commercial real estate work. That's the firm where Helms had worked before he came to O'Reilly, McManus. That's where he could have learned about deeds and mortgages. And notaries.

Helms could be our guy. We agreed to put him on our "A" list.

I then told the group I had asked Phil to investigate Greg Connolly. I gave them a brief, but vivid, sketch of my relationship with him.

"But he's basically running the show over there, now," Carolyn said. "I interviewed with them before I took this job. Why would he get involved in something like this?"

"I don't know," I answered. "But I know he has revenge as a motive. He had access to my notary. And he manages all of Brownstein's files, always has.

Nobody knows more about how Sy runs his business, his holdings, the whole works. He knew my condition. Helms wouldn't have that kind of information. Connolly could be the guy. He goes on the "A" list with Helms."

They looked at me a bit skeptically, but Mindy dutifully wrote "Greg Connolly" under "Vincent Helms" on the blackboard. I stared at his name. It looked right. It felt right. I could see him stamping the deeds. I could see him smile. Revenge.

It had to be him.

Chapter 17

Tuesday's all-day rain gave way to a steam bath on Wednesday. I ran, early. The pavement was damp, the air already thick and heavy. Despite the soupy conditions, I felt like I had a lot of energy, real bounce in my step. I took the long route, the 8 miler. I rarely time myself but I knew my pace had been increasing. I was clearly in the best shape of my life. Physically.

I was feeling pretty well mentally, too. I liked the activity, the hunt. I wanted to find out what was going on. Not be a victim.

The tail end of my run took me past the Presbyterian Church. The gardens looked healthy and lush after the tropical rains. The sign had been changed. The new message was:

C H _ _ C H
What's Missing?

Cute.

My run was productive thinking time. Often it wasn't; I kind of blank out when I run. I never use headphones. I never found them comfortable. I just observe what I see as I go, very in the moment. I find I think better in the shower and in the car.

I got to the office around 8. My students would be with me soon. I put a call into John Gartner; he was supposed to meet with ADA Melendez at the DA's office around noon. I asked his voice mail to have him call me when he finished with her.

I put a call in to Mary Robinson, at her home. I caught her just before she was heading out the door. I thanked her again, and promised to come to her

Church a week from Sunday, which would be the day before Labor Day. Then I asked her for some more help. She said she would do what she could.

I had to respond to the Grievance Committee, in writing, before the hearing, which was now only 9 days away. I still hadn't called the retired judge, and now I pretty much decided that I wouldn't. I'd defend myself, if need be. I was 50-50 on whether I was going to contest the charges or just walk away. The only thing holding me back from resigning was that my team seemed pretty excited and they were getting me pumped up a bit. That, and I didn't want to give Connolly the satisfaction.

I met with Brian and Mindy, this time to actually do work for Joel's firm. Since they weren't admitted yet, they couldn't do depositions or trials. But I felt it would help them better understand the paperwork they were doing if they knew how to, and that they would be a better asset for the firm if they were ready to go as soon as they were sworn in. I had arranged for them both to sit in on a deposition, to observe other attorneys. I told one of Joel's partner, Ed, that they were ready, or would be by D-day. He seemed skeptical, but they were both assigned cases to attend. I worked with them as if they were going to conduct the depositions themselves. I went through the basics of depositions with them, outlining what they should look for, how to properly phrase a question, that sort of thing. I loaded them up with transcripts of similar cases, and sample question sheets. We practiced, with each of us taking turns role playing, with me throwing twists at them. We went for four hours. I have to admit I enjoyed it.

At the end of our session, I felt they were ready. Even though they weren't going to actually conduct the depositions, you could see they were excited. Doing a deposition is a big step towards actual trial work. You learn how to deal with other attorneys; you learn how to ask questions in proper form. You learn how to think and act like a trial lawyer. After doing dozens of depositions, you're much closer to being ready for actual in-court trial work, which is why they had joined Joel's firm.

Carolyn had poked her head in and interrupted us around 9. I asked her to do a couple of things on my case. She said she was off to cover a conference in

Court, but would take care of them before lunch.

After my tutoring session broke up, I went back to my office to see if Gartner had called in yet. He had not. Rita had left just one message, from an old client. I called him. He had heard through the grapevine that I was back practicing. He wanted to know if I would take over a case he had going against a former partner of his in the plumbing supply business he owned. He was unhappy with his current lawyer. I declined, but referred him to Joel, with my highest recommendation. I transferred him to Joel's secretary to set up an appointment. I had been getting more calls lately from old clients, with increasing frequency. I referred them all out. Keeping it simple, simple, simple. Except, of course, this notary business.

I checked my mail. Garbage.

While I waited for Gartner to call, I typed up a bill to Marcia and sent it off. I got a copy of Phil's invoice from Joel's billing clerk, and attached it. I also included my notes about the deal; I wanted her to know I took it seriously, even if I did have my suspicions about The Amazing Derek. I handwrote a note telling her how sorry I was, and asking her to call me when she got settled.

Still no call from Gartner.

I turned back to the Grievance Committee response. I had dictated the letter several times, in several different ways, in my head. Everything from an elegant, lengthy response filled with legal prose and precedent, to a simple fuck you, I quit.

I stared at the beige walls, which yet again failed to reveal any wisdom. Maybe I should paint them a more informative color. I watched my $5 Radio Shack clock tick off several minutes. I gazed at the computer screen for a bit.

Without consciously thinking, my fingers started tapping out a response. I settled on a short one paragraph letter in which I denied the charges completely.

There. I had decided. If they wanted to disbar me, or take any further action, they would have to hold a hearing, with witnesses and evidence. I wasn't going to walk away. Maybe I would keep practicing, maybe I wouldn't. But I was going to decide, not Connolly, not the Grievance Committee.

I finished the letter and checked with Rita. Still no call from Gartner.

Carolyn poked her head in, saying she was back from Court, and she had good news. She was in much better spirits today, feisty again. She told me about her conference, how well it had gone, how much Judge Harley seemed to like her. Her good news was that she had, at my request, contacted the attorneys for the title insurance company. They had agreed to a meeting, at their offices, on Friday, to discuss the case. Maybe we could get some more information out of them then.

I wanted an informal meeting. I had always told clients and attorneys who worked for me, never to discuss their case with anyone. I often said that I learned more about my case and my adversary's case, talking in the hallway, than I ever learned through formal, legal discovery. Too many attorneys, and their clients, liked to discuss the case on the phone, or standing around waiting for a Judge. They liked to tell you what your case's weak points were, to discuss strategy, to discuss their problems. It always amazed me. I learned early to be pleasant, and "chatty", but to be careful not to reveal anything. Let the other guy talk. "Loose lips sinks ships" applies in all walks of life. Many times I used information obtained in friendly banter, or hallway bluster, to shore up my case, or to torpedo the other guy in the courtroom. I only hoped the title company's attorneys were feeling talkative on Friday.

Finally, Gartner called, a bit after 1. He said he had good news, bad news and OK news. Which did I want first? I was in no mood for games–I just stayed quiet. John got the message.

"OK. First, Reid came back with the handwriting analysis. Split decision. The notaries on the deeds are inconclusive, he needs the originals. He thinks it could be a tracing, but he can't be sure. The good news is the notaries signed at the closing? Definitely not you. Brownstein's signatures on the deeds? Harris Mathews on the mortgages? Not you either."

He continued. "I gave Melendez the polygraph report and Reid's report. We talked for almost an hour. She's still not convinced. She said her handwriting expert's findings were "inconclusive" too, but blamed it on the fact that you didn't give them samples. She's going to think about it. She may want you to take a test with one of their polygraphers and she may want fresh signatures from you. Maybe not. She'll let me know next week. But you aren't going to be arrested. Not today, anyway."

As I listened, Carolyn was leaning forward in her chair, trying to read my face, trying to hear John. I probably should have put him on speaker phone, but I just couldn't. I thanked John profusely, hung up, and told Carolyn the news. She was pleased, but perplexed.

I reached into my desk drawer and pulled out my brown bag. I told Carolyn I was going to the Garden for lunch. She said she had never been there, and asked if she could join me. I paused a split second before saying most certainly. I don't think she caught my hesitation.

Before we left, I put a call in to Marcia. I was concerned for her and I told her answering machine exactly that, right after the beep.

Carolyn and I walked together to the Garden. We talked about Kyle, about how Carolyn's old friends from the Bronx DA's office had called her, how she was redecorating her living room, how her mother-in-law was starting to drive her crazy, how she got an invitation to an alumni dinner for Cornell, and she wasn't sure if she wanted to go, how she could never get her flowers to grow like this. God! Look at the colors, what kind of fertilizer do they use, how nice and peaceful the bench is. Actually, I didn't say too much of anything, at all.

We shared my bench, though it was a bit tight. I was starting to feel very uncomfortable sitting next to her, very ill at ease. She smelled nice. No, she smelled great. I had made a mashed tofu and bean sprouts salad, mixed with pickle relish. It didn't smell as nice.

Carolyn asked for a taste; she seemed to like it. Maybe she was just being polite. It couldn't have gone well with the roast beef and Swiss hero she was devouring. Talking, sharing my bench, sharing my food. Being this close to a woman, especially one I had admit to myself I was attracted to, was sending my senses into overload. I stood up and walked away, pretending to look at some low-growing plants across the path. I just had to move.

Carolyn seemed not to notice. She kept up both ends of the conversation. I let her. She was smart, and she was funny, and she was engaging. She made her search for the right wallpaper sound... interesting.

In rehab, they told us to be careful and aware of our emotional state at all times. The Buddhists call it being mindful. Being depressed or scared, like I was most of the time, was dangerous; it made you vulnerable to taking that first drink. But being happy and excited was dangerous, too. It made you let your guard down. I had successfully walled off most of my emotions, except maybe the depression, for the last year or so. Now they were starting to pop out again. This notary business. Marie and the kids. Carolyn. My increasing thoughts of my daughter Patricia. I felt like I was being sucked back into life. I hadn't handled life well, the first time. I had to beware.

We finished lunch. I had to fight the urge, several times, to reach out and take her hand as we walked, side by side, on the winding path out of the Garden, and back to the office. Safely alone at my desk, I confirmed a deposition for the morning. I made a few more calls, trying to get some more background information on Sy Brownstein. In my representation of him, years ago, I had come to know a bit about him, but not much. He held his cards pretty close to the vest. I knew one thing, though: he could be vindictive with people who crossed him.

One of the suits I had handled for him involved a boundary dispute. The facts were simple. Sy bought a large commercial office building. It had about 10 floors and was surrounded by a huge parking lot, with many more spaces than the building needed. Beyond the paved lot was another 30 or 40 feet of dirt and weeds. Just beyond the dirt, the next parcel was owned by an elderly couple who ran a small take-out deli, for years not much more than a counter.

A couple of years before Sy had purchased the large commercial building, the elderly couple had a fire, destroying most of their little building. Taking the insurance proceeds, and most of their life savings, they had rebuilt the building, only a little larger and a good deal nicer. Now they had a few tables where customers could sit and eat their sandwiches. Nothing fancy, but it made a big difference in their bottom-line. What they didn't realize, and neither, apparently, did their now-bankrupt builder, was that the building, instead of being set back at least 10 feet on the couples' property, was actually rebuilt four feet onto the property Sy would come to own. Which meant that 14 feet of this new building was illegal.

Sy had owned his building for a few years, when he suddenly hired us to make the couple tear the building down. Their attorney pleaded with us to let the building stand–they would pay rent. I had told Sy, why bother with this? You're never going to need the land, you can generate some income, and besides, they'll probably agree to feed you for life, too. He wouldn't budge. Faced with total financial ruin, the couple had no choice but to fight us. So we fought. Sy's final bill to O'Reilly, McManus was over $100,000.

We won. They were ruined. I didn't care. It was another victory for me and another large fee for my division of the firm. I'm not sure if Sy cared much either. I think he was in Florida the day the bulldozers knocked the couple's building down.

I never knew much about Sy's personal life or how his business worked. So I made more calls, reaching out to as many people in the industry as I could. Nobody had returned my earlier calls and of those that I reached, not too many people were willing to talk about Sy. Maybe they were afraid of crossing him. Or maybe they just didn't want to talk to me.

I reached a former associate of O'Reilly, McManus, an attorney fresh out of law school who had been assigned to Connolly, but who had really wanted to work for me. I knew he had worked on some of Sy's files; I thought he might be able to give me some insight. He was now a sole practitioner, according to the legal directory. He answered his own phone. When I told him who I was, his voice turned icy. Then I remembered—I had used this guy to feed me information about Connolly, what he was working on, which files he was having problems with. I had used that information against Connolly in partners' meetings. Connolly suspected he was my spy and not only fired him, but then proceeded to blackball him with every other firm around. He begged me to help him; I didn't return his calls. I had just used him and then walked away.

Our conversation was short. I didn't get another word in after my name. He was still cursing me out as he slammed the phone down.

I had better luck with my next call, a commercial insurance salesman who had insured a number of Sy's buildings. He was pretty chatty. I must not have screwed him, though salesmen have much more of a live-and-let-live attitude than most other people. They develop a pretty thick skin in their line of work, and, at the end of the day, a sale is a sale. You never know where your next lead is going to come from; you don't have to like the customer, just get his business. Apparently he no longer had Sy's business, so he was willing to tell me what he knew, and more importantly to me, he gave me his impressions of Sy and his company.

"The old man is a tough son of a bitch, no doubt. I didn't deal with him too much though. I mostly dealt with the sons. Every year, I had to pitch them, wine and dine, the whole deal. Didn't matter, though. They couldn't decide dick without the old man signing off."

"The boys? Typical. Winners of the sperm lottery, if you know what I mean. I worked with both of them. Neither one is too bright, both pretty arrogant. It's like they take abuse from the father, so they dish it out on the help, on guys like me. The older guy, David, is the smarter of the two, meaner, too. I only worked with him a couple of years before he took off for the coast. Him and the old man, they'd argue all the time. David thought he could run the operation better than Sy. He'd try to make decisions on his own—like once, he approved this package deal I set up, without clearing it with the old man. What a fight! I got blamed for it, like I was trying to sneak something passed Sy. In the end, though, the kid just took off."

"The younger one? Avi. Nicer guy, but still had that attitude like he deserved everything. A user. With David it was all business, but Avi liked to have a good time. Went to a bunch of colleges. Didn't fight with Sy, like David did, but Sy was on his ass all the time, anyway. Always thought Avi liked the work, he liked people better than Sy or David, but he eventually couldn't take it either. He left the company right about the time I lost the account. Say, you still have any connections there? I'd really like to make a proposal again this year."

I finished the afternoon by burying myself in the appeal. Unfortunately, I was having a hard time concentrating. I left the office early. I felt like a passenger in a small boat in rolling seas. I attended an AA meeting before dinner. Then another one after dinner. Better safe than sorry.

Chapter 18

I got to the office on Thursday, tired and cranky. I hadn't slept well, again. My morning run had been awful. I just never got loose, never felt right, at all.

I prepared for the morning's deposition and fooled around with the appeal a bit. My students arrived promptly at 8 and we reviewed their drafts and the day's tasks. I actually felt useful. These two were turning around their assignments like lightning. Any managing attorney with a real practice would have had a hard time keeping up with them.

I was just walking out the door, when into the lobby walked Henry. He barely greeted me. He just handed me a large manila envelope, turned and walked away with a grunt. I guess he wasn't happy that I had imposed on Mary again. I put the envelope in my briefcase, gave Henry a minute or two to clear the building, so we wouldn't have any awkward scenes in the parking lot, then headed off to the deposition.

The deposition was awkward in its own right. The opposing attorney had been in charge of the local bar association's holiday party the year I showed up drunk and made a scene. And the court reporter recording the testimony looked familiar and quietly hostile. I vaguely recalled having hit on her back in the day.

At a break, I called in to Rita for my messages. Phil had called. He wanted to meet me for lunch to go over what he had found so far. He named a restaurant and a time; I called his office and confirmed. Then I finished up the deposition, avoiding the urge to cut corners to make sure I got out of there on time. I needn't have worried; I made it with time to spare.

Phil's choice of restaurant's made me smile. Here was this Italian guy from Brooklyn. Where do we meet? At Bombay Garden, a great Indian restaurant in Garden City, tucked behind the Roosevelt Field Mall. Best thing about Long Island, next to the beaches, is the variety and quality of the food. I liked Indian food and Phil had picked a good one. Bombay Garden offers a lunch buffet that is simply wonderful.

Phil was already sitting at a corner table when I got there. We exchanged hellos and took off for the buffet. We both loaded up on tandoori chicken, a flavorful, but mild chicken cooked in a special oven, and a host of other, more flavorful Indian specialties. As I always do at restaurants where the food will be spicy, I asked the waiter for an extra glass of ice water. Phil, his mouth already full, nodded a "me, too" at the bus boy. We ate in relative quiet, shoveling in this excellent cuisine. "I get tired of freakin' macaroni all the time, ya know what I mean? Oh, sorry, I mean pasta. It'll always be macaroni to me, the yuppie bastards."

After we had loaded up our plates for the second time, we were intercepted as we reached our table.

"Phil!"

"Sanjay!" They exchanged hugs.

"Petey, this is Sanjay. He's the owner. Sanjay, Pete De Stio."

"A pleasure." We shook hands.

After asking about how are lunch was, Sanjay turned to Phil. "Have you brought me anything, my friend?" he asked in his sing-song Indian accent.

"Do you have anything for me?"

"But of course! Nothing but the best! Three whole bags, waiting for you out back. When you leave, I'll have them brought to your car."

"Fair enough," Phil smiled. He reached under the table and brought out a black plastic trash bag, maybe a quarter full. Sanjay took it, almost cradling it.

"I cannot thank you enough, my friend! So much!"

"It's prime shit, Sanjay. Took my boys a month, so don't waste it."

"Of course not. I'll leave you to your lunch. Peter," he said with a small bow, "A pleasure to meet you. Phil, I will see you next month at the meeting, no?"

"Of course."

Sanjay left us. I looked at Phil, waiting, but he had turned back to his food, eyes down. After our plates were half empty, he finally looked up at me. I raised my eyebrows in question form.

"Ah, Petey. How can I explain? I'm gonna tell you about this, but it's just between me and you. Only my wife knows about it and I don't want my balls broken, *capisce*?"

"You have my word."

"I gave Sanjay a bag of worm castings."

"What?"

"Worm shit. It's the best fertilizer there is. Black gold. I have, uhm, a worm compost bin. Sanjay gives me garbage, y'know vegetable peels, that kinda stuff. I get used coffee grinds from Starbucks. My boys love it. They eat, they make little worms and they poop. Nice life, huh?"

"What does Sanjay use it for?" I looked with horror at my plate. "He doesn't put it—"

"Of course not, you asshole. Jesus Christ, worm shit in the food, are you nuts?"

"Well, then?"

"Alright, I'll tell you, but I swear Petey I'll freakin' kill you this gets out. Sanjay and me raise orchids. Go to a meeting at the Planting Fields Arboretum every month. Worm castings are great and they're expensive. So we trade. I get garbage and take-out a coupla times a month. Sanjay gets a bag of shit. Got any problem with that?"

He thrust his jaw out at me. I just smiled, said no, no problem, sounds great. We ate in silence for a while, me trying not to giggle at the thought of Phil and his orchids, him glaring at me to make sure I didn't.

As we ate, Phil gave me his report.

"Ready for business? Here's what I got. Harris Mathews? A figment of somebody's imagination. Don't exist. Got a Harold Mathews, but he's freakin' 85 livin' in bum-fuck Egypt Illinois. He ain't our guy."

Phil shoved some vindaloo in his mouth.

"Houston Mesquite?" he mumbled. "It's a New York corporation, formed last May. In time for the deeds. Harris Mathews' listed as Chairman of the Board of Directors. You're listed as the attorney. Congratulations."

"Well I didn't incorporate them, we know that. That all you got on Houston Mesquite?"

"C'mon, Petey, you know the deal. New York don't require dick to form a corporation. You don't have to put a penny into it, you don't have to list the shareholders or officers, nuthin'. Just call up one of the companies that form the corporations, send them 300 bucks or so, and boom! You're incorporated. All you got to give them is an address for service. Guess where Houston Mesquite's is? It's a freakin' 20 story office building in Jersey, Newark, actually. But no suite number. We checked the tenant registry. Never heard of Houston Mesquite, Harris Mathews, or even you, for that matter. Whoever did this just picked out an address."

"What about Tariq Singh?"

"Immigrant from India, here about 6 years. College educated. Worked his way up at the bank. He was a loan officer by the time he got whacked."

"Whacked?"

"Oh, yeah. Professional job. Two to the back of the head. They beat him pretty bad, first. Found him in his car."

"Family?"

"Not married, but lots of brothers, sisters, cousins, etc. Seems he was the man for the family, bringing everybody over, setting them up."

"Sounds expensive. Couldn't have made much at the bank."

"Nope. And he was definitely in on it. He was the loan officer on the deal, big bucks wired to India right after it was done. Not enough to account for all the money borrowed, but a nice commission, that's for sure."

"But whoever did this, whoever is Houston Mesquite, they got their money. Why take out Singh?"

"Good question. I don't have an answer. Yet. And neither do the cops."

"How about my missing attorneys?"

"That was easy. Well, sort of. The guy Johnson is living in a retirement home in Boca. Alzheimer's. Not our guy. Andrea Schneider is now Andrea Goodman and is practicing in Illinois. I think we can rule her out, too."

"What about Helms?"

"Haven't found him yet. I got my guys working on it. I should have something soon."

"Great, Phil. Anything else?"

Phil pulled out a folder. He slid it across the table to me. Our waiter refilled our four water glasses for us; the food was delicious, but spicy.

"Seymour Brownstein. Age 76. Was married 48 years til his wife died about three years ago. Two sons, David, age 46, lives in California, married, two kids, runs an investment company. Avi, age 31, single, no kids. Has a real estate license. Lives in Florida."

"15 years between kids. That's a big spread! So Sy was what, 45 when the younger one was born."

"Yep. Anyway, Brownstein started from nothing, the son of Polish immigrants. Brownstein's just a kid when they get here. When he's maybe 20 years old, him an' his brother, they buy a run down building in Brooklyn, fix it up, sell it. They do that a buncha times, til Sy wants to start holdin' onto the properties, reinvestin' the rents, that sort of thing. Brother says no, keep flippin' 'em. So they split, and not on good terms, neither. Our guy goes on, buyin' and holdin', keeps his debt real low, keeps his expenses down. When the market gets soft, and everybody's sellin', he buys. Buy low, and hold, that's his freakin' motto."

The waiter offered us coffee, which we took.

"Anyways, he checks clean. No debt, I mean none. No criminal record. His buildings are mostly commercial, in decent shape. No rent strikes or that bullshit. Doesn't drink, gamble or screw around, from all accounts. S'been givin' a lot to charity, Israel and cancer hospitals, mostly. Stays pretty much out of the spotlight."

"Does he still work or did he retire?"

"Still goes in, six days a week. Takes Saturday off for schul. That's temple for you goyim."

"Yeah, like you're Rabbi Ruggiero."

"Maybe I am. Maybe I'll give you a freakin' circumcision, how 'bout that, smart ass?"

We both chuckled.

"Anything else?"

"Just that he's pretty much known to be an asshole to work for. Lot of turnover."

That seemed to match my impression. "What happens when he dies? The sons take over?"

"Don't know. I ran some of the buildings we know he owns passed some people. Figure he's worth upwards of 1, maybe 200 million. Hard to tell, it's all private. Y'know that the estate stuff'll stay pretty secret til he croaks. Hell, if he's like most rich guys, he'll change his will ten times between now and then, anyway. He hasn't made any announcements in the press that we could find, anyway. The sons don't work for him anymore, but with the wife gone, I'd guess they collect."

"Anything else on the sons?"

"Not much. They both worked for Brownstein for a while. Helped manage the buildings, low end day-to-day stuff. But now one lives in California and one lives in Florida, so I guess that tells you how well they got along, huh?"

"What about Connolly?"

"Here it gets interesting. Greggie's got the house in Manhasset, right? Worth about mil and a half, I guess. Recently paid off."

"How recently?"

"Last July."

"Last July? Right after this deal went down?"

"Yep. He had about 10 years left on the mortgage, so he must have prepaid it. Maybe he came into some money."

"Yeah, maybe he did. Maybe he got a check from Houston Mesquite."

"Well," Phil said, "Don't get carried away. He coulda hit a big case, or his uncle coulda died. You don't know."

"I don't like coincidences, Phil."

"Neither do I, Petey, so this one makes me more concerned."

"What does?"

"Our boy's wife made a purchase last August. A beach house. Hamptons." Phil slid another envelope across the table. "800 grand."

We looked at each other.

"Petey, she paid all cash. Didn't mortgage a dime."

We finished up. I grabbed the check before Phil could. I told him to send me a bill; he said he'd put in on Joel's tab, I could settle with him.

I was heading back to the office when I remembered the envelope Henry had brought me from Mary. I pulled over into a parking lot and opened it up.

Mary had come through again. I wasn't going back to the office. I was headed to Island Storage and the closed files of O'Reilly, Mc Manus.

******

Island Storage occupied a mammoth, five-story, cinder-block building built to the Lovas brothers' specifications. The entire building was cut up into row after row of small rooms and cubicles, the walls made of aluminum panels, the doors and ceilings from chain link fence. The rooms came in different sizes, from as small as 3' by 5', to as large as 50' by 50'.

O'Reilly, McManus initially rented two medium sized rooms from Island Storage to store closed files. Now they had ten rooms in total, including two large ones. Clerks from O'Reilly, McManus came to the facility at least two times a day, shuttling files back and forth. Sometimes you would be working on a current case and needed to see some documents from a client's old file. Or sometimes you were assigned a case that was similar to an old one, so you'd pull it from storage to see how that case had been handled. Or, many times, a client would lose his copy of the closing papers on a real estate transaction, or need an additional copy of some document, and so the closed file would be accessed.

Each of the rooms had a combination lock, the kind where you could set your own combination. All of the rooms had the same combination. Because I had arranged for the first rooms with Island Storage, as a sort of barter for the litigation the Lovas' were facing, I had set the initial combinations. I had used the first 4 digits of my home telephone number.

Because the clerks who shuttled the files weren't paid very much, there was a fairly high turnover. The Lovas' had suggested we change the combination each time a clerk left, so that nobody not on the firm payroll would have access. During my entire time at O'Reilly, McManus, we never changed the combination. As I drove to Island Storage, I hoped that the breach of security hadn't been plugged.

The filing system was fairly simple. Closed files were put in a box, which was numbered. Sometimes cases took up multiple boxes. The head clerk was in charge of maintaining the system and keeping track of the box numbers. Then the boxes were put on steel shelving, arranged in rows in each storage room. Each room had a number given to it by Island Storage. In each room, O'Reilly, McManus had labeled each row with a number and each shelf a letter. So the Smith estate file might be listed in the O'Reilly, McManus computer as located at 235-5-B-3416. Meaning it was in room 235, row 5, shelf B, box 3416. When the file was closed, it was stamped with this number.

If a file, or a box, was removed from storage for any reason, a bright pink "place holder" card would be left in its place on the shelf, with the date and the name of the person who had requisitioned it, so the files could be traced. The file would later be returned back to its original spot. The system was simple and it seemed to work pretty well.

I pulled into Island's parking lot, finding a space far from the entrance. I looked around. It was pretty quiet. I went straight to the office; a young Hispanic kid was behind the counter, looking fresh in a blue and grey Island Storage polo shirt. I asked if either of the brothers were in. While the kid went to look, I took a peek behind the counter. There were five TV screens, security monitors, actually. Each showed a different floor of the building, the picture flickering every few seconds, the scene changing from one row to the next. Most of the hallways seemed empty. The few people in the building right now were probably in their rooms, communing with their storage.

Ricky Lovas, the younger of the two brothers, the one about my age, came out. As soon as he saw me he broke into a huge grin.

"Peter! So good to see you, my friend!" He came around the counter and gave me a bear hug. "You look great! It's been too long, how are you?"

Ricky, and his brother Bobby, were the eldest children of Portuguese immigrants. Their parents owned a small restaurant in Mineola, a nearby town that not only possessed the county offices and the courts, but also one of the oldest and largest concentrations of Portuguese-Americans in the United States. The Lovas' were a large family, with many cousins and friends in the area. Ricky and Bobby's sisters helped run the restaurant.

I asked how the family was doing, how business was doing. All was well. I got the run down of the new babies, the expansion of the business, the recent vacations. Ricky looked happy. I was glad. I had handled two complicated cases for the Lovas'. Both came out very well. In the first, I had battled local opposition and a bullheaded zoning board to finally allow the Lovas' to build this building. In the second, I had successfully defended them from a former employer who sued to enforce a non-compete the brothers had signed while they managed his self-storage facility; he claimed that the brothers had stolen customers from him when they started this business.

The cases had gone on for months. We had been in almost daily contact. The brothers seemed to genuinely like me. They had offered innumerable times to treat me to dinner. They had invited me and Lorraine to weddings and vacations. To family parties. I never went. I always kept a wall between me and my clients. Old man O'Reilly had tried to talk with me about it once. He had told me I was in danger of missing out on the best part of being a lawyer. Be careful, he had told me. It's a lot more enjoyable being the country family doctor, who becomes a part of people's lives, than the nameless surgical specialist who comes in, cuts something out, and leaves. The surgeon might be appreciated, indeed he may grow very successful on the recommendations of his talent, but he will never be beloved. O'Reilly liked his clients and they loved him. He became a part of their families. I just couldn't. I did my job. My clients were thankful, they were appreciative. Some, like the Lovas, seemed to want to stay connected with me. I just moved onto the next case.

I asked Ricky if we could talk. He took me back to his office. As we walked, we passed a glassed-in room, set up like a shipping office, with Federal Express and UPS signs. There were packing displays set up, it appeared, for a retail trade. I noticed a very attractive woman, thirty-ish or so, behind a counter. Ricky noticed me noticing.

"That's my sister Ines. Yeah, we took your advice and made this a shipping center, too. People can drop off their packages for delivery or they can use us as a drop off point. We can box and wrap anything. We get a lot of traffic around the holidays. It's been great for the rental business, too. We have a lot of manufacturer's reps who get their samples and material delivered here; we hold it for them, put it right in their room if they're on the road. It pushed us from 84% filled capacity to 96%. Plus the profit from the shipping is pretty good, too. And we have you to thank. It was your idea."

"Not mine. If I remember right, I had a client once in the mailbox business. I just suggested it, since you had a staff here anyway."

"Yeah, well that suggestion lets us send our parents to Portugal each winter."

We sat in his office. It was a shrine to fishing. Paintings. Rods. Mounted fish. Photographs of Ricky on docks and boats, arm held high, with the catch of the day hanging heavily. He had a wall full of lures and artificial flies. Nets hung from the ceiling.

"Have any hobbies, Ricky?" I asked as I looked around.

"Like to fish, Pete? I go out on my boat every Wednesday, most weekends. You're welcome to come along. Anytime."

"Thanks. I may take you up on that."

"Please do. I'd love to take you out, do some blue fishing this fall when they come back down, how about it?"

"Sounds good to me. I think I'd like that."

"Good. We'll do it. Now, what brings you here, my friend. Need space?"

"No, no space. I just need to see some old files of mine." I hated lying to Ricky, but I didn't want to involve him.

"You back with O'Reilly?"

146

I paused. "No."

He thought about that for a few moments. "I should ask you if you have permission to go back to the rooms."

I didn't answer.

"You got the combination?"

"Yeah, I think so."

"Go ahead. No need to sign in the book. I didn't see you here. But you got to come fishing with me, you hear?"

I smiled as I stood and shook his hand. "I will. I promise. And thank you."

"Don't thank me. Just be careful, Pete. I don't want you getting in trouble, and I'd rather not lose the account."

I thanked him, told him I'd be careful and that I'd take the fall if anything happened. I left his office and pulled out the envelope Mary had sent over. I took the elevator to the third floor. I walked down a long aisle, the sound of my steps on the concrete floor echoing softly. I made a left at the end of the aisle, and walked down about 75 feet to Room 373.

I took a breath and looked around. I don't think there was another person on the floor, but I did see the security camera. I squelched the temptation to wave. I held the lock in my left hand and twirled the tumblers with my right.

7. 9. 9. 6.

I pulled.

The lock came free.

Lazy bastards still hadn't changed the combination. Lucky me.

I opened the door and stepped into the room. First, I looked for my boxes of stuff. I found one right where Mary had said they would be. It was sealed with tape and covered in a fine layer of dust.

Where the second box should be, though, there was nothing. Nothing, that is, except a bright pink card.

Somebody had requisitioned my box. I held the card up so that the bare bulb would shine directly on it. The date was last May. A month before the fraud.

The name of the person who requisitioned the file?

Gregory Connolly.

Bingo!

I opened the box Connolly hadn't requisitioned, but stopped as soon as I pulled the cardboard top off. My past hit me in the face and I literally staggered back a step. I stumbled back into the hall and leaned against one of the chain link walls. I looked down the long hallway. I couldn't do this. I had glanced into the box– it held the remains of my former life. I could almost smell the desperation, the hunger emanating from the box.

I had to do it. Face your fears, Pete. I took a breath, and got back to work.

I emptied the box bit by bit. It had one of my diplomas, a couple of citations, some old letters. It reeked of my old life. If I spent any time looking through all this memorabilia, I was going to get way too depressed. I sped up my search, rummaging through, without spending much time reading anything, or thinking. I found my pens and scissors and staple remover; it was the contents of the top drawer of my desk, which is where I used to keep my notary stamp.

The stamp wasn't there.

I was tempted to throw everything back in the box and call it a day, but I knew I couldn't do that. I finally convinced myself that I had to do a more thorough search, which I did. The notary stamp was still nowhere to be found. I wasn't surprised. The stamp should have been in this box. If it wasn't, that meant that somebody had removed it. Somebody with access to this box.

Connolly.

Next, I looked at the contents of Mary's envelope again and found row 6. Shelf C, all the way at the bottom. Box 2785. I opened it up. There were five files in the box. I found the one I was looking for. It was entitled "Robbins, Stock buy-back". It was the first file on my list, one of the three lists Mary had gotten for me.

The first list was of all of Sy Brownstein's files, open and closed.

The second list, the one in my hand, contained every case Vincent Helms had worked on during his tenure with O'Reilly, McManus. The list had 346 separate files. A few had been for Sy, though at a quick glance, none of those cases struck me as being very large ones.

The third list was much longer than the first two. It held every case Connolly had ever billed on. Many of those files had been for Sy Brownstein.

I put the Connolly list aside. I was going to have one of my little team look this over, have them search for any references to Houston Mesquite, Harris Mathews or Tariq Singh. Maybe Connolly had worked on loans with Singh before. I figured I would start with the Helms' files and then move on to Connolly's or Brownstein's.

I was going to look at each one of the 346 files on the Helms list. I didn't know what I was looking for, but I had some time; the preliminary Grievance hearing was still 8 days away. Luckily, I had the access. Phil and the rest of my team were busy tracking down other leads. I hoped this might be helpful or, if not, it would at least give me the illusion that I was doing something, that I was on the attack. Plus, this way I could rule Helms out and convince my team to concentrate on Connolly.

I lifted the file stamped 373-6-C-2785 from the box and sat down on the concrete floor. I put a little check next to the name of the case on Mary's list. I opened the file and started going through it, page by page. Searching. Probing. Vincent Helms. Who are you? Did you do this to me? Where are you? I tried to divine the answers from the file, from the copies of correspondence, from the printed documents, from the hand-scribbled notes, from the sheaves of legal paper, yellow among the white parchment.

Nothing.

I put the file back in the box, the box back on the shelf. I looked at the list. One file down. 345 files to go.

Chapter 19

I lost track of time. I had been there several hours and had gone through about 40 files. My butt and back were sore from sitting on the concrete floor, but I had finished all of the files in Room 373. O'Reilly, McManus had two rooms next to each other on the 4th floor, 412 and 413. I figured I'd do the files in 412 next.

Room 412 was at the dead-end of a very long, straight aisle, with no hallways branching off of it. The aisle was wide enough for a couple of people to pass, but not much more. The same combination opened this room, and I settled in to review the 150 or so of Helm's files that were stored in 412.

So far I hadn't found anything, except that Helms was a doodler. He liked to draw on the inside folders, and the legal pads he used were filled with drawings, and sketches. Lots of boxes. Some dirty pictures, like a 13 year old might draw in his Middle School Math textbook. Football plays, with arrows and lines showing where the players were supposed to run to, and whom they should block. Graphics. The files themselves were organized and neat. The doodling was always in the margins, away from the case information. I didn't know what that meant psychologically, if anything. I made a mental note to check it out later.

I was in the middle of the fifth or sixth file in Room 412 when I heard a door crash open and loud pounding footsteps. They were getting closer. They were coming, rapidly. Towards me.

I frantically looked for someplace to hide– there wasn't any. The room was completely filled. I threw the file down and leaped into the hallway. I was just starting to close the door, when I saw Ricky racing down the aisle, a big roll of plastic bubble wrap in his arms.

"Quick, let's go–someone's coming!" he called out in a screaming whisper.

I jammed the lock back in place and started running towards Ricky when I heard the elevator door open and heard the clicking of heels on the concrete. I was still about 20 feet from Ricky, and about 100 feet from the safety of the next aisle, when the clicking heels turned the corner, coming towards us. There was nowhere to go. I stopped running immediately and put my head down. I walked towards Ricky, who was looking directly at me in panic. As I approached him, I glanced over his shoulder. Walking towards us, maybe 40 feet away now, was Catherine Sullivan, my fashion-conscious former partner at O'Reilly, McManus. She was walking a bit tentatively, holding a piece of paper half-up, comparing the number on it to the room numbers. She looked uneasy; the storage facility was clearly unknown territory for her. She must have needed a file badly and had no one around to fetch it for her. It was the only reason she would be here.

I was shielded, mostly, by Ricky's body, and the roll of bubble wrap he had in his arms. I had to do something. If I just stood here, Catherine would see me, and wonder why I was hanging around near O'Reilly, McManus' rooms. If she went into 412, she would see the files on the floor. Even if they couldn't figure out what I was doing, at the very least they would wake up and change the combination on the locks.

I tried to will myself into invisibility. It didn't work. I tried to telepathically order Catherine to stop, turn around and leave. Didn't work, either. Plan three, the best defense is a good offense.

I grabbed the bubble wrap from Ricky's hands. The roll was maybe three feet long, maybe two feet in diameter, bulky, but very light. I hoisted it up on my right shoulder, and brought my left hand up to balance it. Between the roll and my hand, I was blocking my face. Ricky's mouth dropped open as I charged down the aisle, towards Catherine. My face was covered as Catherine and I converged. I kept the roll between us as we passed. I was just another worker; she didn't pay me any mind.

"Excuse me," she asked Ricky, "Can you tell me where room 413 is? I have to get a file.... oh, WAIT!"

She had stopped and whirled around in my direction. I was about four steps passed her, almost free.

"Come back here. Come back here!"

I felt my stomach rush to my throat. I stopped. I turned slowly to my right, still keeping the roll between my face and hers. She took a step or two towards me.

"I'm sorry, I just *love* this stuff!!" She reached out and popped several of the little plastic bubbles. "I'm just like a little kid with this!" She laughed.

Ricky had regained his composure. "Then I will give you a whole sheet when you leave, on the house! Luis, please bring that down to Ines right away, she's waiting for it, OK?" I guess I was Luis. "Now, tell me again, ma'am, what room are you looking for?"

I hustled down the aisle, and took the same staircase down that Ricky had raced up ahead of the elevator, only I stopped between floors to sit on a step and let my heart slow down.

I waited on the second floor for about 20 minutes. I heard the elevator doors start to open and I hopped back into the stairway. It was Ricky, looking for me. I stepped out and thanked him.

"That was ballsy, man. Lucky I saw you on the monitor go into 412. I was getting Ines that bubble wrap from the stock room, when I heard her tell Luis she was with O'Reilly, McManus and she needed a file. I took off up the steps. Good thing I didn't think to drop the wrap! Popping the damn bubbles. Woman makes a jillion bucks a year, dresses like she's on Park Avenue, she's gotta pop bubbles. I almost had a heart attack."

We both laughed. "Me, too, me, too. Lucky she wanted 413, not 412. I couldn't get the file back, I think its still on the floor."

Ricky stopped laughing. "C'mon now. Tell me what's going on."

I thought about it a second. I didn't have a choice; I had to tell him. Standing in the aisle, leaning up against the walls of one of the rooms, I filled

Ricky in on just about everything. He didn't say anything until I was done.

"OK, here's what we're going to do. I'm going to give you a room to use, with a table and a chair so you can look through the files like a human. Me and Luis will pull the files, bring them to the room. You stay out of their rooms. My heart can't take another close call. When you finish with the files, we'll put them back."

"I can't ask you to do that, Ricky."

"You didn't ask. I'm telling you." He shook his head. "I don't think you ever understood how grateful we are to you. You saved us. You gave us this life. We couldn't afford to pay you, not right away. You trusted us. Now trust me. Go downstairs, Luis'll give you a room. And say hello to my sister Ines." He smiled and winked. "She always liked you, you know. And she's single again."

*****

Before I returned to the files, I made a call to Phil. I left a detailed message on his machine. I told him about the pink requisition slip, about how Connolly had pulled one of my boxes from storage. I asked if there was any way he could think of for us to track down that box.

I stayed at the files until after 11. I was hungry and tired and a bit frustrated. Maybe this was silly. I wasn't finding anything, except that Helms had a penchant for short passes to the right and women with large breasts.

I drove home, pulling up to a dark house. Mrs. Murphy either wasn't home or she was already asleep. I parked on the street and strolled up the driveway, keys in hand, my mind on bubble wrap and files and tomorrow's meeting with the title company. I had just turned the corner, a few steps from the staircase leading up to my apartment, when my head exploded.

Something hard had hit me on the side of my head, just above my right ear. The pain was incredible, piercing. It shot through my skull. I crumpled to the ground. Whoever had hit me was stomping on me, kicking me. I tried to ward off the kicks, tried to get up. I wasn't successful with either effort. I started crawling, trying to get back down the driveway. I felt something striking the back of my head, my shoulders, my back. It felt like a club or a bat. I was barely holding on, hardly still conscious. Only the realization that whoever was hitting me was trying to kill me kept me going.

I collapsed again, my arms over my head, the impacts battering my hands, my ribs, hard, heavy, fast. I was just about to give up hope, when the whole area erupted in light. Headlights.

I sensed, more than I heard, car doors opening, and footsteps charging up the driveway. My attacker was gone; I guess he fled.

My saviors turned out to be Mrs. Murphy's son Sean and his boyfriend Roger. I didn't find that out until later, though, because once the attacks stopped, I passed out, a swirling blackness finally, thankfully, overtaking the pain.

*****

I woke up.

Slowly.

I was in a hospital room. There were no windows. My head hurt.

I took assessment. When I prepped a client in an accident case for her testimony, I always told her that when she was asked to describe her injuries, she should start at the top of their head and work down, so that she wouldn't leave anything out. I did that now. The pain in my head was excruciating. I felt my head. There was a huge lump behind and above my right ear. I ran my tongue across the inside of my teeth. They were all there. My neck was stiff and achy. My shoulders, especially the back of my right shoulder, throbbed. I was having a hard time breathing deep. My chest, especially my ribs, hurt like hell. It hurt to move my arms, but I could. I wiggled my fingers. At least one was bandaged. I reached up so I could see my hands without moving my aching head and saw that my left hand was wrapped, with only the fingertips sticking out beyond the white gauze. I could move my legs and wiggle my toes.

I felt like one, big bruise. I was nauseous. I had a blinding headache that hurt worse, if that was possible, when I moved my head.

I knew this feeling.

I felt hung over.

I thought about earlier in the evening. I remembered it all. The files. The attack. Nope, I hadn't been drinking.

I had been attacked.

Mrs. Murphy crossed my mind, in a panic. I hoped she was OK. I was trying to remember the details of the attack, when the nurse came in.

"Ah, look, Sleeping Beauty has arisen, and I didn't even get to kiss you yet!" She was a big, smiling, bleached-blonde woman, probably mid-fifties. "You wait right here, sugar, don't go running off. Dr. Afati wants to see you as soon as you open those baby browns." She peered into my eyes as she spoke and then went out the door with a rush of air.

I closed my eyes. It didn't help the pain. A few moments later, a small, slight man with thick glasses and a mustache that reminded me of the song by Jimmy Buffett, "Pencil Thin Mustache", stood by my bed. With the strands of the song playing in my head, I tried to answer his questions.

"Good morning, sir, how are you feeling?" he asked, a hint of a mid-eastern accent dancing on his words.

I grunted.

"Tell me, sir, what is your name?"

"Peter De Stio."

And so it went. He asked me my date of birth, how many fingers he was holding up, my address, my telephone number. He had me count backwards from 100 by threes. He asked me to name the President. He asked me if I remembered what happened to me. He asked me about my family, their names. I must have answered correctly, or at least acceptably, because he kept nodding along with my answers, saying "Good, good, veddy good" while he felt around my neck and flashed a light across my eyes.

I asked him where I was. He told me I was in the Intensive Care Unit of the South Nassau Communities Hospital. I asked him what time it was. He told me it was around 5 a.m. I said good, I have an important meeting at 10, I have to get home and get dressed.

He kept saying no, no, sir, you cannot, as I tried to get up. I said I have to, it is very important. You don't understand, I have to meet the title insurance people, with Carolyn, it's very important.

He said I couldn't.

I said I had to.

He was right. I couldn't.

I got my head all of six or eight inches off the pillow when it collapsed back and refused to move. My body screeched in pain. I felt like I was going to throw up.

He kept talking; his words finally got through the pain. It was 5 a.m., alright.

Saturday, 5 a.m.

I had missed Friday. I had missed the meeting. How could you miss a whole day? I mean I had missed whole days before, but never sober. I was trying to wrap myself around that thought when I fell back asleep and said goodbye to Saturday morning.

I woke up to find Mrs. Murphy's son Sean sitting in a chair at the foot of my bed. I looked around; I was still in the I.C.U.

"Hey, you're up. My mom just stepped out for a second. They'll only let one of us in here at a time. How you feeling?"

"Like shit. How's your Mom?"

"Fine. A little jittery. It's kind of scary to see someone getting beat up in your own driveway, after all. Who was it, do you know?"

"Not a clue. How did– why were you guys–" Man, my head hurt.

"Roger and I came down for a weekend with some friends out in the Hamptons. We were going to stay with Mom Thursday night, then go out there yesterday."

"So today is still Saturday?"

"Yes. You slept through yesterday, it's almost 2 o'clock in the afternoon now."

"What happened?"

"Well, we pulled into the driveway and saw this guy pounding on you with, well, it looked like a crowbar. I didn't even stop the car and Roger was out running towards you. The guy took off. I'm sorry; we didn't get a real good look at him. We called an ambulance and the cops. They couldn't find anything. They think you walked in on an attempted burglary. Nothing was missing from your place or Mom's, as far as we can tell. Mom's still shaken up, so we're staying with her the weekend."

"Thanks, Sean. Thank Roger for me, too. And thanks for coming here; you didn't have to do that."

"No problem. I'm only sorry we didn't catch him."

I was sorry, too. Sean and Roger looked like twin blocks of cut granite. They were both well over 6 foot and were regulars at the gym. Roger had been in the Marines; Sean was a triathlete. If they had gotten hold of this guy, they would have torn him apart.

I spent the afternoon being pampered by Mrs. Murphy and thanking Sean and Roger for saving my life. The nursing staff took good care of me and by late afternoon I was moved to a regular room. I slept some more after the Murphys and Roger left.

Before they kicked me out of ICU, I was examined by a very efficient, very no-nonsense, very cute resident wearing a name tag. Dr. Nancy Porter. Dr. Nancy examined me in more detail than my sore body could handle, although under other circumstances I probably wouldn't have minded.

"You're a very lucky man," she said. "I can't believe it, but nothing's fractured. Your head and ribs took the worst of it. Looks to me like you have a concussion and a series of contusions that will be sore for a week or two."

"So I'm dented, but not broken."

"Something like that. I'm going to keep you on the pain medication and I want you in here for another day or so. I'm concerned about internal injury, especially to your spleen and kidneys."

"I'll pass on the pain killers, doc."

"Why? I don't take you for the hero-type."

"Nah, if I was, I would have won the fight, right? No, uh, I'm a recovering alcoholic. I'd rather keep the medication to a minimum."

"I don't see why Vicodin would affect your alcoh-"

"Please, doc. If I can't handle the pain, I'll ask for something. But for now, how about some Advil and we call it a day, OK?"

"OK." She smiled. "By the way, the BAC came back negative. Now I understand why you asked for it."

I was confused. BAC? Asked for it?

"Huh?" Ah, such witty repartee with the pretty doctor.

"The BAC. The blood alcohol content test. I was in the ER when they brought you in Thursday night. You were crazy, demanding that they test you for alcohol. The ER doctor didn't want to do it. Now I know why you wanted it. To show you weren't drunk."

I guessed she was right. But I didn't remember anything about it all, not from the time I laid my head on the driveway until I woke up in the ICU. Dr. Nancy and I small-talked a bit more, then she was gone, with an assurance she would check up on me soon.

*****

I slept on and off all Saturday night. I peed a little blood early in the evening, but it cleared up by Sunday morning. I checked myself out. The staff wasn't happy. I felt terrible. I had a blistering headache and my body revolted every time I took a step. My hands were shaking. I felt like I had to throw up.

South Nassau Communities Hospital was only about ten blocks from Mrs. Murphy's house. I walked. Or, rather, I shuffled and limped. With my three day beard, wounded body, and head that hurt so much I couldn't keep it up straight, I must have looked like a bum on a three day bender, like I was a squeegee away from washing windows at a stoplight.

I somehow got home, although it seemed like less and less of a good idea each block I walked. I showered, and then I took a bath. I popped more Advil than I was supposed to, but I didn't care. I shaved, and got dressed. I felt better. A little better. A very little.

I looked at my answering machine. The little light was blinking. I had 9 messages. I didn't play them. Instead, I laid down on the couch. I had three hours or so before I was due at my sister's. I didn't know if I should cancel or not. Before I could decide, I fell asleep. I woke up a couple of hours later, a little disoriented, a little dizzy and still in a lot of pain. I made myself get off the couch. I tried to stretch a bit. It didn't help.

I looked at myself in the mirror. When I was dressed, except for the bandages on my hands, you couldn't see any cuts or bruises on my body. Underneath my clothes, though, ugly purple splotches were starting to spread and deepen on my shoulders, back and ribs. The son of a bitch. I thought of inventive ways for him to die a slow, painful death.

I decided to go to my sister's anyway. I eased myself down the steps and somehow folded myself into the car, taking great care, as if I was putting an ancient, brittle letter back into an envelope. I stopped at Mario's Bakery on Merrick Road for a couple dozen of their excellent Italian pastries. Marie loves cannolis; I got a half dozen just of those.

The drive to Massapequa was excruciating. Every turn, every step on the brake, was an adventure in torment. By the time I was about halfway there, I realized I probably shouldn't have left the apartment. By the time I pulled into the driveway, I realized I probably shouldn't have left the hospital. What little energy I had was fading fast.

Marie came to the front porch after I pulled in. Her smile faded quickly as she watched me unfold stiffly from the car, and fragilely negotiate the walkway. She stood outside her front door and she didn't step aside.

"Are you OK?" she demanded.

"Yeah, I'm fine. Just had a little accident."

"Are you drunk?"

"No, no, nothing like that. I told you, I just had an accident."

Lou appeared at the door, just behind Marie.

"You look drunk." he said.

"I'm not drunk, I swear it!" I said, perhaps a bit too forcefully. The words sounded familiar in my mouth– I had said them before. This time they were true. Maybe I needed Drummond's polygraph with me all the time. I saw their reaction as I said it; no way were they going to believe me.

Lou stepped forward onto the stoop. "You look drunk, or at least hung over. You're not coming in here, in front of my kids, like that. Get the hell out of here."

I looked at Marie. She looked like she was going to cry, but she didn't say anything. Nothing. Not a word. I couldn't argue with Lou; I felt hung over. I could try to explain about the attack, but I realized it would sound just like the elaborate excuses and lies I used to use. I couldn't blame them. One babysitting assignment successfully completed doesn't undo an adult life of alcohol and abuse. I had no deposits in the bank of credibility upon which I could draw.

"If you don't leave, right now, I'm calling the cops." Lou looked defiant, and a bit victorious. Marie just looked hurt.

"I really am OK," I said softly. I could see the boys at the bay window, waving to me. I gave them a little wave, then painfully, and slowly, bent down and put the pastry box on the first step. I lifted myself back up unsteadily. I shuffled back to the car and left. I heard my sister crying. I didn't turn around.

Chapter 20

Back in my apartment, I couldn't bring myself to listen to the messages on my machine; there were 14. I called Joel's office and left a message on the general mailbox that I wouldn't be in Monday morning until after Court. I had Jamaal's case in Family Court and I knew there was no way I would be able to get up early Monday morning and deal with my eager students.

I was feeling sorry for myself, a dangerous mind set for an alcoholic. Probably dangerous for anyone. I had a few choices; I could go to an AA meeting. I could listen to the messages and return the calls. I could sit on the couch and pig out. I could drink.

I did nothing of the kind. I laid down on the couch and I slept. I woke up a few times, took some more Advil and fell back to sleep. Maybe the pain killers the hospital had given me were still in my system. Or maybe my concussion was worse than I thought. My pee was clear, though, even if my head was fuzzy.

Monday morning came earlier than my body expected. I had a real hard time getting up. It took me forever to get out of the bathroom. I just couldn't get moving.

Luckily, Family Court runs on Island time. Not the hectic, go, go, go of Long Island time, but more like the Caribbean, no-worries-mon, relax it'll get done when it gets done Island time. When I dragged myself into the courthouse at 10, not a single case had been called yet. It took me a half an hour to track down the County Attorney. We stood in the hallway. She had about 10 files slipping around in her arms. She juggled the files around until she found

Jamaal's, mostly thanks to a deft use of her thighs. She looked at the probation report. If he would plea guilty to the theft, she would recommend an extension of the probation he was already on. I guess five strikes and you're still not out in this game. I told her I would recommend it to Jamaal.

I went to the Courtroom. Waiting outside in the narrow hallway was Jamaal and his mother. Goldtooth was nowhere to be found. I didn't mind.

My head was still killing me and I felt stiff, but the Advil and all the sleep had helped, a little. At least I could keep my head up straight.

I pulled Jamaal over.

"Listen, Ace, the County is offering an extension on the probation in exchange for a guilty plea. I think it's a good deal. What do you want to do?"

"Ah'll take it."

"I'll tell them. By the way, what happened to your Mom's boyfriend?"

"Oh, man, is he pissed. She went to that shelter you told her about, an she got an Order of Protection on his ass. Cops threw him in jail the other night. He got right out next day, but he is one mad mutherfucker. His boys told me he ain't done, he's gonna get his."

"What does that mean?"

"I dunno, but it don' sound too good, does it?"

"No, it doesn't." I started to walk away to tell the Court officer we were ready for the plea, when a thought hit me.

"Jamaal, when was he arrested?"

"I dunno, some night las' week. Hey Ma, when was Albert busted?"

Mom looked at us. "Wednesday. Wednesday night. And they released him Thursday morning." She just shook her head.

Released Thursday morning. Mad as hell. Was Goldtooth my Thursday night attacker? Or did it involve Houston Mesquite? Or was it an attempted burglary? I stopped thinking–my head hurt enough as it was.

I didn't have time to dwell on the thought, anyway; our case got called. Mom, Jamaal and I stood in front of the judge, to his left. The County Attorney stood to his right. The small courtroom had a court reporter taking down the proceedings on her little stenographic typewriter. A couple of court officers. A court Clerk shuffling the papers around. And a couple of bored attorneys sitting in the 10 or so chairs bolted to the floor in the back of this tiny room.

The County Attorney rattled off the deal. "Your honor, on docket number 58390, People versus Jamaal Washington, the People would offer a reduction of the charge of petit larceny, to the charge of attempted petit larceny, in exchange for a plea of guilty to the charge as amended, concurrent with a two year extension of the Defendant's probationary period, as recommended by the Department of Probation."

"How does your client plead to the amended and reduced charge?"

"Guilty, your honor."

"Very well." The judge addressed Jamaal directly. "Mr. Washington you have heard the offer of the People, and your attorney's response that you plead guilty. Is anyone forcing you to take this plea?"

"No, sir."

"Anyone make you any promises?"

"No, sir."

"You understand this plea is the same thing as having been convicted after a trial, that you are giving up your right to a trial, to have witnesses called against you, to have your attorney cross examine those witnesses. You understand you are waiving those rights?"

"Yes, sir."

This part of the proceeding is called the "allocution." Jamaal had been through it several times before. It was standard stuff. My mind was wandering, to Goldtooth, to Houston Mesquite, to Marie. To Carolyn. To all the messages on my machine at home. I should have been paying more attention to what I was doing.

"Now, Jamaal, on March 11th, at approximately 3:30 p.m., did you take a certain, what did he take? Wire cutters, from the Home Depot in Hempstead, without paying for same?"

Silence.

"Mr. Washington, did you hear me?"

"Yes, sir, I heard you, y'honor, sir."

"Then what is your answer?"

"No, sir, I didn' take nuthin'."

There was immediate silence in the room. I snapped to attention. I had half heard it, but I didn't believe it. I knew what was coming next.

"Off the record," the Judge barked. "Jesus Christ, *counselor*, I can't take a plea from a boy who says he's innocent, what's the matter with you? This is America, for Christ's sake, we don't take guilty pleas from innocent people. This isn't some Gulag where we force guilty pleas to keep things moving. Pick a trial date, *Counselor*."

I got my bearings. This was embarrassing. I could feel the smirks of the attorneys behind me. Having a client blow an allocution was terrible, a real amateur mistake. I should have prepped him in the hall, but between my complacency that he had been through this before, and the pain in my head, and my concerns about Goldtooth, I had just forgotten. My headache got instantly worse.

"Your honor, could we have a second call on this?"

"Why, so you can browbeat the boy into a confession? Not in my Court you don't, Counselor. Pick a trial date."

"Please, Your Honor, give me five minutes."

"Five minutes. But watch what you say to him. He comes back in here saying he's guilty, I'm going to want to know why. *Counselor*."

I got Jamaal out in the hall, half dragging him away from the courtroom.

"What's the *matter* with you? You've been through this before. Why'd you say you didn't do it? You want a trial?"

Jamaal just hung his head. I waited for a response.

He leaned in, his voice barely audible.

"My ma. She was in the Court."

"Yeah, so what?"

"So I couldn't say I did it in front of her, man. She thinks I'm innocent, only takin' the plea so we can get outta here."

I shook my head.

I went over to Mom and asked her to wait outside. She looked at me curiously, but said OK. Then I went back into the Court and asked for a sidebar, a private conference with the judge and the attorneys, away from the earshot of the rest of the room. Actually, that's just in theory. This courtroom was so small the whole room heard our conversation anyway, as I could tell from the titters coming from the attorneys in the back row. I told the judge what the problem was. I don't think he believed me. Maybe I did need Drummond's machine with me *all* the time.

He called the case again and asked Jamaal all the same questions. When he got to the part about the crime, he took a different tact.

"OK, sir, did something happen at the Home Depot in Hempstead on March 11th?"

And Jamaal told him. "Yes, y'honor, see I went into the Home Depot to steal some wire cutters, cause me an' my friends been stealin' bikes an all, an we needed the snips to cut the chains, and--"

Thankfully the judge cut him off before he confessed to more misdemeanors and felonies. The judge accepted the plea and restored him to probation. The look the judge gave me as we left the Courtroom told me I would be remembered by him the next time I came in this courtroom. Wonderful.

I made it back to the office a bit before noon. Rita was at her desk. She didn't smile, or even acknowledge my "Good morning." Strange.

I was still a little shaky, and a lot stiff. My headache had started to subside. I found that the Advil kicked in about 20 minutes after I took it and that with each dose the headache stayed in abeyance for a little longer. I shuffled down to my office to see what awaited me.

The first thing I noticed was that my desk was almost clear. Mail, and messages, were piled on a chair. I didn't see any files or drafts from my students for me to review. Instead, there was only an envelope, with my name typed on the outside, sitting in the middle of the desk. The return address told me the envelope was from Levine, Johnson, Majors & Smolinski. There was no stamp.

I nudged the envelope aside, dumped the mail and messages on the desk, shut my door and sat down. I looked at the messages first.

The messages I had missed on Friday, while I was dozing in the I.C.U., were from my sister confirming Sunday dinner, a couple of calls from Barnaby's, presumably about an assignment they had for me, and a call from Phil Ruggierio. And a message from Rita, asking me to see her, "important".

Monday's messages were from Detective Fisher, another call from Phil, and a return call from Marcia Simpson. I put the messages aside.

I looked at the mail next. Mostly garbage. Except for a business card from Detective Fisher. Apparently he had stopped by earlier that morning. Not good. Not good at all.

I buzzed Rita on the intercom. "You wanted me to see you?"

"I can't talk to you about it. Talk to Mr. Majors, he'll tell you."

"Rita, what is it?"

"Please, please just forget the message, please. Just talk to Mr. Majors." And she hung up.

Ronald Majors was one of the original partners of Levine, Johnson, Majors & Smolinski. He was the only one of the partners I hadn't known from law school. Unlike the other three, Majors stayed far from courtrooms. He had developed a nice corporate and real estate practice. Since he was the one who was mostly in the office, the day-to-day duties of running the firm had filtered down to him over the years, although Joel was regularly voted the managing partner by his peers. It had been a point of contention for Majors over the years.

Ronald Majors was also the only member of the firm with which I had a confrontation when I was drinking. It had been at a bar association seminar. I had shown up drunk; he was one of the organizers and had asked me to leave. It hadn't gone well, although no blows were thrown. I had been nasty, as I recall, and Ronald had not been happy with Joel's private rehabilitation program. Joel never told me anything, but the word was Ronald was giving Joel a hard time, at almost every partner's meeting. If Rita wanted me to see Ronald Majors, it couldn't be good.

I dialed Joel's extension and asked his secretary if I could speak with him. I was told he had left after the meeting that morning and had gone to Court on his trial. She didn't expect him back; I asked her to have him call me when he got the chance.

I looked again at the unopened envelope. I closed my eyes and counted my breaths to ten. Then I did it again.

I opened it. It was a letter.

Dear Mr. De Stio:

On behalf of the firm of Levine, Johnson, Majors & Smolinski, I hereby demand that you vacate this office no later than September 30. We would appreciate an earlier vacancy. All ancillary rights, such as reception services, use of the photocopy equipment, etc. are hereby terminated, effectively immediately.

Please be advised that any prior agreements you may have had with this firm concerning services to be provided by you, including but not limited to the training of our staff and your appearances on litigation matters, are also hereby terminated. Attached hereto is this firm's check representing all fees due you through this date.

Annexed hereto is a statement for professional services rendered to you by our associate staff, as well as a statement for disbursements and investigative services billed to this firm on your behalf. Please forward your payment for same promptly.

Finally, our staff and attorneys have been directed by the partnership committee to cease all work for you, whether on firm time or not, and to cease all professional contact with you as well. Your cooperation in observing this stricture is greatly appreciated.

Yours very truly,
Ronald Majors

So I was being evicted. I looked around at my office. I could leave today. It would only take a box or two. I read the letter again. I guess my disappearing act on Friday had been interpreted by everybody as a fall from the wagon. When I didn't return the calls at home, they must have assumed I was on a bender. Would they believe the truth any more than Marie had? Majors had acted quickly. Even if I got Joel to believe me, it was clear his partners wanted me out. The next to last thing I wanted in the whole world was to cause Joel problems. The last thing I wanted was to lose his respect. It looked like I had done both.

I reached in the desk and took out my checkbook. I knew I was basically paying Joel's firm with Joel's own money, but I didn't want the bill to be outstanding. I wrote a check to Levine, Johnson, Majors & Smolinski for the amount on their invoice, covering Carolyn and the other associate's time.

I weighed returning the calls. I dialed Phil.

"Petey. How you doin'?"

"Been better Phil."

"Problems? I mean real problems?"

"We'll see." Then I told him about the attack on Thursday, and Goldtooth. I also told him about Marie's reaction and Majors.

"So you feeling' sorry for yourself?"

"Yeah, a bit."

"You gonna drink?"

I thought about it. "Not today."

"Good boy. You want some protection?"

"I don't think so. I'll just be more careful, I guess."

"Wanna hear what I got on Vincent Helms?"

"Shoot."

What he had wasn't much, but it helped fill in the picture.

"Vincent Helms, age 33, grew up in a small town outside of Chicago. Single. No family. He was an only child, parents passed away while he was in college. Good grades in high school, no sports, but he was President of the chess club. College at the University of Wisconsin, good grades. Family had no

168

money, but Vinnie seemed to get through OK. Worked at an Indian Casino during his summers."

"How'd you find that out?"

"Vee haf ways, young man. Shall I continue?"

"Please do."

"Wisconsin led to Harvard. Middle-bottom of his class. Again, summers at the casinos. He clerked for a Federal judge in Connecticut. Then on to Manhattan at Kremer, Ludley and Finch, for two years. Then O'Reilly, McManus. So far, so good."

"Anything else?"

"Anythin' else? You kiddin'? This is where it gets good. Guy's making serious money, right, plus no wife an' kids suckin' him dry. Should be doin' OK, right? Wrong. Guy owns no real property. Was living in a studio apartment in a crappy area of Queens, fourth apartment in three years. Evicted each time. His freakin' credit report looks like a train wreck. He owes everybody, and I mean every freakin' body. Credit cards. Personal loans. Get this– he owes the casinos in AC over 50 grand."

"What do you think?"

"I think the guy's got a gamblin' problem. His landlord hasn't seen him in over a year, maybe last June, beginning of July, he ain't sure. Helms stuck him, bounced a bunch of checks. Judgments? How 'bout 5 of 'em so far, plus a few on the way."

"Any before June 1?"

"Yeah, one, and he cut a deal to keep them from garnisheerin' his salary at O'Reilly. Made a coupla payments, then bounced a coupla checks. By the time they tried to get his salary, he was gone."

"Mail?"

"Still coming to the old address. Nothin' interestin', just a lot of unpaid bills. No forwarding address. No new telephone number. Didn't change his driver's license, either."

"Car?"

"According to DMV he owns a seven year old Mazda. The insurance has expired, so have the plates. We did a national search for him, nothin'. No phone, no car. Nothin'. Like he disappeared."

"Anything else?"

"Nothin' yet. I reached out for his phone records, but they ain't come in yet, but you didn't hear that part, it ain't exactly Kosher without a court order."

"Where is this guy?"

"I dunno yet. Could be at the bottom of a river somewhere. Sure as shit, if he owes this kinda money legit, and he's a gambler, he owes one or two bookies. Maybe a loan shark, too. Could be in Witness Protection. If he is, we won't find him unless he fucks up. But if he's in WitPro, he's got more problems to worry about than some freakin' title insurance company, that's for sure."

I thanked Phil, and told him to send his bill to my home address, which I gave him. He offered some protection, again. I thanked him, but declined. Even if I wanted it, I couldn't afford it. My income, small to begin with, had just taken a serious hit, thanks to Majors' letter.

I looked at the other messages. I still hadn't checked my messages at home. What to do next?

I decided to take a walk.

I dropped off the check Majors had asked for with Rita, who didn't even say hello, and I made my way to the Garden, walking slowly because my body demanded it, and because I was in no rush. I had no place to go.

I followed the path to my bench, without thought, mostly out of habit. So I was more than a little startled to see Carolyn, sitting on my bench.

It looked like she had been crying.

Chapter 21

I jumped a bit. "Jesus, I didn't see you, you scared me!"

She just looked at me, with a stare similar to the one she had given me the first day we met.

"Where the *fuck* have you been?"

"I'm sorry, it's a long sto–"

"I don't want to hear it! Do you know what you've done? Why didn't you call me? I would have come over. We all would have. Why did you have to do it?"

"Do what? I didn't do anything!"

"Oh, Peter, that's bull shit. You're drinking again. Your sister even told Joel that you came to her house all hung over. Oh, my God, do you know what went on here Friday– and this morning! Joel got his balls crushed this morning, because of you! Goddammit, say something! Or are you drunk right now?"

"What do you mean, Joel got his balls crushed?"

"This morning, the partners held an emergency meeting. When you didn't show on Friday there was hell to pay. The title company's attorneys were screaming at me. Then they asked for a partner. Majors was the only one around, so Rita put the call in to him. Then came the death threat. Then the police came by looking for you this morning, right as the meeting started. Majors said you had to be cut off, thrown out. Joel wanted to wait until he spoke to you. We both had tried reaching you all weekend and again this morning. The partners' meeting got heated, with Joel defending you. We could hear it all in the hallway. Then your sister returned Joel's call, Rita put it through right into the meeting room. When she told Joel you had been on a bender, he had to give up. They voted Joel out as Managing Partner. It's Majors now. Joel left talking about leaving the firm altogether." She caught her breath and frowned at me.

"Peter, tell me the truth. Where have you been?"

I told her about the attack, and the hospital. I told her about the blood test. I unbuttoned my shirt and showed her the bruises. She winced. I told her that my sister and Lou had been wrong. I told her about Majors' letter.

"Yeah, we've been told that if we are even seen with you, we're fired."

"You mentioned a death threat. What were you talking about?"

"Friday morning Rita took a call for you. Anonymous. Said if you didn't keep your nose out of it, you'd be dead sorry."

"That's what he said, dead sorry? Keep out of what?"

"That's all Rita remembers. Joel was in court, we couldn't find you, so she went to Majors with it. They called the cops, but there is nothing they could do, especially since you are the potential complainant."

I stood, she sat, in silence.

"So when are you going to tell Joel?"

"I'm not going to and I'd like you to keep quiet about this, too."

"Why? If you weren't drinking, don't you think everyone will want to know that? It changes everything!"

"No it doesn't. The best thing for everybody involved is if I just go away quietly. There's been too much damage. Some things you just can't fix, no matter how much you want to. Remember from law school– you put a drop of ink in a glass of milk, there's no way to undo it. I've caused Joel enough trouble. I'm just going to leave."

"But you owe him an explanation!"

"No, I don't. I owe him some peace. He doesn't need me to be giving ammunition to his enemies in the firm. I've been there. You don't understand. It's war. Majors will use anything he can against Joel. I don't want my every mistake to come back to haunt Joel."

"But aren't these guys all friends?"

"In law firms, everybody starts out friendly, but as the firm grows, or especially in tough times, the friendships start to fade. It becomes about ego, and money. Especially money. It starts out an adventure, it winds up a business. You know, like in The Godfather."

"I hate that movie." She made a disgusted face, as she swiped at her nose with the tissue in her hand.

I smiled. "How can you hate The Godfather? Godfather III, OK, I agree with you, but not I or II. All this in-fighting among the partners? It's not personal, it's business. It's just what happens."

I looked at her, at her bright blue eyes, a bit puffy from the tears. I felt a tremble, an emptiness in my gut. I sighed.

"Go back to the office. You're going to be fine. Don't contact me again, I don't want you losing your job. I'll be fine, don't worry. I'm not going to drink. Go. Go get Sophie some money. Go on, get going."

Carolyn stood and came over to me. She gave me hug and a kiss on the cheek.

"You be careful." And she was gone.

My arms and ribs ached from the hug. My heart ached from the kiss goodbye.

*****

After Carolyn left, I realized I had no place to go.

They wanted me out of my office. I'd lost my team. I was facing a Grievance hearing in only 8 days. I had a good polygraph report, but an inconclusive handwriting analysis. I had suspicions about who did this, but so did the cops. Unfortunately, they suspected me.

There was little else I could do at the moment, so I decided to go back to Island Storage. I don't know why. My career pendulum had swung back again; I was seriously considering just turning in the license and heading West. Maybe Colorado. Go wash dishes in a restaurant, maybe do a little skiing. Not that I felt like doing either right now. Everything still hurt.

I went directly to the new room Ricky had set up for me. A big table, a comfortable chair, a desk lamp. Add my $5 Radio Shack clock and I could call this place home.

Ricky and Luis had brought in all the Helms files and all the Brownstein files. They were neatly piled up, awaiting my review. I got started.

Again, I found Helms to be neat, with the exception of the doodles and drawings. I leafed through the files, page by page, hindered by my bandaged hand and a wandering mind.

I had thought a lot about my daughter Patricia in the last few days. I wondered if I had lost her forever.

I guess I was always an alcoholic. Early on I limited my heavy drinking to home, to weekends. But even before the alcohol took over, my work, or rather my obsession with my work, consumed my life.

When a kid is growing up, she has needs. She needs love, of course, and time and understanding. She needs consistent discipline, a certain structure. I just wasn't there. It probably was worse for Patricia that I did come around once in a while, because when I did I was distracted, or drunk, or hung over, or anxious about the time I was missing from work. So here this kid thought she had a father, when all she had was a self-centered idiot who was sometimes there physically, but never emotionally. Now she wouldn't speak to me. Each month, on the 14th in honor of my first day of sobriety, I wrote her a letter. I told her how sorry I was, what was going on in my life, what I was doing, how much I would like a second chance, even if I didn't deserve one. Each letter was part apology, part diary, part wish list.

She returned every one. Unopened.

I saved the returned letters in a box in my office. At first, I told myself I was saving them to prove to her that I indeed did write them. Now I just kept them out of habit.

I wrote Lorraine similar letters, also enclosing 17% of whatever I had earned the month before. Her letters never came back, but she didn't cash the checks, either. For all I knew, Lorraine tore hers up.

After a while I switched from Helms' files to Brownstein's. I started with the most recent closed file and worked my way back. Some of the files were massive, completed complex purchases of large buildings. Others were thin, inquiries that never reached transaction stage.

I found four will files. I looked at the most recent. I didn't expect to find the signed original will in there. The office policy at O'Reilly's was to have the client take the original home with them, or else we would store it in the office's safe. Original wills were too important to be left in a file, though an unsigned copy of the draft would usually be maintained for future reference.

Sy's most recent Will file had about four pages of Greg Connolly's handwritten notes, a cover letter sending the draft to him, and an execution sheet filled in indicating the date and place Sy signed the will, and the names and addresses of the witnesses. According to the notes, Sy had signed his will in O'Reilly's big conference room, in front of Connolly, Vincent Helms and a secretary about three years ago. Helms was a witness? I thought about it. Helms had reported to Connolly, so that wasn't too strange. Still. I took a mental note to look for other files that the two of them had both worked on.

I looked at the file again. There wasn't a draft copy in the file, but from the notes I saw Sy had left his entire estate to a charitable trust. The two sons were specifically disinherited.

If the notes were accurate, Sy was appointing Greg Connolly as his Executor and as one of the Trustees of the charitable trust. Naming your attorney to these positions, especially if he is the person who drafted the will, is greatly frowned upon in New York. Too many unscrupulous attorneys had hoodwinked little old ladies out of their estates, or put themselves in a position to garner huge fiduciary fees. The rules had been changed to discourage this practice. It wasn't prohibited but it would be looked at very closely by the Surrogate's Court when this will was probated. Talk about walking a line. Connolly better have a good explanation for this when Sy dies, I muttered.

I took a break after several hours. I was the only person in the building, besides the evening attendant, an old man with "Sam" embroidered on his Island Storage shirt. I walked down the block to a 7-11 and got coffee and cookies for me and Sam. I was feeling a bit more limber and the headache was starting to recede a bit.

I called Phil. He was in.

"Petey, I been lookin' for you, where the hell are you?"

I told him. "Anything new on your end?"

"Yeah. I just don't know what it means."

"What've you got? Something on Connolly?"

"Not exactly. Kinda. Y'know that box he got out of storage?"

"Yeah, did you find it?"

"Sorta. That box was pulled by Connolly, but only so he could have it delivered."

"Delivered? To who?"

"That's what's weird. My info, and it's from a great source, don't ask, let's just say it's from somebody at O'Reilly's who knows, my info is that Connolly pulled the box and had it shipped to Levine, Johnson, Majors & Smolinski."

"You're kidding? When?"

"Let's just say it was before you went into rehab. Way before your stamp was used, kiddo."

"Really?"

"And this is the interesting part, Petey. The box?"

"Yeah?"

"It was delivered to Joel Levine. He signed for it himself."

*****

I tried to settle back into Helm's files. Why was the box delivered to Joel? Why didn't he tell me? What was in that box? Where was it now?

I knew I had to concentrate on one thing at a time. I re-focused on the files. They all dealt with corporate buy-outs, or mergers, or the purchase or sale of corporations. Helms wasn't very high on the food chain, so any file on a deal of significant size had a number of attorneys working on it. The smaller, Mom-and-Pop type deals, like the purchase and sale of a transmission shop, or a restaurant, those deals often only Helms worked on. It was the files that were truly "Helms" files that had the doodling and drawings; the larger files were pretty clean. I guess Helms felt comfortable in his own file, but not if a bunch of other lawyers were going to have access to it.

It was after 10 p.m. I had looked at over 200 files, including the files from Thursday. I was tired, ready to call it a tough, disappointing, depressing day. I decided to look at the last three files in the pile in front of me, when something caught my eye.

The file open in front of me dealt with the purchase of some stock from a minority shareholder in a small medical supply company. It was a Long Island based company; all of the shareholders lived here as well. I had gone through most of the file, when I reached four or five yellow sheets, clipped together. The main portion of each page contained draft terms, calculations, notes. The margins were covered in the Helms drawings and doodles I had become accustomed to. Except that the second sheet had a number written sideways in the margin, crossing over a doodle of a plane dropping bombs. I had gotten to the fourth page before I realized what I had seen.

I turned back to the second page. The number was a telephone number, with an area code I wasn't familiar with. What made it strange was that in the 200+ files I had already looked at, Helms never had written any words or numbers in the margins. Only drawings.

I looked through the rest of the file. It was one of Helms' last deals. He had worked on it the last month he was with O'Reilly, McManus. The last month before he disappeared. I copied the telephone number and went downstairs. I asked Sam if I could borrow a phone. He said sure, no problem. I guess since Ricky was paying the phone bill and Sam had gotten coffee and cookies from me, he figured generosity was in order. I thanked him, told him I'd be quick. He said he had to go to the head, would I hold the fort? I told him, sure, no problem. Trusting guy.

I punched in the telephone number. It rang four times, then an answering machine picked up. A woman's voice came on: "You have reached Foster Realty, the home of the friendly real estate agent. Leave your name, number and a brief message after the tone, and Arlene or Lucy will call you right back." I hung up as the tone sounded.

Sam was still using the facilities, so I called information. I gave them the area code and asked if they could tell me what area it covered. I waited a bit. I could hear Sam returning. The operator came back on the line, and told me the area code was for Pennsylvania. Western Pennsylvania.

Why would Helms need the telephone number of a real estate agency in western Pennsylvania? That was a silly question. A wave of excitement coursed through me. The real question was, did I really find it? Is this where Helms had run to? To whatever town Foster Realty in western Pennsylvania serviced so friendly? Would Arlene or Lucy know where he was? Or did this telephone number have absolutely no relationship to the notary whatsoever?

Chapter 22

So many thoughts were raging in my head, that even though I was so tired and hurt so much, I figured for sure there was no way I was going to get any sleep. I was wrong. I barely had my head on the pillow, when I was gone. I had been having a lot of dreams lately, but if I had any that night, by the time I awoke any traces had vanished.

I knew where I was going, but I wanted to wait until the morning rush hour had passed. Of course, merely waiting until after 10 or so on a Tuesday is no guarantee that the traffic leaving Long Island would be any lighter, but it's best to play the odds. The night before, back at Island Storage, Sam had let me use a computer. I searched for Foster's Real Estate. It was located at 567 Main Street, Transom, Pennsylvania, a little town outside Pittsburgh. I printed out the directions. I threw a few things into an overnight bag. I counted my cash, which didn't take too long, and made sure I had my wallet and license.

I was ready to leave, but I felt like something was missing. I thought about it as I watched "Good Morning America", waiting for the time to pass so I could start my quest for Vincent Helms. It hit me along about the third commercial. I was going on a trip, and I had no one to say goodbye to. I was leaving my itinerary with no one. If I got to Transom, and liked it, and chose to stay, other than Mrs. Murphy, who would be out her rent, no one would notice, much less care. I guessed this was true freedom, but if it was, it didn't feel good. In fact, it felt terrible. I wondered if this was how Vincent Helms felt when he disappeared. No family. No close friends. No job. No responsibilities. No real life.

I tried to shake off the feeling. I thought about going for a run before I left, but my head still felt sore, inside and out, and my body was still stiff. At least the blinding pain seemed to have passed. Maybe it was best I took it a bit easy, especially with a long drive in front of me.

I looked around at my apartment, as if for the last time, and started on my way. The day was hot, but overcast. I always prefer to drive on overcast days, when there is a lot less glare, or at night. There is something about driving at night, especially late at night, on a long trip that makes me excited, like I'm doing something illicit.

So off I went, in search of Vincent Helms. I played with the radio, looking for a talk show where people weren't screaming at each other, or some soft music not interrupted by blaring commercials. Back in my previous life, I was an unabashed car singer, blasting rock from my youth, pumped up and singing at the top of my lungs. I barely turned the radio on anymore. I appreciated the quiet.

I gave up trying to find a station and shut the radio off, just as I was zipping through the tollbooth for the Midtown Tunnel, my EZ Pass allowing me to bypass the traffic backed up waiting to pay cash. I love this device, where the toll is automatically read. It was my one concession to modern technology-- an EZ Pass is the only sane way to drive around New York.

Somewhere around the Jersey-Pennsylvania border I slid a CD into the dashboard and listened to John Gorka, a great contemporary folk singer. One of the counselors in rehab played him all the time, and I got hooked.

Gorka's songs are funny and poignant, and exquisitely written. One of his refrains struck me deep, and I thought about it often, both in and after rehab:

"There's a bar room for every way the wind blows,

And Temptation in every substance known;

You pull your own weight or else it pulls you,

And it gets harder the older that you've grown."

The southern tier of Pennsylvania steadily passed beneath my tires, with only a couple of quick rest stops. On the long stretch between Harrisburg and

Pittsburgh, I kept glancing at the clock. I had left New York at 9:30; it was 3:30 now. I really wanted to get to Foster's Realty before 5:00, if I could. Unfortunately, traffic came to a complete stop, just outside Pittsburgh. An accident *and* a construction zone. Looking beyond the graying concrete road barriers, I had a magnificent view of one of the rivers for about an hour, before traffic moved along. No way was I going to make Transom before the real estate office closed.

I was tempted to simply check in at the Marriott, right in the heart of the city. I like Pittsburgh. I've been there a few times on business. I like the bridges, I like the architecture of the new buildings, as well as the old. The restaurants are good, the bars even better. I used to take a suite at the Marriott, charging it to the client of course. However, on this excursion, "the client" had limited funds. I decided to drive on through to Transom, anyway, have a look around, and find a Motel 6. Some place relatively clean and definitely cheap.

I followed my directions and found Main Street, then Foster's, around 6. To my surprise, I could see people still in the narrow storefront. I slowed as I passed Foster's, and then continued past. Cars were parked all along Main Street. I stopped suddenly, too quickly really, and swung my car in a tight U-turn right into an open spot I had seen, at the last second, across the street. A black sedan, coming up from behind, missed me by only inches. He didn't honk, which I thought was unusual, given his New York plates and the bonehead move I had just pulled.

I got out of the car and tried to stretch. It felt like rigor mortis had set in and my mouth was gummy. I needed a shower and a toothbrush, and a bed to stretch out in, but since the agency was open, I figured I'd try my luck.

As I walked into the storefront, it was clear the young black male and the older white woman were packing up for the evening. The door had a set of bells attached to it, that rang far too loudly for such a small place.

"Can I help you?" asked the woman with a smile fake enough for a beauty queen.

"Yes, I hope so. I'm looking for a friend of mine. I believe he rented a house or an apartment from you sometime in May or June last year."

She didn't lose a watt from her smile, but a frostiness started to creep in.

"Well, I'm sure if he was a friend of yours, you would know his address, now wouldn't you?"

"Yes, well, you see, my friend has, well, my friend is..." I stopped. I had anticipated this line of defense, as any good trial attorney would, and had worked out a story in the car. I hoped it would work. I hung my head. "Well, you see, my friend is, well...we were *very* close, and he has...well, he doesn't have much time...and I think he thinks he gave it to me...and he left our apartment in The Village over the summer, I think he wanted to be alone when he..when he...." I stopped, and tried to get myself under control. "I think he's hiding because he's *so* upset, but I want to see him one last..one last..time." I sniffled.

Ice Queen bought it. The young guy clearly didn't, as I could tell from the smile on his face. Ice Queen wanted no part in helping me find my "friend", but she also had that small town impulse to help. So she did what most employers do when faced with an uncomfortable situation. She directed the young man, evidently named Anthony, to help me, and gave me a wide berth as she glided out the door.

We both watched her leave.

"That was pathetic, man. What are you, a cop?"

We both smiled. "Nope, just somebody who has to find somebody."

He started to get up. "I don't get paid overtime."

I reached in my pocket and pulled out a twenty. "This help?"

He looked at the twenty, then back at me with a smile. "Never liked Andrew Jackson, too much. He was from South Carolina. This is Pennsylvania. Ben Franklin is our man."

I shook my head. I wasn't giving this kid $100, no way. "But Ben wasn't even President. Not like my friend U.S. Grant." I put the twenty away and held up a fifty dollar bill.

"Man won the war, how can I turn him down?" Anthony took the $50 and sat back down. "What do you need?"

"I'm looking for a man name Vincent Helms, though I don't think he used that name. Called here, maybe came here, over a year ago, sometime in May or June. I figure he rented, rather than bought." I showed him Helms' photo from the O'Reilly, McManus brochure.

Anthony thought a bit, and nodded. Without saying anything to me, he went over to a loose leaf book, one of several on a set of file cabinets. He leafed through it.

"This place may be small, but we're pretty busy. This is the rental book. Everybody that comes in here gets a page. Let's see what we got."

While he looked, I made small talk. "I really appreciate your help. What do you do around here, anyway?"

"Me? I'm just here part time. I'm a senior at Lamont College. I'm thinking about going to law school next year."

"Really? That's great."

"Yeah. This place isn't so bad, but I want to move on, you know? I've got my real estate license, sold a few houses. I get a finder's fee from the apartments we rent out to college students. Helps pay the bills." He shrugged, as he kept looking, pulling out another book, and rifling through it.

He didn't look up. "This guy with a family or alone?"

"Figure he was alone."

Anthony turned through the pages. He stopped and read closely.

"Got a guy here....nah, I remember him, too old. Let's see...maybe...no, no, this guy was with a family and a dog. Your guy got a dog?" I told him I didn't think so.

He kept looking. He stopped, started tapping a page. "Yeah, yeah....this could be your guy. Called in, said he got us from the Chamber of Commerce referral line. First called last year, June 10th. Came in on June 26th. Signed a lease for July 1. Paid all cash, one year lease....hmmm, that's strange."

"What is?"

"He paid all twelve months rent, in advance, all cash. Our fee and the security, too. No credit references. Rent is high for this neighborhood, too. Looks like Arlene saw him coming."

"Got a name and an address?"

"Yeah, you know, I think this was your guy. Short, kinda nervous. Didn't have a New York accent though."

"Anthony. A name and an address?"

"Yeah, right here. Said his name was Thomas, Richard Thomas. Apartment 2C, 10 First Street."

"Can I get there from here?"

"Sure."

"Do you know where it is?"

"Yep."

I waited a bit. "Anthony, give me a break."

"I live in the complex. My dad is the super. Your guy doesn't live there anymore."

"Damn!"

"As a matter of fact, he moved out in the middle of the night, sometime this March or April. April, I think. I was just back from Spring Break. I helped my Dad move his stuff to the basement."

"Anthony...."

"Y'know, I'm on my way home. But I've got lot's of studying to do..."

"Could President Jackson convince you to hold off on that studying until I see the stuff in the basement?"

"I don't know. President Grant is a persuasive guy..."

"You already got $50 from me for three minutes work. That's $1000 an hour–which is a lot more than you could charge as a lawyer, my friend."

Anthony thought for a bit. "OK, $20. But I'm not carrying any of the stuff to your car– you're on your own."

"Deal."

Anthony and I walked to the apartment complex, a series of garden apartments, maybe 50 or so units. I told him I was a lawyer. We discussed what he could expect over the next three years at law school. As we walked on the grounds of the complex, we passed a lot of college-age girls; school must have started already. They all seemed to know Anthony.

"You seem pretty popular, Anthony."

"Well, housing is tight around here. People know I have a connection, I can help them get in here. These are about the nicest apartments in town."

"So let me guess. You get a finder's fee from Arlene, and you get a commission from these young ladies looking for decent housing."

Anthony laughed. "I guess you could call it a commission. Some pay me in money, and some are…y'know…"

"Nice to you."

"Yeah. Nice. I'm going to miss this place next year."

"And probably for a good many years after that, my friend."

We arrived at Helms' old building. Anthony unlocked a metal door, and led me down to the basement. He turned on the light, and pointed to a corner area. There was a pile of furniture and bags and boxes. Not too much. Looked like a couch and a chair; there was a mattress and box spring leaning against the wall behind the couch. Piled on the couch were some clothes, still on hangers, and some boxes. There were a couple of shopping bags dumped on the chair.

"Why'd you keep this stuff?"

"The guy just took off. There was still a couple of months left on his lease, but he was gone. Dad wanted the place cleaned out, but he was afraid the guy would come back and want his stuff. So we piled it here."

"How'd you know he was gone?"

"I didn't, but my Dad did." Anthony pointed to the shopping bags. "The guy stopped picking up his mail. It was piling up, big time, so we put it in those shopping bags. We went into the apartment with a buddy of mine, a cop. We had an old lady die on us once, man, did that suck! Smelled and everything. But when we went into your guy's place, I mean there was some stuff left, but it looked like pretty much everything was gone. You know, most of his clothes, underwear, toothbrush, all that, cleaned out. Like he left in a rush."

I picked through some of the stuff. "Mind if I look through the mail?"

"Nah, I don't care. I got some work to do, though, and my Dad'll kill me if he finds you down here. Listen, I've got my own place. Why don't you come up to my apartment and go through this stuff?"

"Won't your Dad miss it?"

"You kidding? He's been asking me to clean out this crap for months. If Thomas ever comes back, hey, we had a flood, you know what I mean." He winked.

I smiled. Over the years, I had more than a few clients who lost key, invariably harmful, documents in a "flood". It happened so often, I was sure that Noah had to build an ark because a bunch of his neighbors were facing tax audits.

We went up to Anthony's apartment, with him peppering me some more about law school and being a lawyer. I sat at his kitchen table and dumped the bags out. Anthony told me to throw out anything I wasn't going to use; he gave me a big plastic trash bag for the garbage. He went off into the living room to do some reading for a class.

The sorting went quickly. Most of the mail was junk, lots of advertisements and thick envelopes addressed to "occupant" and "resident".

I made a small pile of envelopes to look through. I left the pile unopened until I had gone through it all. There were no personal letters, no credit card bills. No rental agreements from a future apartment. The only things of interest to me were his cell phone bills and his bank statements. There were three of each, covering April, May and June of this year.

I knew that by opening these envelopes I was committing a felony, a federal felony at that. I weighed that thought for about a second and half, and ripped open the last cell phone bill, the one for June, just two months ago.

There was no activity. No calls, no payments. The bill said the account was suspended and would be terminated. I leafed back through some of the mail I had tossed out; I found the termination statement, dated July.

The bill for May, likewise, had no activity.

The bill for April, though, was revealing. All outgoing calls ceased as of April 20th. Before the 20th, there wasn't that much outgoing activity on it. Three or four numbers appeared 6 or 7 times each. Local calls.

On the 20th, though, there was a series of calls, maybe 8 or 9. Some 1-800 numbers. The others were long distance, to an area code I was unfamiliar with.

I have trouble reading cell phone bills; they always confuse me. I shuffled the bill around a bit, and found the list of incoming calls. Or, rather, incoming call. One. From a long distance number that was blocked. It lasted 16 minutes. I compared the time to the outgoing calls on the 20th. The call had come in at 6:03 p.m. It set off all of the other calls Helms had made that night. The 20th had to be the night Helms fled, and that incoming call had sent him running.

I had just finished looking at the cell phone bills, when Anthony came in the kitchen, opened the refrigerator, and pulled out two beers. He held one out to me. It looked good. Too good. I shook my head. "I'll take some water if you got it."

"You sure?"

"Yeah, but thanks."

I took the water and drank deeply.

"Anthony, any idea why I don't have any regular telephone bills in here?"

"Sure, old man. Most kids don't bother getting a land line anymore. The cell is easier to get, easier to move with. Cheaper, too. If your guy wasn't planning to stick around, the cell phone made more sense." He looked down at the open bill. "Find anything?"

"I think so, but I'm not sure."

"Can I help?"

I thought about it. Why not? Anthony sat down, and I explained the situation to him.

"So you think this guy forged this guy Sy's name and yours and took off? With millions?"

"Yeah, but I don't know if he got the money or not. Something's not right."

"But it looks like the cops are going to clear you, right? I mean, if they can't prove you signed anything..."

"Probably."

"So why you looking for this guy? Seems to me the title insurance company should be looking for him, not you."

I thought about it. "You're probably right, but..."

"But you're hooked now. You want to clear your name."

"Something like that. It's the challenge, I guess. I don't like to lose, and not knowing how this ends would seem like losing to me."

"Be careful. You start talking millions, that's when people start getting hurt."

I sat quietly. I hadn't told Anthony that somebody apparently already had been killed. I felt the ache in my head. I had kind of convinced myself my mystery attacker was a burglar or maybe Goldtooth. Anthony made me remember what Phil had said–maybe it hadn't been Goldtooth who had attacked me. Maybe it was the guys who offed Singh. Maybe it was the same guys who caused Helms to flee in the night. I shivered. What had I gotten dragged into?

I looked back at the cell phone bill in my hand and showed it to Anthony.

"Recognize any of these numbers?"

Anthony glanced at the bill and laughed. "Sure, I do. That one is the pizza place. This one is Chinese." He reached into a drawer, chock full of paper, and pulled out a huge handful of take out menus. "Here, look through these."

In about ten minutes we had identified all of Helms' pre-April 20th numbers. It seemed Vincent didn't cook much for himself.

I turned to the bank statements. They were from a local bank, Pleasant Valley State. I opened the April statement first. It was a joint checking and savings account entitled Richard Thomas. No "in trust for".

The balance at the end of April was $485,237.52.

Bingo.

The checks were few. The cell phone. A few stores, all local. No credit cards. No plane tickets.

The account had ATM access, but before the 20th there was no ATM activity at all. On the 20th, though, and for each day until the end of the month there was an identical withdrawal of $400. The 20th had been done here in Transom. The rest were all in Hershey, Pennsylvania, at the Giant Supermarket #2367. $400 per day. Every day.

I opened the May statement. And the June one. All the same. $400 per day, everyday. All at the same ATM machine.

Anthony spoke first. "Man likes cash, huh? And it looks like he's in Hershey, now. What do you think?"

I thought for a few minutes, twirling the statements on the kitchen table.

"You use an ATM, Anthony?"

"Sure."

"What's the maximum you can take out in one day?"

"Me? $400."

"Anybody ask you for ID when you go to the ATM?"

"Hell, no. You just swipe in the card, punch in your pin code, and, boom, it's like winning a slot machine."

"Except it's your money, right?"

"Hell, yeah."

"OK, suppose Helms, or Thomas, has to hide. He can't use his real name, he can't use Thomas for some reason. He takes off. He dumps his cell phone, he clears out of his apartment. But he needs cash to live."

"But he can't cash a check, 'cause he's not Richard Thomas anymore."

"Right."

"So why doesn't he just get a new fake name, and write a check to himself?"

I thought about it.

"Anthony. You're a smart guy. You're a hustler. I want a new ID. Where do I go?"

Anthony thought about it. "I don't know. There's a printer near school who'll make up a fake driver's license for you, if you're underage and need proof for the bars."

"But I'm talking about me. How do I, a 40 year old guy, or Helms, a 30 year old or so guy, how does he get a fake ID? Especially since 9/11?"

"Ask around I guess."

"C'mon, if I just walked in anywhere, they'd figure I was a cop. Helms went to Harvard, for Christ sakes. Anyone would figure he was undercover. So where does he go? I mean for real proof, proof that would let him get a bank account, credit, all the things he's going to need?"

189

Anthony sat still for a bit. He took a long pull on his beer bottle. It looked too good. "I don't know."

"Neither do I, Anthony, and I'll bet neither does Helms. Or at least he didn't in May or June. Maybe now, but it took him a while, it had to."

"So he's living off the ATM."

"Exactly. It's just too bad these statements only go until June. I'd love to know where he is now. If he's still living off the ATM, it'll show me where he's at. If he established a new ID, I'll bet you're right, there's a check from "Thomas" to his new name. And then I can find him."

Anthony pulled out his cell phone and started texting. A few minutes later, he looked at his phone and smiled.

"Tomorrow morning, meet me at the Pleasant Valley State branch right on Main Street. The assistant manager, Tina, is going to help us."

"Anthony! Thank you! Tina a friend of yours?"

"Yeah, she graduated last year. Lives in Apartment 43D. I helped her get the apartment. She thinks she owes me a favor, but as I remember it she paid me back already." He smiled.

"Anthony, I can't thank you enough. Can she do this? I don't want her to lose her job, or anything."

"Nope, she said tomorrow would be perfect, her manager's on vacation. Besides," his smile got broader, "You're going to open an account tomorrow."

I chuckled. "Mmmhmm. And is there a fee for opening this account?"

"You remember my friend Ben Franklin? Tina and I are *both* big fans."

I pulled out two one hundred dollar bills. "Anthony, you should seriously reconsider law school. I think you're going to be taking a pay cut."

Chapter 23

I found a little roadside motel down on Main Street and crashed there for the night. The place was....well, it wasn't the Riverfront Marriott, but it was OK. I was still hurting from the beating and tired from the long drive. I fell asleep quickly.

Nine a.m. found me at the front door of Pleasant Valley State Bank sweating already, even in the shade. I waited a few minutes for Anthony. We headed straight for a drop-dead gorgeous young blonde girl, maybe early 20's, sitting at one of the platform desks. She was on the phone, but beckoned us with a killer smile.

We stood by her desk and waited for her to finish her call. When she was done, she stood and came around the desk. She shook my hand, introducing herself as Tina Young. She gave Anthony a big hug and a kiss on the cheek.

We sat down. Tina took over, punching at the keys to her computer as she spoke.

"I pulled up the account you gave me. It's still open. It's just like you said. Most of the activity is ATM withdrawals. Always $400. Always at the same ATM. I pulled the address for you," Tina said as she slid a piece of paper with very crisp, clean handwriting on it, to me. "The withdrawals are all just before 5 in the afternoon, give or take a few minutes. See?" she said pointing at the screen. "4:52, 4:54, 4:48, 4:47. They're pretty much all like that. Let's see....last one we have on our records is....yesterday."

"You said most of the activity is withdrawals. What else do you see?"

"Well, there have been, let's see one, two, three, four, five, five checks that have cleared the account. All made to cash. The first one was in early June, then late June, then two in July, then two so far in August. The first two checks were for $1,000. The third was for $5000. The last two were each $10,000."

"Can you tell who cashed the checks?"

"No, sorry, our system doesn't do that. I would have to order the checks." Tina looked at me with a little frown. I figured ordering checks from Thomas' account without his permission would cause problems for her, if she could even do it, and besides, I didn't think I had the time. When I told her not to bother, she relaxed, visibly relieved.

Tina tapped through a few more screens. "He changed his mailing address, by the way. The statements are going to a post office box in Harrisburg."

"Anything else?"

"His balance is a little under $400,000."

It would take Helms a long time to empty this account, $400 at a time. Then again, that gave him $12,000 a month to live on. But these checks made payable to cash, they just didn't make sense. Why would he risk cashing Richard Thomas' checks, and who was cashing them for him?

"Anything else you can tell me? Do you know how he opened the account?"

"Let's see. Yes, he showed a Florida driver's license and had his signature guaranteed by a Florida Bank. He made an opening deposit of $1,000,000 even. No other deposits."

"Any large withdrawals before April?"

"Let's see." She scrolled through the screens. Her voice dropped a bit, like she was passing on gossip. "Let me tell you, he spent a lot of money on American Express." Tina counted, moving her lips as she did. "Over $200,000. But the last American Express check was in October last year. After that, not much spending. He did make large cash withdrawals from time to time."

She looked up from her screen, pushing her hair behind her right ear. "I hope that helped."

"It most certainly did. I can't thank you enough."

"I really shouldn't be doing this, you know. But Anthony said it was important, and that you would keep this confidential."

"Absolutely. I was never here. We never met. Thank you, Tina, thank you *very* much for your help."

"You are most welcome. And you," Tina said, turning to Anthony, "You, I will see Saturday night." They smiled at each other, parting with another full-bodied hug.

We went outside. I turned to Anthony.

"Saturday night?"

"Yeah, we're going into Pittsburgh, dinner, like that."

"How come I think both of those Ben Franklins are still in your pocket, my friend?"

He just laughed. I thanked him, and gave him my card. I told him to call me if he ever needed anything in New York. He said he would and I believed him. I think Anthony kept close track of favors in and favors out.

I got in my car and headed back across Pennsylvania, winding my way along US 76, bearing north to Harrisburg, then off the interstate, following the signs for Hershey, the home of The Great American Chocolate Bar, and a world-class amusement park. Or so I had heard. Lorraine used to take Patricia there; I was always too busy, bowing out at the last minute, and letting them go alone.

I thought about Helms, and his bank account. I was pretty sure I knew what was going on; the next several hours would probably tell the tale. I found a roadside motel with a "vacancy" sign, right down the block from a series of factory outlets, clustered together in mini open-air malls. From the door of my second floor room I could see the roller coasters of Hershey Park rising high into the bright, hot, glaring Pennsylvania sky. I turned the air conditioner in my room on high; it choked out a mild stream of barely cool air that tried to squeeze through the stifling thickness of the room, like a creek pushing its way through the Mojave. I had checked in at about noon. I had a few hours to kill. My first plan, to hang out in the room, wasn't going to cut it– it was too damn hot, and the AC was going to take way too long to cool off even this little room.

I decided to explore the town. I went back to the front desk and got directions to the Giant supermarket where the ATM was located. It was close. I wanted to check out the ATM early and find a good place to perform my very first surveillance. I followed the motel clerk's directions and found the Giant with no problem. The supermarket was fronted by a large parking lot, half empty on this Wednesday afternoon. From my car, the Giant was straight ahead of me, stretching to the left. To the right, connected to the supermarket was a small strip of storefronts. Starting at the Giant, from left to right, there was a florist, a hairdresser, a movie rental shop and a sports bar. Wally's Sports Bar.

Bingo.

I wasn't a betting man, but Vincent Helms was. Phil's report painted Helms as a gambler and apparently not a very good one. The debts, the Atlantic City accounts in default. Phil was right.

And so I'd bet the ranch, if I had one, that Helms' afternoon trek was to the ATM in the Giant and then on to Wally's Sports Bar for an evening of betting. Those checks made payable to cash? I'd bet the house, if I had one, that the checks went to a bookie. Why would Helms risk exposure as Richard Thomas in this supposed hide-a-way? Because as bad as drunks can get, and I should know how bad that is, there is nothing as bad as a gambler.

Gamblers, bad gamblers, problem gamblers, combine all the worst characteristics of alcoholics and crack addicts. They come from all stations and classes of life. They are line-walkers, always living for the next bet, the next rush. When they win, they're big spenders, like it's found money. When they lose, they try to make it up on the next hit, the next game, the next long shot. They get desperate. They lie to themselves and to everyone else. They'll lose everything they've got and go back with everything they can borrow or steal, and that's still not enough.

A drunk walks into a liquor store without a dollar in his pocket, he walks out without a bottle. A crack addict tries to buy a hit without money, she's out cold on her ass, unless her ass is good enough to sell, but that's another story. But with gamblers, there's always some bookie who'll take the bet without looking in your pocket. Gamblers can lose not only everything they've got, they can lose money they'll never, ever, have. All in one night, or on one game, on one roll of the dice, on one sure thing. And then the bookie comes looking for his money, introducing the threat of violence, and often the actuality of violence, into the picture.

A gambler's desperation. It's enough to make a man do crazy things. Like throw away a promising legal career. Like commit forgeries. Like risk blowing a hide-out to pay off a bookie. What if Helms was desperate and Connolly knew it? Maybe Connolly had used Helms as a pawn in this. Helms was the key.

I got out of the car and walked across the parking lot, waves of heat rising from the scorching blacktop. I entered the crisp, jarringly cold air in the Giant. I felt my sweaty shirt, sticking to my back, freeze. It felt sensational. I walked around the store, looking at the layout, pretending I was shopping. As I approached the checkout, I spied the ATM machine. I looked around; there was only one way for the public to go in and out of the store. I could watch the doors from my car, out in the parking lot.

I steeled myself for what I had to do next. I walked out of the Giant and headed to Wally's Sports Bar. Helms could already be in there, but I doubted it. Except for maybe a day baseball game or two, it was too early for any action. I moved from the bright sunshine of the sidewalk to the darkness of the bar. It felt familiar; I had entered a lot of bars in the daytime, not leaving them until the deepest of nighttime.

The first thing that hit me was the smell. Stale beer, mixed with stagnant air; pungent and sweet at the same time. Smoke lingering in the wood of the bar. Nothing else smells like an old man's tavern.

There was a huge man behind the bar, well over 6'5" and long past 350. He was maybe around my age, but with his shaved head and bushy goatee, it was hard to tell. Wally's Sports Bar was maybe 15 feet wide and from what I could see, maybe 40 or 50 feet deep. The bar was in the front of the room, taking up the left half as I walked in, stretching back about 20 feet, fronted by a dozen or so stools. Further along the left wall, going back to what looked like a storeroom and the restrooms, were 5 or 6 booths, each with their own swag lamp dripping small circles of light on stained, initial-carved, dark wood tables with high backed, attached benches. Everywhere you looked, from every angle, there was a TV. There had to be 15 of them. Right now only 3 were playing. Two had the Cubs game; one was showing some horse track.

I sat at the end of the bar, closest to the booths, away from the door. The booths were empty; only one ancient guy nursed a beer on a stool back near the door. The mountain behind the bar came over and asked me what I wanted.

"For my wife to hurry up so we can get to the park sometime today," I said with a smile. The Mountain didn't find me amusing.

"Um, just a Diet Coke, please."

"No diet."

"Just a Coke, then."

He wasn't impressed. I didn't care. I was sweating. I tried to tell myself I was feeling the heat, but I knew that wasn't it. Or that I was scared, so close to actually facing Helms. I was scared, alright, but that wasn't why my stomach was fluttering, my heart was pounding, and my pores were leaking like a Congressman with a secret. I was "freaking out" as the kids would say because I was sitting in a bar, all by myself. Sitting and drinking a Coke. It would be so easy to tell Mountain, hey, let me have a beer. Or, how about having a shot of Jack with me, whadayasay? Just one for the nerves. Just one. I promise, just one, to kinda fit in here. So I don't stick out. Hey, I'm supposed to be on surveillance. Who walks into Wally's Sports Bar on a hot Wednesday afternoon and doesn't have a Rolling Rock or two?

Me, that's who. I sipped half of the flat Coke, laid a couple of bucks on the bar, and went back to the bathroom. There probably was a back door through the storage room, which was latched with a combination lock. But there was no rear public exit, to my surprise. That had to be a fire code violation, but since I planned a one-man stakeout, a single entrance suited me fine.

I peed, because one thing I have learned since I turned 40 was to never pass up the chance to pee. Then I headed out. Mountain didn't say goodbye or encourage me to come back. Perhaps I should have reported him to the Hershey Chamber of Commerce.

I drove around the town for while, getting my bearings. The street lights on Main Street are all in the shape of Hershey Kisses. I think I knew that. I think a six or seven year old Patricia had told me that once. I grabbed a sandwich at a cozy lunch shop, with an ice cold fizzy Diet Coke, and then meandered down the block. I could smell the chocolate in the air from the factory when the wind was still, but I got a nice whiff of cow manure when the breeze blew in from the west. I was still sore and my head was starting to pound again. I popped into a pharmacy, one of the chains that seem to have dotted America like chicken pox or Starbucks. I bought some Advil and a large bottle of water.

Then I headed back to my motel room, in the hopes it had cooled enough so that the water I had just purchased wouldn't boil. The room wasn't much better than when I left it, but at least the air wasn't as syrupy as it had been. I stripped down and took a shower. The water pressure was as weak as the air conditioning, but the water was colder. I threw on a pair of shorts and lay on top of the bed, watching some really bad courtroom TV show while I slugged down the Advil and the entire bottle of water.

I called my sponsor. I don't like calling him at work, so I kept the conversation short. I just wanted to touch base. Wally's Bar had left me edgy.

I lay on the bed, feeling wisps of almost cool air slide across me. I thought about Helms, about Connolly, about Marie, and about Carolyn. I thought about Joel and my box. The same questions haunted me. If Joel had the box, why didn't he give it to me when I moved into the office? Why did he ask Connolly for it? The thought that maybe Joel was so supportive because he was guilty about something tried to dance into my head, but I dismissed it brusquely. There was nobody in this world I trusted more than Joel Levine. Period. End of discussion.

I thought about Patricia. Would I ever see her again, if for no other reason than to apologize? I had flittering memories of her, a little girl smiling at her Daddy, a picture of her on a carousel, I think. I wondered if she would ever open one of my letters, or if she would just keep returning them. No matter; I'd keep sending them.

Anthony's friend, Tina, said the ATM withdrawals were mostly just before 5 each day. I got dressed, bought a copy of the local paper from the machine in front of the motel office, picked up another big bottle of water, and by around 3:30, I had positioned myself towards the middle of the parking lot, facing so I could clearly see the Giant and Wally's.

I was ready. I hoped.

I sat in the car with the engine running for the air conditioning, while I read more than I ever wanted to know about Penn State football and the Derry Township library battle. I actually didn't read much. Mostly I watched.

At a quarter to five, my heart leaped from my chest. I saw him! Helms, unmistakably Helms, was walking towards the doors of the Giant. He had a newspaper under his arm. It seemed like an eternity, but in about 5 minutes he walked back out, and right down the sidewalk to Wally's Sports Bar.

Bingo.

I had plotted out my attack back in the motel room. I was going to wait. Let Helms have a couple of drinks, let him get settled. My guess was he was in for the night, setting his bets on the early games, planning to stick around for the games from the coast that wouldn't finish until around midnight here, or later. Win a few, lose a few more. I wanted to let him get loose before I confronted him. Besides, if I was wrong, he had to come right back out in front of me, and I'd follow him home.

I waited in the car, with the engine running and the AC on, until 8 p.m. I was going to wait longer except that I had a gas tank that needed to be filled, and my own tank which needed to be emptied. Keeping the car on this long had used up a lot of gas. Drinking two big bottles of water was more than my middle-age bladder could handle.

This seemed so silly, but I couldn't face Helms dancing around and trying to keep my legs crossed. And I couldn't just walk passed him to the bathroom in Wally's. I knew I was taking a chance that Helms would leave, but I had to go, badly. I had to balance the risk. I went into the Giant, and half-ran to the restroom, which was thankfully unoccupied.

I finished up, took a deep breath and strode down the sidewalk to Wally's.

From the window, I could see ten or so guys in the bar, which went along with my count from my car. I saw Helms. He was at the end of the bar, right near where I had been sitting earlier that afternoon, at the far end from the door, close to the booths. He was intently watching a ballgame on the TV directly in front of him. He didn't look happy.

I walked in and sat at the stool closest to the door, keeping seven or eight guys between me and Helms. My heart was hammering and I was glad I had just taken care of business. The Mountain was still behind the bar. He came over. I didn't think he had specially ordered any diet soda for me since this afternoon, so I just asked for a Coke. He eyed me up and down; I figured he thought I was a cop. He didn't look happy; Helms didn't look happy. None of the guys at the bar looked happy. Come to think of it, I wasn't real happy, either. Maybe Wally's just wasn't a happy place.

I left a five on the bar, leaving my drink after one sip, and slid behind the guys at the stools until I was standing right behind and a little to the left of Helms. He had just finished cursing out the pitcher for giving up a double, when I leaned in behind him, putting my right arm under his left. He started to pull away from me, but I had a death grip on him.

I put my mouth right next to his left ear. "Let's you and me have a talk in one of these booths, *Vincent.*" He jumped, and tried to turn to see who I was.

"Don't make a scene. You don't want the cops here, do you?"

He shook his head. I half pushed, half lifted him away from the bar. I glanced back. The Mountain was talking with two guys at the other end of the bar, arguing over the spread on the upcoming Penn State game. I led Helms to the rearmost booth, placing him furthest from the door. I slid in the other side, but not too far, in case he made a run for it.

"Who the hell are you?" he demanded. He must have regained some of his composure. "Why'd you call me Vincent, huh?"

I hadn't had much to do with Helms at O'Reilly, McManus. We were two ships passing, I guess. I looked at him now. If he was 5'4", it was a lot. Maybe 140 pounds. He looked like shit, all drawn and pallid. He was nervous to the extreme, his hands, his eyes, his face, his whole body twitching and darting and rocking. He was like a downed, live electric line, sparking and jumping in his seat, his hands twisting and tapping the table. He was making me nuts.

"Take a good look, Vincent." I leaned in, so my face was under the swag light. Through the rapid blinking of his eyes, through his beer-induced haze, through his unquestionable panic, across the two years since we had seen each other, and beyond the disorientation of seeing somebody in an out-of-context-place, he looked at me. And then he remembered. He tried to leap from the booth, but I had stretched my leg under the table, putting my foot on the edge of his bench, blocking his exit. He almost tripped over me– I put out my arm, and shoved him back in his seat.

"I'll call Wally!" I assumed that was Mountain.

"Go ahead. I'll tell him you still have over 300 thousand in an account at Pleasant Valley State and that you're wanted by the cops in New York. Who do you think Wally's going to care more about, me, or the easiest blackmail target since Monica got her dress dirty?" My, I was talkative, and eloquent, tonight!

He slumped in his seat. "Is that what you want? The rest of my money? And how did you know?!?" He looked like how I probably did when ADA Melendez had shown me that deed, which now seemed like a lifetime ago.

"I don't want your money. I want some answers."

"About what?"

"Vincent, you want to play stupid, that's fine with me. I'll walk out of here and call the cops. They'll find you soon enough. Unless there's somebody else you're worried about. Maybe the guys that killed Tariq."

His eyes got huge. If his body was jangling before, now it was like he was sitting on an electric chair and I had just thrown the switch.

I sat. And waited. He squirmed, and changed positions on the bench every few seconds, like it was on fire.

"Alright, alright. What do you want to know?"

I stayed still. He kept up his rocking and twisting.

"OK, OK, OK, I'll tell you. You found me, you probably know anyway."

I just kept staring at him.

"Listen, I'm sorry I pretended to be you, but I didn't have a choice.

200

Besides, you were out of there, last I heard you were drunk, sleeping on floors. Nobody was supposed to get hurt. Nobody, I swear to God."

I waited.

"So, what do you know, huh? You going to turn me in? C'mon, Pete, uh Mr. De Stio, please, I swear, nobody was supposed to get hurt. The money was supposed to be paid back, I swear it. Oh, God, how did I get into this? Oh, God! Please, Jesus Christ, say *something*!"

I nodded. "Calm down, Vincent. Keep it cool. Tell me everything, from the start. You owed the bookies, right?"

"Yeah, I always win, but I don't know, you know it was bad luck. I got on a cold streak, see, craps is my game, I came up with a system back in college, and I always won, but then I hit a cold streak, and, and I got shut out of the casinos, I just couldn't pay them. So I started, you know, with some basketball, and then the next thing I know, I'm, I'm tapped out, and I owe this guy almost 200 thousand, with the vig and all. And I couldn't even keep up with the interest much less pay down the loan. I tried to borrow from the firm, but Connolly just laughed at me, the asshole. I thought he was my 'mentor', the prick."

"So Connolly knew you owed money on the street?"

"Well, no, not really, I told him some story, hell, I don't remember what I told him, but he said, no, no way. I mean, I didn't know what to do, you know? You been there, right?"

"What happened next?"

"C'mon, why should I tell you? Right, like you want a big confession, huh? Well fuck you! That's all, I'm not talking anymore."

I stared at him. I kept my voice low. I hoped it sounded menacing. "Here's the deal Vincent. You tell me everything. And no bullshit. Remember, I found you. You don't know how much I know, and how much I don't. Lie to me, refuse to answer my questions, and I'll get up and walk out of here. But Vincent, when I do, I'm calling the cops and I'm calling the boys."

I didn't think it was possible, but his eyes got bigger.

"Don't think I don't have connections with the boys, Vincent." Now came the riskiest part of my bluff, but I needed to push him over the edge if I could. "Don't forget, you were at the closing when the money was borrowed. All I have to do is show your photo to the title company, and you're dead."

He slumped. Bingo.

"How do I know you haven't done it already? And why won't you do it anyway?"

"You don't know. But here's my promise. You tell me what I want to know and I won't tell the boys anything and I won't tell the cops where you are. That'll give you a head start. With 300 grand you should be able to hide again."

He thought about it, drumming his fingers, shaking his legs under the table. A caged rat looking for an escape route. He couldn't find one.

"OK, I don't have a choice here, do I? I have your word? You swear to God?" I nodded. "Shit. OK. Alright. OK, so like I said, I owed a ton to this bookie, right? So he says he's got a proposition. He's got another guy who's in the hole, but he's got an idea. They got a connection at a bank who can loan them money, but they got to show collateral. He tells me this other guy has a plan, but he needs some help. If I help out, they'll wipe out my debt. So I meet with the guy, hear out his plan."

"Harris Mathews."

"Yeah! Mathews! You know him?"

"No, Vincent, I don't know him. Who is he, really? Harris Mathews doesn't exist."

Vincent looked away. "Really? I didn't know that."

"Don't bullshit me Vincent. Who is Mathews?"

"Jesus, man, I don't know! I swear to God!"

"Go on."

"Anyway, Mathews and I meet. He tells me, look, I know this property that's free and clear. He wants to forge a deed into a dummy corporation, then borrow off it. I tell him, it won't work, the owner will find out when they do an inspection or when the tax bills stop coming, whatever. But then I think, hey, if we time the transactions right, and deed the property right back to the true

202

owner, the tax bills will keep going to him."

"So that was your idea, deeding back the property?"

"Yeah, well I had a deal once where we flipped properties back and forth, you know? And we realized we did it so fast, the tax bills just kept coming without interruption. I thought that was interesting, you know? Funny what you remember."

"So you decided to do the deal, huh?"

"Not right away. This guy, Mathews, he tells me he can take care of the inspection, no problem, he's got access to the building. I told him I didn't want any part of it, because as soon as the first payment was due, the bank would start foreclosure proceedings and then the bank would find out who the true owner was and then they'd be after us. But Mathews, says, no, he's going to pay the mortgage every month, so nobody would ever know."

"He said he would pay the mortgage?"

"Yeah. But I said, what if the owner wants to sell or mortgage the property himself? Our mortgage might not be in his name, but it would still be a lien on the property. As soon as they ran a check on the place, they'd find out. And we'd have no control over that, you know."

"But he said he knew the owner very well, no way was he selling or borrowing on it. And then he said he was going to be coming into some big money soon, anyway, and he was going to pay the loan off."

"And you believed him?"

Again, he looked away. "Yeah, I did."

"So you got a million dollars."

"It wasn't set up like that, at first. Ah, man, this is where we messed up. See originally Mathews was going to borrow about 900K on this one piece of property. It was all going to go to the bookie, to get me and Mathews straight and clear. We met with the guy from the bank, that Singh guy, and gave him some bogus documents. I mean, he knew all about it, he was in on it. Then Singh and Mathews start talking, and the next thing I know it's a multimillion dollar deal, spread over two properties."

"Did the bookie know?"

"No way. All he knew about was the first property, the smaller one. When he found out later, he was pissed. I mean, why the hell should he care, he got his money? But Mathews said it was because we tapped out Singh at the bank. I think they were going to use him on other deals. Then when the foreclosure started, they went right to Singh, you know, cause it was his loan at the bank."

"Go back. When you did the deal with the two properties, what happened?"

"Well, the bookie got his money, the 900K. I got a million, I know Singh got some big dollars, maybe a couple of million. Mathews was supposed to take his money and set up a fund to keep paying off the mortgage, until his windfall came in. I figured it would at least buy us four or five years, let things cool off."

"But it didn't work that way."

"No, no it didn't. I quit O'Reilly, McManus right away, and moved out. I owed a lot of money, credit cards, the casinos, like that. I didn't want my money just going to creditors and I didn't want to file bankruptcy. Too many questions, y'know? I figured I was straight with the boys, so they wouldn't come looking for me, y'know. I wanted a fresh start. This was my chance to start over, clean."

"So you became Richard Thomas of Transom Pennsylvania."

"Yeah, Mathews got me the fake ID."

"Why Transom?"

"I had a cousin who went to college there. I visited him a couple of times. Seemed as good a place as any. Suburban. Quiet. I figured I needed to slow down, take a break, you know? I thought, you know, if I could get away from places where gambling was so easy, I could, you know, stay clean. Didn't work out too well, though."

"Go on."

"I kept in touch with Mathews. I just knew something was going to go wrong. Then Mathews stopped paying the mortgage back around February. The bank started an investigation of the file and found out the supporting documents were phony. They started looking at Singh. He panicked and told the bookie about the whole thing, our side deal, and everything. Told Mathews he was going to go to the cops, cut a deal. Next thing you know, bam! He's gone!"

"And Mathews calls you and tells you to run."

"Yeah. He found out they were looking for him and me, too, now that they knew how much money we borrowed. So I said, what do they want? He tells me they want like $5 million. So I tell him to give it them, he should have plenty left. But he tells me it's invested. Invested, right. Says he needs some time to cash in some holdings, then he can make it all right. Told me to lay low for a little bit, he'd take care of it. So I came here."

"Why here?"

"I came here when I was a kid. It's a nice place."

"Wally over there, he take book?"

Silence.

"Vincent."

"Yeah."

"Takes checks made out to cash, too, right?"

His eyes got big again. "How the hell did you know that?"

"So where is Harris Mathews?"

"I don't know. I had a cell number for him. But it's dead now."

Something was missing. I believed Helms mostly. Just one thing he said didn't ring true.

"How was Mathews going to come into big money?"

Helms' twitching ratcheted up another notch.

"I don't know, I swear. C'mon, Peter, you're not going to turn me in are you? Can you give me a couple of days? If they find me, they'll kill me, whether I'm in jail or not. You got to help me."

"Who is Mathews?"

"For Christ sakes, I'm telling you, I swear on my mother's grave, I don't know!"

Helms had gotten loud and had attracted Wally's attention. He ambled over to our booth, towering over us. He looked at Helms.

"Mikey, this guy giving you a hard time?"

205

"No, Wally, no, man, not at all."

I looked up, and up, and up, at Wally. "No, me and Mikey used to work together. I'm in town with the wife, just catching up with my old friend Mikey here."

Wally wasn't buying it. "You a cop?"

"I get that a lot, but no, not a cop."

"I don't like cops in my place, gives it a bad reputation."

Helms chimed in, his voice unnaturally high from the stress. "No, no Wally he isn't a cop. Say, how are the Mets doing?"

"They lost, 4-2."

"Ah, shit. Well, I'll make it up on the Giants, what do you say Wally? Double down on San Francisco?"

Wally glared at me, certain I wasn't Mikey's friend. Taking no chances he said, "Don't know what you're talking about Mikey. I don't know nuthin about bettin'. I run a clean establishment."

He walked away slowly. I could feel the gravitational pull as he left.

I looked at Vincent. He sat across from me, all alone in the world. No family. No friends. No career. In the throes of a vicious addiction. Except for the active addiction part, we were in the same boat. I was one drink and a few felonies, from being Vincent Helms.

"OK Vincent, let's say I believe you. You don't know who Mathews is. Fine. What does he look like?"

"What?"

"Describe him for me. Height, weight, age, color of his hair, color of his eyes. Right handed or left handed? Does he walk with a limp? Any scars? Tattoos? Piercings? C'mon, Vincent, tell me. You met him. What's he look like?"

"Peter, please, I c-can't"

"Sure you can. Where did you guys meet? What kind of car did he drive? Does he have an accent? Was he ever with anyone?" My voice was rising, it was my old cross-examination voice, the angry one. I hadn't used it in a while, but it was still there. "Does he wear cologne? Did you see him days or nights?

Is he married? Ever talk about his kids? When you talked, what was the sum and substance of your conversations? How often? Vincent, what does he eat, drink, wear? C'mon Vincent, tell me, or I swear to God you'll be dead by morning!"

"Stop! Stop it– I can't tell you!"

"You better tell me, Vincent, right now!"

"Listen, Peter, I can't tell you! He's the only one that can get me out of this. I told you, he said he's working on a plan to raise the money; he just needs time to liquidate some things. He's my only hope. I can't give him up. I don't care if I go to jail; if he doesn't make it right, I'll be dead wherever I am. I can't afford to let you find him, too. Please, I'm begging you. I answered your questions. Tell them I forged your signature. That gets you off the hook."

He was almost in tears. "Just don't make me tell you who Mathews is, I just can't do it."

We sat in silence for a few moments.

"Vincent, I don't know what I'm going to do. I want to kill you myself for putting me through this, but I don't know. I have to think about it. But I gave you my word—I'll give you some time. Just one more thing."

"Shoot."

"Is Greg Connolly Harris Mathews?"

Helms stopped drumming. His body stilled. He looked me straight in the eye.

"No."

I stared back and then started to slide from the booth.

He thanked me, again and again. I left the bar around 9, got back to the motel and checked out. I was on the interstate by 10. I was heading home, certainly with more information than I had before, but not much more peace.

Around 11, I pulled into a rest stop on US 78, just before the Jersey border. I had made up my mind. I was going to tell the cops about Helms, but I would give him a day or so head start. My compromise with myself. Since I didn't have any direct connection with "the boys", it would be easy to keep that part of my oath of silence.

I called Carolyn collect from a payphone at the rest stop. Not having a cell phone was becoming very inconvenient; I thought I might have to take another step towards becoming a part of modern society again and pick one up. She answered the phone on the sixth ring. After I apologized profusely for the lateness of the call, and repeatedly promised to pay her for it, we spoke for about a half an hour. I filled her in on the highlights of my Pennsylvania trip.

She had some information for me. She had conspired with Rita to search for my box, the one Joel had signed for. They had found it.

"Where?" I asked.

"It was in a back closet, under a pile of old books. Peter, I showed it to Phil. As best we can figure out, the box hasn't been opened. It's still taped up with the shipping stickers in place. We cut a hole so we could look in– it looks like tax returns and some books. Nothing like the stuff that would come from a desk, you know staplers, things like that."

I thanked her and asked her to thank Rita for me. I asked her if she could reschedule the meeting with the title company. She said she would try. She told me to be careful. I apologized again for calling so late. She told me again to be careful.

I drove the rest of the way in silence. I headed south when I hit eastern New Jersey and took the Goethals Bridge, the ugliest bridge ever built, from Jersey to Staten Island and the Verrazano Bridge, the most magnificent bridge ever built, from Staten Island to Brooklyn, and then the Belt Parkway onto Long Island.

I knew some things for certain that I didn't know when I crossed the bridges the day before, at the start of my trip. I knew that while Vincent Helms was a tortured, addicted soul, I believed he did this out of desperation, not necessarily malice. I knew most of the story now, because Helms had mostly told me the truth. I knew Helms was lying about one thing in particular, though: he knew who Harris Mathews was.

And, now, I believed I did, too.

Chapter 24

I reached my apartment a little past one. I'd made pretty good time, even with the stop to call Carolyn. When I opened the door, I felt something strange. This apartment actually felt comfortable. In almost felt like... home. In the year or so I had been living there, it hadn't ever quite felt that way.

There were 10 messages on my machine. This time I listened to them. There were three calls from Carolyn; three calls, starting on Monday, from Joel; a recorded solicitation about home mortgages; two calls from my sister, Marie; and two messages from Detective Fisher of the Nassau County Police Department. They all wanted a return call. They might each get one, I thought, but not tonight. I took two Advil and climbed into bed.

Morning came early. I was tempted to run, but my head and my ribs still faintly ached. One more day, I thought.

I had a court appearance on an assigned counsel case scheduled for 9:30. I was representing a crack addict in a proceeding by the State to terminate her parental rights to her three kids. My client didn't care, and hadn't shown for the last two appearances. I didn't think I would see her in court that morning, either. Nobody was going to miss me at court until 11 or so. I looked at the clock; I had five or so hours to kill, and a theory to test out.

I drove to Island Storage. It would be empty this time of the morning; I could get into my room without being seen by anyone. As I drove, I passed the little white church. The sign had changed again:

They Are Commandments
Not Suggestions

It seemed that since the "body piercing" message, the sign guy had gotten much more conservative. He must have taken some heat from the congregation.

I arrived at Island Storage before 7:30. I was surprised to find Ricky sitting at the front counter, with his sister Ines. They insisted I sit and have a cup of coffee with them. I did. It was good coffee. Ines was pleasant and attractive and funny. She was an arm toucher, reaching out and lightly squeezing my arm as she laughed. It was an enjoyable 10 minute oasis of peace.

I went up to my room and looked through the lists I had left on the table. There were five Brownstein files that both Connolly and Helms had worked on together. I pulled them and scoured them, looking for a connection.

Nothing jumped out at me.

I went through the files a second time, to make sure. Helms had assisted on the files, doing pretty much minor assignments. It seemed the contacts with Sy were all handled by Connolly. Maybe as a result of my raids on his other clients, Connolly tried to wall off Sy from anyone else in the firm. According to the notes and the correspondence, Helms mostly interacted with Sy's employees, including both of his sons, David and Avi, his accountant, his CFO, and other management level people. But never with Sy. Helms' only direct contact with Sy seemed to be when he witnessed the old man's will. Helms' correspondence with the underlings seemed cordial; Connolly's letters, even with Sy, seemed rigid, almost forced.

I locked up, and headed back downstairs. Ricky was finalizing his plans for the Labor Day weekend. It sounded like a three-day fishing party. I told him I was done with the files, and that I would be back to re-shelve them. He refused; he told me his guys would take care of it. He didn't want me getting caught putting the files back; one close call was more than enough. I offered to pay him, but he waved me off impatiently. I asked if I could use a phone; he brought me into an empty office and left me at the desk.

I called Phil Ruggiero. He wasn't in, but I left a pretty detailed message on his voice mail. So detailed, in fact, I had to call back twice, because I kept getting cut off. I filled him in on my Pennsylvania trip and my conversation with Helms.

John Gartner was next. I caught him in the office early, getting ready for a hearing that morning. I filled him in on Helms and his whereabouts. He told me he would contact the ADA; I told him OK. I didn't tell him about the Transom connection or how I had found Helms. I figured that would give Helms as much time to take off as he deserved. If he was smart, Helms would be at the bank in Transom this morning when Anthony's friend Tina opened the doors. If I were he, I'd empty the account and be gone by 9:15. But it was up to him. I was going to give him about a half a day's head start.

I pulled his card out of my wallet and dialed Detective Fisher. Another detective told me Fisher wouldn't be in until around 4. I asked the detective if she would take a message for me, involving the Brownstein case. She grunted like she knew about the case and that she didn't relish taking a message for Fisher.

She seemed more interested as I laid out my information. I told her about Helms, about how he had done it. I told her Helms was in Hershey, last seen at Wally's Sports Bar. I didn't tell her about the Transom bank account, either. My compromise, I guess. Maybe Vincent could straighten out and start fresh. When I finished I figured it was 60/40 whether Fisher would get the message at all and maybe 3-1 against him getting the full message. I made a mental note to call him back after he came on duty.

It was a few minutes after 9. I called Carolyn at the office. She had just hung up with the title insurance company's lawyers. At first, they wanted no part of setting up another meeting. Then she told them I had information on who actually committed the fraud and where they could find $300,000 of their money.

The meeting was set for 2 p.m. that afternoon. Apparently, *now* they were interested in meeting with me. I thanked Carolyn, who then informed me that she would be at the meeting, don't try to argue. I did, but I didn't have my heart in it. A friendly face would be helpful in the room. I called Phil back, leaving a message about the time and place of the title insurance company meeting. I asked him to meet me there, if he had the time.

The Grievance Hearing was scheduled for the next morning. At least now I had something to say beyond, well, I don't think it's my signature. Still, I didn't want to take it for granted. I had to find some time to prepare my remarks and I had to get copies of the reports to hand out. Come to think of it, I would need them for the meeting this afternoon, too. I called Carolyn back. She said she'd bring the copies with her to the title insurance company's office.

Finally, I called Marie back. I got the answering machine. I just left a message that I was returning her call. That left only Joel and the recorded mortgage solicitation unreturned. I couldn't face Joel. Maybe later.

*****

Family Court went exactly as I thought it would. I got there around 11:00, and sat around until 12:30 when the Judge finally declared my crack-addict client in default and issued an order terminating her parental rights. That would allow the kids, who had been left to the vagaries of the foster care system, to be adopted, if a home could be found for them. I guess I technically lost the case, but it was at least a chance of a win for the kids. I was OK with that.

I got to the offices of the firm representing the title company a few minutes early. The attorneys weren't employees of the company; they were outside counsel, hired to work this case. Carolyn was in the waiting room already, talking with Phil. They were chatting away, comfortable and relaxed, sitting catty-cornered in two of the ten or so chairs that circled the room, all facing the receptionist's station. Behind the receptionist, on either side, were doors which led back to the offices and conference rooms. They were both shut when I got there. I sat next to Phil, directly facing the receptionist.

They made us wait about 25 minutes. During that time, every once in a while, somebody would come out of the back office and talk to the receptionist. Or pretend to. I noticed it right away; so did Phil. When one of the pretenders left the waiting room, Phil whispered to Carolyn what we had noticed. She wasn't happy.

"They're doing a show-up? What are they, crazy? Why? They could never get it into court now, even if they wanted to!"

A "show-up" is the term for when a cop catches a fleeing suspect, and

212

brings him to the victim. Is this the guy that robbed you, the cop asks, holding the handcuffed suspect up by the back of his neck. Courts hate show-ups, because they are too suggestive and prejudicial. What's the victim supposed to say? Nah, release him officer, it may look like him, but that's not the guy. Rarely happens. Usually the victim says to himself, hey, if the cop chased this guy down and handcuffed him, he must be the guy, right?

No, the more preferred way was a fairly run line-up, where the victim is shown several people roughly matching the description of the suspect. A line-up is marginally more reliable, but still not very good. People just have a hard time describing, and really remembering, other people. I used to make new associates play a little game. I'd have one of the secretaries come in the room, sit in on a meeting for a few minutes, then leave. I'd then have each associate write out the secretary's description, without consulting with anyone else. The results were always bizarre and never very close to each other. It was my lesson that eyewitness identifications sucked and that they shouldn't be afraid to attack them.

Carolyn was upset because Phil and I had caught the title insurance company pulling a show-up. The people coming to the receptionist area must have had contact with Helms or Mathews. They were checking me out, to see if I was either man. It was dumb, but then again, they were out $13.4 million dollars. Maybe Helms wasn't the only person feeling a bit desperate these days.

We finally were called into the conference room for the meeting. We exchanged introductions all around. There were a couple of suits from the title insurance company, and three of their lawyers, and a couple of suits from the bank, with two of their lawyers. They were about evenly split, male and female, and they sat all along the far end of the table, wrapping around both sides. We sat at the foot of the table, me on the end, Phil to my left, Carolyn to my right. The door was behind me.

Directly across from me, sitting at the head of the table was a sleek 50-ish year old man, a thick head of silver hair. He wore an expensive suit, and designer glasses. He was smooth, shaking my hand with a nice, strong grip, looking me directly in the eye as he did. Their end of the room seemed to defer to him, if only by body language. He introduced himself as Patrick McIntyre. He was the President of New Amsterdam Title Insurance Company. He was the fellow who had signed the letter to the grievance committee.

We all settled in. McIntyre spoke first. "Well, Ms. Peterson, it looks like you found your client today. That's good news, yes?" The suits all chuckled. Phil said something under his breath that sounded a lot like "asshole". "It's your meeting. Why don't you proceed, counselors?"

One of the lawyers jumped in. "Before you do, I want to advise you that we do not consider this a settlement conference. Any information you provide today will be used in this proceeding."

Carolyn started to object, but I lightly touched her arm. "That's fine," I said.

And I started. I told them about Helms, his background, and his gambling problem. I referred to Phil when I discussed Helms' finances. I walked them through Harris Mathews' plan, and the involvement of the late Tariq Singh. The suits, all except McIntyre, were writing furiously. When I got to Singh's involvement, the bank suits started looking nervous; their insurance proceeds might be jeopardized by their own employee's fraud.

I walked them through the transaction and the distribution of money, as related to me by Helms. I told them that the initial plan only involved one property; that's why one deed was forged on June 8th, and the other one not until the 10th. I told them that the original plan called for Mathews to pay the mortgage, which was why they got payments for several months before the mortgage went into default. I told them I had thought that the fact the mortgage was paid for several months was unusual, as was the re-deeding. I told them Helms' explanation for that; it brought a few nods at the table.

"But do you have any proof?" one of the insurance suits asked.

"We have this. Peter didn't notarize those documents." Carolyn said as she tossed them copies of the handwriting expert's report, and the polygraph report. "I'm sure once the experts compare Helms' writing to the forged notary, they'll find a match."

I continued. "I don't have access to Singh's accounts, but you might. He might have been murdered before he spent all the money or before he could clean up his tracks. I also don't have access to the money trail from the mortgage proceeds check, to Houston Mesquite, to Helms and Singh and Mathews. I assume you do."

The suits looked at each other. McIntyre answered. "The money went into a Houston Mesquite account in Florida. It was then wired to the Caymans. We don't have access, yet. We might not ever."

"Maybe not. But if you check Richard Thomas' account with the Pleasant Valley State bank in Transom, Pennsylvania you may be able to back-track the funds. Same thing with Singh." There. I had given Helms a fair chance. It would take the title company a day or so to get a Court order freezing the account. It was as much charity as I could muster.

"Who is Richard Thomas?" one of the suits asked.

"He's Vincent Helms."

McIntyre looked at me. "That still leaves Harris Mathews. How do we know you aren't Harris Mathews? How do we know two dysfunctional attorneys at the same firm didn't team up to commit this massive fraud?"

Phil leaned forward. "Cause you had all your freakin' people checkin' him out while we cooled our heels in the freakin' lobby, that's how."

Carolyn pulled out a blow up of Helms' photograph from the O'Reilly, McManus brochure. "Have them look at this photo. See if this is the guy who called himself Peter De Stio at the closing." McIntyre nodded and one of the suits left the room with the photo.

"And, besides," Carolyn continued, "Why would anyone be so stupid as to create an alias and then use their own name and stamp to notarize the document? And then have their accomplice use his name at the closing. Does that make any sense?"

McIntyre shook his head. "No, it doesn't." He looked at the suits to his right. "You're right, by the way. Everyone who met with the fellow calling himself "Peter De Stio" and with Mathews did take a look at you. Everyone except Singh, that is. You don't look anything like either of the two men, at all. Am I right Georgette?"

"Yes, sir. They're all certain Mr. De Stio is not either of the men who came to the closing."

McIntyre turned back to me. "So tell me, Mr. De Stio. Who is Harris Mathews?"

I breathed in slowly. "I don't know for sure. I think I have an idea, but I'm not certain yet."

"Care to share?" he asked with a smile.

I returned the smile. "Not just yet. But I'm not done."

"Really? What's in it for you?"

"I don't know," I told him. And I really didn't.

The suit who had taken Helms' photo out of the room came back in and whispered into McIntyre's ear.

"I see. You're sure?" The suit nodded yes.

"You're right, Mr. De Stio. They all identify Vincent Helms as the man impersonating you at the closing." He adjusted his tie, sat up straight, and leaned forward, with his hands folded before him on the table. "I think we can all agree that we have inconvenienced you unfairly." He held up a hand to stifle the lawyers' protests. "I'm not saying we didn't have grounds to proceed, initially. But enough is enough. We're big boys. We got taken, and I think it's clear we can't prove Mr. De Stio was involved. Anybody disagree?"

He stood. Carolyn reminded him about the Grievance Committee, and the hearing scheduled for the next morning. McIntyre assured us that the Grievance Committee and the DA would be notified immediately that they were withdrawing their complaints and that the lawsuit would be discontinued. We shook hands.

"No hard feelings, then, Peter?" McIntyre asked with a smile.

"No, Patrick, no hard feelings. Thanks for not letting this drag on." I meant it. Many bureaucrats would have let the cases continue, on the odd chance that something might pop up. It took confidence and intelligence to make the call McIntyre just made, in the way he made it. No committees. No cover-your-ass- memos. I was impressed.

In the hallway, there were hugs all around. In the elevator, I invited

Carolyn and Phil to an early dinner to thank them and to celebrate. Phil begged off.

"Lobster?" Carolyn asked.

"Whatever you'd like."

"Let me call Luz and tell her I'm going to be late."

******

I drove my car, Carolyn hers. I led us to the Freeport docks. Freeport was one of the first villages on the South Shore of Long Island. It was once a thriving seaport, back in the days when Long Island's population clustered around its protected harbors, and only sheep farmers populated the large, flat plain that made up the middle of the Island. Freeport's canals, which emptied into the Great South Bay, now housed party fishing boats, and dockside restaurants serving the best seafood this side of Seattle. We lucked out and found two parking spots right behind each other, and we walked, side by side down several blocks, peeking in at the restaurants, and the little shops that lined the street. The wind off the water smelled fresh and clean, the coming night promising a bit of a respite from the oppressive heat of the last few days of summer.

We talked as we walked, about Kyle, about college, about law school. Carolyn talked a bit about her ex-husband. We doubled back after we reached the end of the row of restaurants, settling on one with open-air tables right on the dock overlooking the water.

We talked about our families, sharing stories of growing up in different parts of this Island. Carolyn's family had money; she had gone to private schools, and had summered in the Hamptons and in Europe. My youth had been spent working, with little of what we today call "discretionary spending". We laughed. We shared. I didn't ask about Steve and she didn't bring him up.

When we ordered, I saw that Carolyn was uncomfortable when the waiter asked for our drink orders. I told her to order some wine if she wanted to. She laughed it off, a little uncomfortably I thought, but then again I might have been oversensitive. She did order the lobster, though, and a large shrimp cocktail. And she had some of my Little Neck clams on the half shell. And a

217

whole basket of bread. I was amazed. She ate like a longshoreman, but she didn't have an ounce of fat on her, as far as I could see, and I was looking closely.

We ordered coffee and dessert. Carolyn excused herself to go use the ladies' room; I asked if I could borrow her cell phone.

It was after 4. I figured Fisher should be on duty by then. I called him. He picked up on the first ring.

"Fisher."

"Detective, Peter De Stio."

"Where are you, counselor?"

"I'm calling to see if you got my message from this morning."

"Where *are* you, counselor?"

"Detective, did you find Helms?"

"You bet, counselor. Right in the dumpster where you left his body. Now, where the hell are you? Don't make this more difficult than it has to be."

"Wha– Detective, what are you talking about?"

"Counselor, I need you in here and I mean right now."

I hung up.

Helms was dead.

And the cops thought I did it.

Carolyn would be coming back any second. I hadn't planned on making the next call right away, but I didn't have a choice now or much time.

I dialed the number from ancient memory, a private line few people had. I told the person I needed a meeting, right away. I told him who should come and what they should bring.

I told him I would be at his office at 7 p.m.

I told him it was a matter of life and death.

I put the cell phone on the table, along with enough cash to pay the bill and the tip. I dug out a pen and left a short note: "Sorry, emergency. Had to go. Will call. Pete".

And I fled the restaurant.

Chapter 25

I got in my car and stomped on the gas. My heart was racing faster than the engine in my little Honda. A block away from the restaurant, I turned down a residential street and pulled over.

I was on the lam.

I had never been a fugitive. What do I do now?

It was almost 4:30. I had to stay clear of the police for 2½ hours. I needed to take this meeting.

Helms murdered. Jesus. Was it Wally? Or was it the same guys who whacked Singh? My money was on the New York hoods. How did they find Helms?

It hit me. I must have been followed. I thought back. I never looked to see if I was being tailed. Hell, I wouldn't even know what to look for.

I immediately glanced into my rearview mirror. No cops. No hoods.

I remembered the car that almost hit me in Transom. Was that the hit men? I tried to remember something about the car. I just couldn't. The only thing I remembered was that it was dark, it had New York plates, and it didn't honk when I made that U-turn. Not much to go on. It sounded like a Sherlock Holmes tale–the hound who didn't bark. Could I have been followed? Why? Could my telephone be tapped? Had I lead his murderer to Helms?

I had to get rid of this car. I had never practiced much criminal law, but this I knew: murder investigations got top priority in Nassau County, and no resource was spared. I had to assume Fisher had run my plates and that the cops had been looking for my little Honda even as Carolyn and I had enjoyed our dinner.

Carolyn. Ugh. I hoped she'd understand.

I had an idea.

I drove carefully, hoping not to draw any attention, to a nearby supermarket shopping center. I parked the car, dwarfed by the vans and SUV's, in the middle of the lot. I grabbed my running gear, and an old backpack that I kept in the trunk. A towel, too.

In the bathroom of the supermarket I changed into my running uniform, carefully folding my workday uniform into the backpack.

I yanked a St. John's baseball cap onto my head, pulling the brim down to hide my face as best I could without looking ridiculous. And then I hit the streets.

The office I had to go to that evening was in Garden City, about 10 miles or so from the supermarket.

I walked a bit, jogged a bit. I kept to side streets as much as possible; where I had to use busier streets I picked up the pace. Blend in. Head down. Just a 40 year old guy out for an early evening walk or run.

I stopped a few times where I saw larger stores. I wandered around in them, mingling with the shoppers.

A couple of times I saw police cruisers, white with the tell-tale blue and orange Nassau County lettering. Though my heart jumped each time, they seemed to ignore me.

I arrived at the building a little early for my meeting. I looked up at the building and headed for the main doors. My plan was to wash up in the lobby bathroom and change back into my suit. I was more than a little surprised to see Carolyn and Phil waiting for me in the lobby.

Their reactions were surprisingly similar.

"Where the fuck have you been?" from Carolyn.

"You gotta be freakin' kiddin' me," from Phil.

"You know the cops are looking for you, don't you? And you leave me at the table, you don't ask for my help? Or Phil's? Or Gartner's? What's the matter with you? Haven't you learned anything, you idiot? Where have you been? Why are you here? Don't just stand there, you moron, answer me!"

I looked at Phil. He wasn't going to be any help.

"I'm here because I have to talk to these people. As soon as I'm done, I'm going to go to the precinct. Do you guys know about Helms?"

They nodded.

"How did you know I'd be here?" I asked.

"After you left me sitting at the table, I looked at my cell. I dialed the two numbers you had. Fisher told me about Helms and the arrest warrant. Then I called and found out about this meeting."

She looked at me. "What are you wearing?"

I told them about my trek from Freeport and my intent to clean up before I went to the meeting.

"Well, then, go. We'll meet you upstairs." I started to protest. "Peter, Phil and I are sitting in on this meeting. End of discussion. Go clean up."

I used the first floor bathroom to wash and change, then the night security guard let us through. We took an elevator to the 5th Floor. For the first time in over two years, I entered the law offices of O'Reilly, McManus.

It felt extraordinarily strange. I had known these offices so well, for so long. I had spent the better part of my adult life toiling away for endless hours here, spending many more hours here than at home. Yet, it felt unfamiliar. It even smelled differently. I felt awkward, unbalanced. I looked at Carolyn. She seemed very tight. Phil, who still did work for O'Reilly, seemed a bit more at ease, but not much.

I called out, hello, anybody here? And out of the Main Conference Room came old man O'Reilly.

"Peter." He had a thin smile on his tanned, lined face. "I see you've brought some guests." He turned to Phil. "Phillip, I'm surprised you're involved in this."

Phil just shrugged.

O'Reilly looked at Carolyn. His smile widened a bit and he cocked his head to the side as I introduced her. "Ms. Peterson, I seem to recognize you. Have we met?"

"Yes, sir. You offered me a job a few months ago."

"Ah, but you went elsewhere, I see. Our loss."

He turned to me, the smile fading as he spoke. "We're ready for you in the conference room, Peter. Are you sure you want to do this?"

"Yes, sir. I think I have to."

"Very well, off we go."

We walked down the hall and entered the Main Conference room. It was huge. The conference table, which didn't take up but maybe half the room, could comfortably seat 40 people. There were small tables, couches, and comfortable chairs, as well as a bar and a serving area, beyond the table. Original art, worth hundreds of thousands, if not more, lined the walls. There was a working fireplace. The room was designed to impress and intimidate. I had used it for both purposes. This meeting was only going to involve 6 people; it could have been held in an office. Somebody was trying to use it as a home field advantage. I knew who it was.

Gregory Connolly sat in a club chair on the far side of the room. He didn't rise as we entered, but rather glared at us, and then turned his attention back to the man in the chair opposite him, a man with his back towards us. As we approached, Connolly finally stood, as did the much older man. I shook hands with both, though Connolly gave me just a perfunctory shake, and the old man a very weak one.

I introduced Carolyn to Connolly; Phil just nodded. They knew each other. I then introduced them both to Sy Brownstein. Sy looked angry, but brightened a smidge while shaking hands with Carolyn. She seemed to have that effect on men, young and old.

O'Reilly suggested we sit at the conference table; he took the head chair. Sy and Connolly sat on either side of him. We moved down the table three of four chairs, then sat down next to each other. I shifted my chair so I could face the three of them directly.

"Sy, I asked Mr. O'Reilly to call you to this meeting because I think it's a matter of life and death."

"So you said," Connolly interrupted curtly. "What is it?"

I ignored Connolly. "You know that somebody forged deeds on your property and then mortgaged them."

Connolly jumped in again. "Yes, I believe the title insurance company thinks it was you, correct?"

I looked at O'Reilly. He turned to Connolly: "Gregory. Enough. Let Peter speak." He nodded back to me. "Go on, Peter."

I plunged in. I told them how the plan was developed, about Helms posing as me, and then Richard Thomas. About Singh. About Harris Mathews. I told them about the change in the plan. I told them about how the mortgage was paid for a while and about how it was supposed to be paid off when Mathews came into a lot of money.

I told them about Singh having been murdered, which they knew about. And about Helms having been murdered, which they didn't know.

"Sy, may I ask you a personal question?"

"You can ask. I may not answer it."

"How are you feeling?"

"Well, right now I'm tired and getting angry. Why am I here?"

"How is your health?"

Sy looked at me. "Alright, young man, I'll play along. My health is fair, right now. I've had a few operations in the past couple of years or so. I had prostate cancer and colon cancer. It's all in remission right now. I have some other things wrong, too. I'm 76 years old. Things start to break down, right, Michael?"

"Can we get to the point here?" snapped Connolly. "Some of us have families to get home to."

"I know who Harris Mathews is."

O'Reilly turned to me. "Really? Would you mind sharing with us, Peter."

"Yes, sir. First of all, whoever Harris Mathews is, he had to have intimate knowledge of the Brownstein properties. I know it's all public information, but Mathews knew the first building didn't have any mortgages on it, and he knew too quickly that the other building was free and clear, too, when they changed the plan from one building to two."

"Second, Mathews told Helms that he knew that the true owner, you, never sold, and wouldn't be borrowing any money. Not he thought, or he hoped. He *knew*. Again, intimate knowledge."

"Third, the bank needed appraisals and information, like rent rolls and income statements. Somebody had to meet the appraiser, show him around. Somebody with access, who none of the tenants or staff would question."

Connolly tried to interrupt again, but I cut him off. "Up to this point, Greg, you fit the bill nicely. You have intimate knowledge of Sy's holdings and access to the necessary documents. And no one would question Sy's lawyer if he did a walk through with some bankers."

"You son of a –"

O'Reilly again cut him off. "Enough, the two of you. Still like children. Peter, go on, get to the point."

"Then there was this whole business about paying the mortgage back, waiting for some big money to come in. That's why I asked if you were sick. If you die, your estate will be extremely large." I looked at Connolly. "The fiduciary fees alone should make someone wealthy." Connolly's face reddened and he stole a glance at O'Reilly. As I figured, the old man had no idea Connolly was worming his way into Sy's estate—he would never have stood for it.

"But, surely, even if someone were to be Sy's fiduciary, the fees wouldn't be enough." O'Reilly looked at Connolly with narrowed eyes. "Not to pay off 13 million dollars, Peter."

"I realize that," I said. "But an inheritance would be large enough."

Connolly started to interrupt, but this time Sy stopped him. "Go on."

"Let's say Harris Mathews was one of Sy's beneficiaries. Sy dies, and let's say he gets half of the properties. He makes sure he takes the properties with the mortgages and he just pays it off from his share. The other beneficiaries won't care—they're getting all their money. Nobody would ever know about Houston Mesquite, or the bank loan or anything."

"Interesting theory, Peter. But, really, do you have any proof as to whom this Harris Mathews is?" asked O'Reilly.

"That's why I asked how you were feeling, Sy. Again, I figure Mathews knew you well enough to know you were ill. Seriously ill. He must have thought that he wouldn't have to wait too long before he'd get his inheritance."

Connolly couldn't contain himself anymore. "You're an idiot. Sy's Will leaves everything to a charitable trust. Nobody gets a dime. Your imaginary Harris Mathews gets nothing. You must still be drinking, *Counselor*. You're hallucinating"

"I don't think so. Sy, is that your will?" He nodded yes. "Where have you been keeping it?"

"In my safe at home."

"Would you mind looking at it?"

As Sy opened the envelope and removed the will, Connolly kept up a tirade against me. He only stopped when Sy said, "Oh, my God!" and dropped the will as if it was on fire.

"It leaves everything to your sons, doesn't it?"

Connolly yelled, "Impossible!" at the same time as Sy whispered, "How did you know?"

I looked Sy straight in the eye. "Sy, I think your son Avi is Harris Mathews. I think he has or had a gambling problem. I think he stole this money. I think his life is in danger as we speak."

Connolly exploded. "Are you out of your mind, you drunken bastard? How dare you come into our office and level such a baseless, defamatory charge? I'll see to it you don't have a license, not that you care. Sy, I'm sorry, we should never have agreed–." O'Reilly snapped at him to be quiet.

I had never taken my eyes off Sy. He kept looking at me. "I don't believe you," he whispered.

The room was silent. I continued.

"When I asked Helms if he knew who Mathews was, he said no, but I sensed he was lying. Quite frankly, I thought it was you, Greg. Actually, I wanted it to be you. Especially when we found out about the money you spent on the Hamptons house, and that you had paid off your mortgage in Manhasset."

"W-what?" Connolly twirled to look at O'Reilly. "My wife's father died! He left Sarah everything. We paid off—"

"Greg, stop. I know it wasn't you. But Helms had to know Mathews' true identity. I thought it was a little coincidental that a bookie would put these two together. I figure they cooked up the plan themselves and then went to the bookie."

I turned to O'Reilly. "I went through all of Helms' and Sy's closed files. You have to change the combination on the locks to storage rooms, by the way. Helms did work for Greg on some of Sy's cases, but he never dealt with Sy. Only Sy's assistants."

"If you go through the files you'll see Helms worked with Avi a lot. I looked at their correspondence and the hard copies of their emails. They seemed to be fairly friendly."

"Then I looked at Sy's will file. I saw Greg's notes, but there was no copy of the will in the file. That was strange, no? Why would someone take the copy of the will from the file? I figured it was so that there would be nothing to compare the doctored will to. Helms witnessed the will. He must have read it and told Avi about it. Avi took the will from Sy's safe; Helms re-did the bequest pages, and exchanged them for the charitable trust pages. I'll bet if you look in the computer, the original will file has been changed or deleted. Then Avi put the will back. Who would complain? Not your other son. He would just figure you changed your mind and decided to leave your estate to your family. Nobody would have looked that closely, and besides, the new pages are on the same embossed paper, using the same printer as the original. He just had to put on a new cover so the staple holes would be covered. Without the draft or the computer file there would be no proof that the will had been doctored."

"Sy, I think Avi is Harris Mathews. If I'm right, his life is in jeopardy."

We sat in silence for a while.

O'Reilly spoke first. "Sy, if Peter is right, Avi may be in real danger. Two other people are dead." Sy seemed to have crumpled, as if there was a force sucking his chest into him.

He spoke softly. "Suppose you're right. You still have no proof."

226

Carolyn spoke for the first time. "But we do, sir. Your son went to the closing. All we have to do is show his photo to the bank and the title company. They'll recognize him. The police will match up his signatures. And once they know who they're looking for, it's a lot easier to find the money trail."

No one said anything. The ticking of the cherry wood mantle clock echoed.

Sy looked down at his hands. "You're right. It has to be him. Avi has always had problems. Drugs. Stealing. Gambling. He's a spoiled, immature kid. I gave him everything, but it wasn't enough. He's in hiding now. He came to me in the spring. He told me his life was in danger. We've been through this before, but I had told him a few years ago, no more. No more! I wasn't going to give him another penny. He was a grown man; he had to take care of his own problems." Sy stopped. He looked close to tears.

"He begged me. I made a deal with him. I've got him hidden away, he's getting help. I told him I wouldn't pay off his debts until I knew he's straightened himself out. He's been in there six months. He seems like a different man, not so much a boy. I cannot believe he did this," he said, pointing at the Will that lay on the table.

"Peter, remember that case you handled for me, that breakfast place I made you put out of business? I know you thought I was a heartless bastard. Do you know why I wanted them ruined? Because that nice little couple let bookies and loan sharks work out of there! They thought I didn't know, but I knew. Avi got in trouble there a few times. That's why I wanted them gone, the vipers!

We all sat quietly for a few moments. Sy broke the silence, again.

"Peter. What must I do to save my son?" he asked me softly.

"Sy, I think you cut a deal with the title insurance company, make them whole. They don't want this publicity, that's for sure. The cops? They don't know about your son yet. They might not ever. Carolyn, what do you think?"

"If Avi comes in voluntarily and agrees to testify against the bookie and if full restitution is made, I think a deal could be made with the DA. I'd make it. They've got nothing right now and they're not looking at Avi, not at all. No one, other than Peter, was thinking that way. But he'd have to testify. No guarantees, but it's probable, I think."

"I don't know if he will."

I leaned forward. "Then no deal. Sy, he's got to come clean, and you have to make full restitution. If not, I tell the cops what I know. They think I killed Helms. If Avi doesn't point them in the right direction, I've got a problem. And if I have one, so does Avi."

"Yes. I see. I'll talk to Avi. He'll do what I say. Peter, will you handle this for me?"

I paused. "O'Reilly, McManus can handle this, Sy. You have good attorneys here. Let them take care of this."

"You could have turned my son in without this meeting. You had enough evidence. You're right. If they hear my son's name and they show a photo of him to the people who met this Mathews, it's all over, no? Why didn't you?"

I shrugged. "Enough people have been hurt," I half-smiled. "I'm a lot more sympathetic to second chances now, I guess."

Sy thought a while. "No, Peter, I would really like you to do this for me, if you would, please." He turned to O'Reilly. "I hope you don't mind, Michael. I just feel much more comfortable with Peter." Sy looked at me again. I nodded, yes.

I didn't look at Connolly. I couldn't. But Carolyn told me later he looked like someone had hit him in the face with a brick.

I didn't see the look on Connolly's face because at that moment the door to the conference room swung open and two Nassau County uniform cops charged in, followed closely by Fisher. I found myself spread eagle on the floor, my arms pulled behind me.

As they put the handcuffs on me, I heard Fisher say:

"You have the right to remain silent..."

Chapter 26

At the precinct, I refused to talk to anyone until my lawyers arrived. They wouldn't let me use the telephone, but I knew Carolyn and Phil would be right behind the squad car, and that Carolyn would have John Gartner meet us as soon as he could.

They left me alone in a holding cell. Hard benches lined the walls. I tried to lie down, but settled for slumping in a half-seated position.

After about two hours Fisher came and led me into a conference room. As we walked down the dingy hallway, he whispered in my ear that he hated it when people hung up on him. I told him I got the message and I apologized.

Gartner and Carolyn and ADA Melendez were already in the small room, sitting on opposite sides of the table. There was another man in the room in a suit and tie. He was introduced to me as Detective Porter of the Derry Township Police Department. Hershey was his jurisdiction. Fisher put me in the seat next to Gartner.

"Counselor, so good of you to join us," Melendez said with a wincing smile. "You know why we're here. Tell us what you know about the murder of Vincent Helms."

Over the objections of both John and Carolyn, I walked everybody through my hunt for Helms. I left my suspicions of Avi out of it, for now. I didn't give up Anthony's friend Tina, either. I just told them I found the bank records and followed them to Hershey.

"Counselor, how about I ask a couple of questions, OK?" asked Porter. "When do you say you last saw Helms?"

"It was about 9 o'clock or so. I left him at the last booth at Wally's Sports Bar. I think he was going to watch the Giants' game."

"And he was alive?'

"Very."

"Why didn't you call the police from Wally's? Or when you located him?"

"I don't know. I didn't want to hurt him, I just wanted information."

"Didn't want to hurt him?"

"No."

"This guy steals your notary stamp, forges your name, gets you in trouble with the bar, gets you sued, has the police looking at you, and you're OK with it? No problems? Don't want to hurt him?"

"I realize it sounds funn–"

"Then why, counselor, did you threaten to kill him?"

"What? I never–"

He pulled out his book, flipped a couple of pages. "Two witnesses, counselor. 'I heard the guy from New York say I swear to God you'll be dead by morning!'"

"Do you deny saying that?"

"Well, no, but I wasn't talking about *me* killin–"

"Were you hitting him up for some of the money he stole? Is that it? You found out he had money left, wanted something for your trouble?"

"No, no."

"How'd you get those bruises, by the way?" He pointed at my hands.

"I was attacked by someone last week."

Fisher chimed in. "Really? And when were you going to report that?"

"Perhaps," Porter said, "Perhaps Helms fought back, huh, counselor?"

Carolyn could be still no more. Her face and posture reminded me of the morning we first met in Joel's conference room. "Enough. Stop it." She turned to me, "You be quiet, you moron."

She turned to the cops. "First, he did receive those injuries last week. I can give you the hospital records. Second, what do you have as a time of death?

Because Peter called me, collect, from the road. I think it was about 11 o'clock. We spoke for about a half hour. I'll give you access to my phone records."

Then she looked at me. "Peter, where did you call me from?" I told them the name of the rest stop and its location.

"When you came home, did you go through any tolls, on the road or the bridges?" I nodded yes.

"Did you use your EZ Pass?" Again, I nodded.

"There, detectives. Go get those records, too." She looked at Fisher. "Peter called you this morning and told you all about Helms, right? You had no clue he was involved in the fraud, did you? And since Helms was using an alias, my guess is, Detective Porter, you would have had some difficulty in ID-ing Helms, no? Why would Peter let you know where Helms was, and what his connection was with the case, if he had just killed him? Does that make any sense?"

Before either detective could say anything, Carolyn concluded. "Tell me, detectives, if Peter was at that rest stop around 11 and used the EZ Pass in New York and New Jersey for tolls right after that, could he have possibly killed Helms? Does the timing make sense? Does any of it?"

A half hour later I was a free man.

*****

I woke up late, but it was the first day my head hadn't hurt in a while. I raced to the Grievance Committee hearing. Even though the complainant was withdrawing the complaint, the Committee was still charged with looking into my conduct. I spent about an hour walking them through the facts. Coupled with McIntyre's letter that had been hand-delivered that morning, my testimony was enough to have the charges dismissed as unfounded.

I didn't have any reason to go to my soon-to-be-former office. I didn't have any appearances in court scheduled until the following Wednesday. I thought about going in to clean out my stuff, but I decided not to.

I made a few telephone calls. The first I made was to McIntyre. I told him I could get him all of his money back, plus expenses for his attorneys' fees, if he agreed not to ask where the money came from, and agreed to ask the DA to close the case. The D.A. certainly wasn't going to actually close the case—too much money, and now two murders, were involved. But it might help with plea bargaining and, ultimately, sentencing. It took him a half a second to agree. He asked me how I did it; I told him I couldn't tell him. I told him I'd draft the agreement and have it, and an escrow check, on his desk by Tuesday. He seemed happy. Very happy.

I called Phil. After I was escorted from the room, they all had agreed that Sy would work with Phil and John Gartner with the logistics of cutting a deal for Avi. We spoke about how the evening at the station had gone, and Carolyn's rescue of me.

I hesitated. Something had been on my mind. I asked Phil if he thought I had anything to worry about. Could I be the next target?

He thought about it.

"I don't know, Petey. I mean, we're talking stone cold killers here, y'know. I don't think so, though. Look, let's be friggin' logical. Why would they kill Singh? Had to be 'cause they were afraid he'd talk. Plus they wanted more money, right? For bein' cut out of the big pie. Helms? Same freakin' thing. You, though, you didn't get any of the money. And you don't know who they are, right? So you can't rat on 'em like Singh was gonna do. Besides, even if Helms told you who they were, you couldn't testify, it would be hearsay, right?"

"Right."

"Anyway, if they were worried about you learnin' somethin' from Helms, and then talkin' to the cops, they coulda whacked you in P A the other night. Why take the chance of you talkin' to the cops today, like you did? Lot's of freakin' open space in Pennsylvania. They coulda taken you anytime they wanted to, if they freakin' wanted to."

He paused again. "I dunno, Petey, maybe you should lie low a coupla days, so they realize you ain't told the cops nuthin' that's gonna hurt them. Nobody knocks on their door for a few weeks, they gonna figure they're home free. Tell you what. Why don't ya stay with me a few days, let this blow over?"

"Thanks Phil, but no– I'll be careful."

"How about I reach out, let some people know you ain't got nothin'?"

"Can you? That might help."

"Sure thing, Petey. You just lie low for a bit, OK, maybe stay away from your usual places, watch your friggin' rearview mirror every once in a while. Use your freakin' brains for once."

I smiled. "You got it. Thanks for everything. I mean it."

"Keep doin' it, Petey. I'm very prouda the way you're handlin' all this. It's tough to stay sober anyways, without freakin' beatin's and murders and investigations and shit. You're doin' good, real good. Stay strong. Healthy, y'know."

"I know. One freakin' day at a time."

Phil laughed and we hung up.

I finally got up the nerve to call Joel back. He wasn't in. His secretary said he was gone for the Labor Day weekend.

I called Marie.

"Peter, I want you here Monday for a barbeque. I won't take no for an answer, do you hear me?"

"Marie, are you sure– "

"What did I just say? See you at 2. Bring a dessert."

As I put the telephone down, it rang. It always seems like magic when it does that, although it's not as creepy as when you pick up a phone to call out the instant an incoming call is about to ring. It was Michael O'Reilly. He asked how everything had gone with the police. I told him. He told me how well I had done on the entire matter, congratulated me. Told me I still had it, I was the best he'd seen in 50 years of practice. He thanked me for not pointing out that Helms had been an O'Reilly, McManus employee, who had used his access to information at the firm to commit the fraud. And he offered me my position with the firm back. Just like it had been. Simply turn back the clock, how does that sound?

I told him, no. Thanks, but no. He sounded disappointed, but he understood, I think. I felt badly turning him down, but I was feeling healthy these days, shaky, wobbly, but healthy. I didn't want to risk that. I did ask him to keep an eye on Connolly. I told O'Reilly I had gotten my information on my own. I didn't want any retaliation aimed at Mary Robinson. He told me Connolly was not going to be a problem, anymore. We wished each other well; we both meant it.

My work done, I decided to take a nice, slow run. It had been over a week, the longest time I had gone without running since rehab. I wound my way through the streets of Oceanside, until I found myself alongside the little white church. I couldn't see the sign because somebody had dumped a huge pile of jet black dirt on the lawn in front of the sign. A huge pile, maybe 6 feet high. I slowed to a walk.

As I passed the pile, which smelled like manure, I saw the large gardener, struggling with a wheel barrow. He stopped to wipe his brow, and caught my eye.

I called out to him. "You the man in charge of the sign?"

He walked over to me. He had a wary look on his face. I guess he was preparing for criticism. I was sure the only reason he came over, though, was he wanted to take a break.

"Ah am," he intoned in a deep voice, dripping with the South.

"I love 'em. I think they're great. Even the body piercing one."

He rolled his eyes. "Ah was goin' for whimsy, but my flock wasn't, shall I say, impressed. Jim Baxter. Ahm the Reverend here." He stuck out a huge paw.

"Peter De Stio. Nice to meet you." We shook.

"What have we here?"

"One of my congregants has a small farm upstate. He offered to bring me a load of manure for the garden. I told him, fine, only he didn't tell me he was coming, and I didn't realize it was going to be so much. He just dumped it here. I really don't know what to do with it."

I looked it over. "It seems pretty well composted. You can put it right in the garden, just keep it away from the base of the plants." I took a whiff. "Mmmm, that smells great!"

We both laughed. "Are you sure about spreading this in the garden? Ah've got to get it away from the building or everyone will leave services this

Sunday."

"Yep. My landlady has taught me a lot about this stuff. She has her own compost heap."

"Well, thank you then, my friend. Ah was going to move this pile to the back of the parking lot, but Ah think Ah'll spread it around instead. Have a blessed day!" He turned to go back to the wheelbarrow.

I watched him take a few steps. I don't know why, but I called out to him. "Would you like a hand?"

He turned back to me. "Excuse me?"

"I'd be happy to help. Why don't I bring the manure to you and you spread it out around the gardens?"

"Are you sure? You have time for this?"

I smiled. "Yes, Rev. Right now, I've got lots of time."

So I filled the wheel barrow and rolled it to the Reverend, dumping it at his feet. He spread it out, taking care not to touch the stems of the plants. After an hour or so, we took an iced tea break.

"De Stio. De Stio. That sounds to me like you belong over at St. Anthony's Catholic Church, instead of helping me here."

"Why? Is that Presbyterian manure?"

He laughed. "No, I imagine it's probably Unitarian, but don't quote me!"

Jim told me that he gave away most of the food he grew in his garden. He told me about some of the charity programs in town. The Outreach program, helping to feed the poor, and the homeless, and the elderly shut-ins, sounded interesting. I told Jim I would give some thought to volunteering some time. We talked a good deal over the afternoon. I was sweaty and grimy, when we finished, but it was the best I'd felt in quite a while.

Chapter 27

I spent the Saturday of Labor Day weekend quietly, trying to get back into my old routine. I meditated early, followed by a light run. I spent a couple of hours drafting an agreement between Sy Brownstein and me, and another agreement between me, as Sy's agent, with the title insurance company. I didn't use Sy's name in the second agreement at all; only I would know who put up the money.

After I was done, I grabbed the book I was reading, a biography of Grover Cleveland and headed up to Teddy's house. Teddy Roosevelt, that is. His home is beautifully preserved in Oyster Bay, on the North Shore of Long Island, with rolling hills, and plenty of open space. It must have been an incredible place for his kids to grow up in. I spread out a blanket and spent the day reading and walking and napping.

Sunday was payback day. I rose early, meditated, a light run and off to church, Mary Robinson's Holy Baptist Church. Services started at 10; I got there in plenty of time. Henry was waiting for me on the front steps, looking uncomfortable in his suit and in his location. We spoke for a while, with me filling him in on what I could. He seemed relieved.

He also told me that it had been announced the day before that Gregory Connolly was going to leave the firm at the end of the year. Wanted to spend more time with the family. I love that line. Everybody being pushed out of a high-powered job or being fired, says they are voluntarily leaving this job they had worked for all their lives, to spend time with the family. It's ridiculous. You never hear an assembly line worker come out of the boss' office and tell his buddies, I've decided to leave the factory, so I can spend more time with my family.

People were arriving in clusters, joining up in the parking lot, and entering the large brick church in talkative groups. There were more women than men, maybe 4 to 1 or better. Same ratio as a Florida retirement village, I guessed.

Henry and I walked into the church, taking seats in the very last pew. "Easier to sleep back here," Henry grumbled. I noticed two things as the choir filed in from behind the front altar. The people in here were decked out. Every man and boy was in a suit and tie. Every woman had on a good dress, many with hats. There were no jeans, or T-shirts, or khakis. The other thing I noticed as the choir started singing was that I was the only white person in the building. I forgot about that, though, once the choir hit full force. The sound from the congregation rose up to meet the choir, and filled the room, so strong, and beautiful, it felt like a substance, as if the air had been replaced by something thicker than oxygen. It was simply glorious.

The Pastor came out, a tall handsome man, maybe in his thirties. Henry whispered to me that he was new, but Mary liked him a lot. She had been the head of the search committee, and pushed hard for him. "He's single, too," Henry said with a grin, "So all these hens are clucking around him like he was made of corn."

The service was alive. Even though we were all the way in the back, the area, according to Henry, that Mary called "Heathenville", I felt the excitement, the energy flowing over us. The pastor approached the podium, as the last strains of the choir shimmered in the air.

"In the Gospel according to Luke Jesus tells us: 'If you had one hundred sheep, and one of them strayed away and was lost in the wilderness, wouldn't you leave the ninety-nine others to go and search for the lost one until you found it? And then you would joyfully carry it home on your shoulders. When you arrived, you would call together your friends and neighbors to rejoice with you because your lost sheep was found. In the same way, heaven will be happier over one lost sinner who returns to God than over ninety-nine others who are righteous and haven't strayed away!'"

"That's right, my friends. God treasures his sinner who comes home to Him, praise Jesus! And we are all sinners, all of us. But we have an obligation, a sacred obligation, to forgive the sinner who repents, to welcome back that lost sheep, yes we do."

The congregation was working with him, with "Amen" and "that's right" rising up from the seats.

"Jesus continues, in case you weren't paying attention, maybe looking at your text messages during the sermon." To the laughter of the choir, he turned and fixed a comic stare at a young woman in the second row. "Jesus says, 'Suppose a woman has ten valuable silver coins and loses one. Won't she light a lamp and look in every corner of the house and sweep every nook and cranny until she finds it? And when she finds it, she will call in her friends and neighbors to rejoice with her because she has found her lost coin. In the same way, there is joy in the presence of God's angels when even one sinner repents.' Praise the Lord, my friends, praise Him. There is JOY in the presence of God's angels when even *one* sinner repents!"

"So I say to you, my brothers and sisters, we have to open our hearts, we have to open our minds, we have to open our homes to the repentant sinner, for if he can make the angels rejoice, shouldn't we find a way to let him bring joy and hope to our meager lives? And I say to you, my brothers and sisters who have let the Lord release you from your sinful ways, you, too, have an obligation. You owe the community of Christ, to work with your brothers and sisters, to not only repent your sins, but also to help repair the damage caused by your sins. It is your obligation to help the community, to volunteer your time, to donate your money, to give some of the gift that the Lord has bestowed upon you, to others. We all must remember that forgiveness is a blessing that helps the forgiver as much as the forgiven."

His sermon went on from there. I thought I saw Mary looking at me, but maybe I was just self-conscious with all this talk of the repentant sinner. Before the end of the service, they passed a basket. I made sure Henry saw the amount of folding money I was putting in; he winked at me, a silent confirmation that he had seen my contribution, and would report it to Mary. The pastor ended the service with some announcements, which included changes in the Bible study start time on Tuesday, the new children's chess club, the bake sale next week, and other housekeeping items.

After the service, we headed downstairs for punch and food. I spent about two hours, with Mary showing me off, beaming that I had come. I was beaming, too. Even Henry looked almost cheerful, with a plate of food and a little huddle of Mary's friends catering to him.

I took Mary and Henry aside before I left, and thanked them again. I told Mary that O'Reilly had assured me all would be OK. She just smiled, and thanked me again for coming. The pastor came over and invited me to come back, anytime. I thanked him for his sermon, telling him it had hit particularly close to home. He and Mary looked at each other, and laughed. Imagine that, he said.

"Say, Peter, a thought just crossed my mind," the pastor said with a straight face. "I believe Mary had mentioned to me that you were an avid chess player, is that right?"

I smiled. "Sorry, Pastor, I haven't played chess since, I don't know, law school I guess."

"But you had such a nice chess set in the office, I thought for sure you knew how to play," Mary said.

"That was just for show. It was a gift." I could see where this was going, and so could Henry, who was starting to grin.

It was the Pastor's turn. "That's too bad, because we have 23 youngsters signed up for our chess club, but I haven't found anyone who could run it. You see, I wanted to give these children an opportunity to use their minds. Every time somebody talks about a program for our children, they start rolling out basketballs. I find it offensive. Chess, now that's a game that builds strong minds, don't you agree Peter?"

"You haven't found anybody?" Mary asked. "That's a shame, it seemed like the children were so excited."

I sighed, with a smile. "OK, OK you two. When does the club meet?"

"You'll do it? Praise Jesus!"

"But Pastor," I said, looking at my friend Henry who was barely containing his laughter, "That's a lot of kids. I think I'll need an assistant. How about Henry?"

Henry's face fell instantly, but it was too late. The Pastor and Mary swooped on him like hawks on a sparrow.

So now I was Peter De Stio, volunteer chess coach. It sounded good.

*****

Labor Day promised to be beautiful, in the 80's, low humidity, clear skies. The oppressive weather had finally broken. My weekend had been just about perfect so far. I hoped my luck would last.

I headed down to the beach, early. I didn't have to be at Marie's until 2, and I didn't want to just hang around the apartment.

The beach crowd was still a few hours away when I spread my blanket on the sand. I was all set. I had a bagel and coffee; I had a cooler filled with water and cold fruit. I had one of Philip R. Craig's J.W. Jackson mystery novels waiting to be devoured. I had my running shoes. I stretched and headed out on my first long run in quite a while.

As I ran along the surf's edge, I thought about Labor Day, and where I was now. I always had considered Labor Day America's true New Year's. I think the Jews, with Rosh Hashanah coming in September, had it right. This was the weekend we said goodbye to summer, to vacations, to reduced schedules, to casual business attire and attitudes. Everything about our society said that this was the start of our annual cycle. Forty million school kids start anew, with clean empty notebooks and the promise of a fresh start. The new TV shows come on. New movies come out. The new cars are introduced. The new court year starts, with summer recesses behind. Football season starts. The whole rhythm of the country changes, the tempo increases. Few of us take vacations in September. It's a month for new beginnings.

I decided to make my New Year's resolutions on Labor Day. It just made more sense. First, I was going to have to find a way to support myself. I was getting tired of the day-to-day, assigned counsel routine. After a year of holding back, I was ready to start again. I knew I didn't want to go back to the pressure and insanity of my former professional life, but maybe I was ready for a steady gig, ready to feel a part of something again. Maybe in law, maybe not. I decided to start my search on Tuesday.

As I dodged a wave that broke high on the beach, I shifted my thoughts to my personal life. Maybe it was time to really reach out for Patricia. I had pretty much left it to my unopened letters to show her I was concerned, but maybe Marie was right. Maybe I had to be more assertive to show her I cared. I decided to think about it some more. Carolyn and I had talked about it some; maybe I would pick her brain again, see what she thought.

Carolyn. I thought about her a lot. But she seemed pretty serious with this guy Steve. After all, when you're over 30, do you see somebody for a few months if it's not going somewhere? And as much as I felt attracted to her, she hadn't shown me anything back, as far as I could see. But maybe it was time to get back out there. I thought of Ricky's sister Ines. I decided I'd give her a call. Just a cup of coffee. I wasn't ready for deep water, yet, but, maybe, a toe in the surf would be OK.

I realized then that I hadn't resolved to stay sober! I let out a "Ha!" as I ran, which scared the old couple I was passing at just that moment. They all said that there would come a day when staying sober would become a part of me, like my arm. Was I approaching that day? I reminded myself to stay on guard, to be mindful.

I thought of Baxter and the Pastor at Mary's church. I liked the feeling I got on Friday, shoveling the manure. It was a healthy feeling of helping out, not getting paid for it, not expecting something back, just helping out. I found I was excited about the chess club. I decided to I'd check out the Outreach in Oceanside. I had the time. I wanted to become a part of society, in a way I hadn't been before.

I ran long, and I ran hard. My bruises were fading, and the stiffness was gone. I ran, and I ran. My body felt loose, my lungs felt open. I sensed a strange feeling inside, one I hadn't had in a long, long time.

I felt happy.

*****

I picked up cannolis and other pastries at Mario's and headed to Massapequa. I was a little unsure how this was going to work out, but I figured I had a good shot of getting past the front porch today. There were a few cars parked in front of the house when I arrived, but Labor Day is a big party day, so I didn't give it any mind.

The front door was open. I poked my head in. I heard voices in the back room, so I made my way back there. The front room was clean; I guess Lou had kept the boys out of there this morning.

Marie was in the kitchen with one of her friends. She came over and gave me a big hug.

"Peter, I'm so glad you came. So glad." She was smiling, but when she pulled away, I saw tears on her cheeks. She wiped them away, saying, "Don't mind me, I'm being silly. Do you remember Bridget?" We shook hands. I handed her the pastries.

"Everybody's out back, go on ahead. I'll be right out."

Just as I approached the sliding glass doors leading to the backyard, a whirlwind flew in the door. Chuckles, and a kid who looked familiar, flew by me, one on each side of my legs. The Assassin, Michael, was right behind. He stopped chasing them when he saw me. It took a half a second, but he yelled "Unca Pete" and through his arms around my legs. I picked him up and gave him a kiss hello. I tried to put him down, but he didn't want me to, so I carried him outside.

There may have been 10 people in the large backyard. There may have been 10,000. I don't know. Because as soon as I got outside I saw two people sitting at the patio table, talking lowly, and looking in my direction.

Carolyn.

And Patricia.

I just stood there, trying to breathe. Carolyn saw me and smiled, with a little wave. Patricia's face got tight, with not quite a smile, as much as the nervous beginning of one, an awkward line of pressed lips, forming on her face. Marie came up behind me. She was crying now. "Surprise," she whispered. "Your friend Carolyn told us everything. She brought me the letters you had written Patricia. I had a talk with Lorraine and Patricia. She's read the letters now." She gave me a light push. "Go say hello."

I walked over, though I don't know how I got my legs to move. Michael held on tight to me.

Carolyn stood up and pulled Michael from my arms. She gave me a peck on the cheek. "C'mon, Michael, let's go find Kyle and Jeffrey," and she was off.

I looked down at Patricia, who looked so much older than she had when I last saw her. "Can I sit?"

"Sure." Her voice, I hadn't heard it in a long time. I found that for me, the voice was what I lost first after separation with someone. I could still picture my grandparent's faces, even remember how they smelled. But voices I couldn't find in my memory. Patricia's voice sounded new, a little familiar, a little like Lorraine's, but different.

"How did– It's great to see you. Um..I've thought about this moment so much...I don't know what to say. Thank you for coming."

"It's OK. Aunt Marie has been on my case for months now. And your friend Carolyn gave her a bunch of letters you wrote. Aunt Marie said I had to read them. I didn't want to, but.. Well, you know Aunt Marie."

We both smiled.

We took the afternoon slowly. We didn't hang on each other, but I didn't let her too far away from me either. We talked a bit alone, but we spent most of the time in the groups that form when family and friends get together. Lorraine came for her about 7. I walked her to the car and thanked Lorraine. Patricia gave me a little hug, quick, and was gone.

I watched the car until it was off the block, then turned to find Carolyn and Marie at the bay window, watching from behind the curtains. I smiled.

*****

I started off my New Year the day after Labor Day. I still hadn't gone back to the office and I wasn't planning on doing so that Tuesday, either. I wrote a short list of things to do and checked them off as I did them.

I met Sy Brownstein at his office. I went over the agreements with him.

He signed where he had to; I had someone from his office notarize his signature. He wired $13,500,000.00 into my escrow account. He thanked me, again and again. Avi was doing very well.

John Gartner had cut a deal. The title company had already told Fisher they were dropping charges in exchange for full restitution. As I had thought, the D.A. wasn't ready to let the matter drop, but they were willing to deal. Their offer left Avi a choice. He had to voluntarily turn himself in, confess to the fraud, and provide information about the bookie. If he agreed to testify, he'd get only probation. If he refused to testify, he faced a prison term.

Avi chose not to testify; he told his father he was willing to pay for his crimes and he didn't want to have to look over his shoulder forever. Phil arranged to pass on the word that Avi was going to keep his mouth shut. An additional "insurance payment" may have been involved, but they kept me out of the loop on that. Anyway, Phil felt confident that Avi would be OK.

Phil, Carolyn and I had discussed the deal among ourselves. None of us was satisfied. It bothered all of us that the murderers of two men might never be found or prosecuted. Even if Avi testified, though, we realized that there still wasn't enough evidence to convict the bookie, or anyone else, on the murders. Unfortunately, life doesn't always tie everything up with a neat little ribbon. Phil spoke for all of us when he said he hoped the killers would screw up and get what they freakin' deserved.

I told Sy I understood Avi's decision not to testify. I told him I wished both he, and Avi, the best of luck.

As I was leaving, Sy handed me an envelope. "Your fee. I can't thank you enough." I put it in my pocket without opening it up. He embraced me, something he certainly hadn't done before. He felt frail in my arms. We wished each other well.

Sy Brownstein. Check.

I ordered flowers to be sent to Marie, to Carolyn, and to Lorraine. It was nice of her to let Patricia see me.

Thank you's. Check.

I went to McIntyre's office. I met with his lawyers for a bit, who made a couple of meaningless changes to the agreement, just enough so that McIntyre would know they had read it carefully. McIntyre joined us. He read the agreement over, pulled out a pen and signed it. I handed him my escrow check for $13,500,000.00.

He handed me a check. "This is a finder's fee."

"I can't take that. I don't represent you. I represent someone else."

"Who won't mind or care. You didn't represent them when you risked your life for us, did you? Tell you what. Forget the finder's fee. Call it settlement of your claim against us for falsely accusing you. Take it. It's yours. I insist."

I told the lawyers to get me a General Release, which is a standard document that ends all claims you might have against another person. They came back in a few minutes later with two: one from me to the company and one from the company to me. McIntyre and I signed simultaneously. McIntyre smiled, looked at the attorneys, and pointed to the form. "I assume one of you is a notary, yes?"

I put the check in my pocket without looking at it. Now I had two mystery checks in one pocket.

I shook hands with McIntyre. Out of earshot of the others, he said he was going to call me about doing work for his company. I told him to call Joel. He said he would.

McIntyre. Check.

I looked up the address of the Outreach program. It was in the basement of the Congregationalist church. When I got there, there were three older women trying to pull out beat up, caked racks from the big commercial oven. Lunch was over, and they wanted to start getting ready for dinner, but the racks wouldn't slide out. I introduced myself and told them Jim Baxter had sent me. They were thrilled. I spent the rest of the day cleaning and fixing and chopping and serving. I felt so good I thought I would burst.

Outreach. Check.

I got home tired and fulfilled. I started to get undressed, when I found the envelopes in my pocket. I looked at McIntyre's check. I looked again.

I opened Sy's. The check was wrapped around a personal, handwritten note. It was touching, a thank you from an old man who had rediscovered his son. The check left me speechless.

These two checks left me with a lot of options. I couldn't retire, but I certainly wouldn't need to rush out and just take the first job. Target would have to do without me.

I called my sponsor. We had a long talk. It felt good. I felt strong.

Staying healthy. Check

I called Patricia when I got home. Just a short, hey, how you doing, kind of call. She sounded friendly on the phone. It was the best part of my day.

Patricia. Check.

Epilogue

I woke up very early on Thanksgiving. I had a full day planned. I stretched, and went out for a light run. It was cold. The sun wasn't up yet, and I could see my breath in the light of the street lamps. It was clear and icy sharp, with lots of stars still visible.

It had been an interesting two months since Labor Day. I went over them as I pounded the frozen streets. I hadn't gone into the office until the Thursday after Labor Day. I found my room completely empty. Nothing in there, not a box, not a file, not even my $5 Radio Shack clock. Before I could get angry, Carolyn snuck up behind me, Joel in tow. They led me down the hall, and around. With a "Ta da!" Carolyn threw open a door to a partner's sized office, furnished, with a wall of windows.

Joel asked her to leave and motioned me into a chair.

"First of all, buddy, return my damn phone calls. I was going to tell you that Majors had jumped the gun. He didn't have authority to do what he did. I told him that I wanted to talk to you first, to find out what was going on. I'm sorry you got that letter."

"It's OK, I appreciate everyth–." He cut me off.

"Just listen, OK? Carolyn and Phil have kept me apprized of everything. I got to tell you, you live an interesting life, buddy. Here's the deal. Mindy and Bryan went to bat for you. Carolyn, Jesus, she barged into our partner's meeting last Friday and gave us all hell. Showed us the medical chart from South Nassau, the one with the blood test. Told us we were nuts for not having you do more for us, instead of throwing you out. And she told us she had just settled Sophie's case. Do you know how much she got?"

I shook my head. Carolyn hadn't told me. Joel did. It was for more than I told her to hold out for.

"She told us how you handled that case, told us all about it."

"Really, Joel, seriously, I didn't do...."

"Be quiet for once, will you? Here's what we want to do. We'd like you to join us. We want you to train our new attorneys and help everybody here analyze their cases. Do EBT's if you like, cover conferences. If you ever feel ready to try a case, we'd love to have you do it. You pick and choose. We'll keep the pressure to a minimum, I promise."

He mentioned a salary. It was a nice one, more than fair.

"Listen, about the box. I'm sorry, man, Marie had asked me to get your stuff before Connolly threw it out. I just forgot about it, completely. I heard there was a second box. The idiot was supposed to send me everything. Too bad he didn't; if he had, maybe Helms wouldn't have found your notary stamp in the other box before they sealed it and sent it to storage. Listen, buddy, take all the time you need to consider our offer. Just don't turn it down until you talk to me again. Oh, by the way, your share of the fee for Sophie's case is in that envelope on the desk. Don't say a word. You earned it. Besides, in the last week Sy Brownstein walked in here with all his work, starting with his estate planning. And I met with Peter McIntyre. He said he wants to use us as his counsel, provided he sees your name on the stationery."

"We have to bring you into the firm. If we just paid you referral fees, it would break us."

I accepted. For the past few months I've been training the newbies and reviewing files with the rest of the staff. I decided to try a case or two. The cases I've chosen have all settled so far, but maybe one will go all the way. I'm enjoying this a lot, more than anything I've ever done, work-wise.

One of the bigger surprises came from Marcia Simpson. She showed up in my office at the end of October, no appointment, all full of good cheer and hugs. She had confronted Derek with my information back in August. He had broken down and confessed. They had cried and they had talked. He had explained why he had taken on the alias; she understood.

They were now married. She was Mrs. Marcia Johnson.

And they had gone on with "Landsculpting." She showed me article after article from fitness magazines. They had 125 personal trainers working for them in three states. The numbers were incredible. They wanted to go national. They had lined up financial backing. They needed somebody to do the filings, to set it all up. I walked her down to Ronald Majors' office and introduced them to each other. Ronald and I had smoothed things over; I was in no mood to hold grudges. I left Marcia to Ronald and walked back to my office with a smile.

The chess club was doing very well. An anonymous donor, one who had come into some unexpected money, had provided dozens of chess boards and chess clocks, and tournament entrance fees. The kids had refreshments at every meeting and the club was growing. Henry and I got a real kick out of these kids. I just smiled all the time.

I finished my run. I had a great Thanksgiving Day planned.

I was starting my morning by helping to cook 25 turkeys and all the fixen's. The Outreach program served up a big dinner, open to all. They, no, we, had dozens of volunteers who helped cook, and serve and ferry people who needed a ride. I was a regular at the Outreach now. It was a great group of people.

I couldn't get into the shower when I got back to the apartment because my guest was hogging the bathroom. I waited patiently until she emerged, using my big white cotton bathrobe, her hair wrapped in a towel, steam billowing behind her.

"About time!" I barked in mock anger.

"If you want me to get up at this hour and help you cook, you have to let me wake up. I need long showers!" she retorted with a smile.

I smiled as she headed to the bedroom to get dressed.

My helper.

Patricia.

Patricia had stayed over the night before. She was going to spend the morning with me; I promised Lorraine I'd have her back right after we served the noontime dinner. Patricia and I were slowly bonding. I went to all her school soccer games. We had gone to a few movies. She had every other Sunday dinner with me at Marie's. We talked a lot, and had even started e-mailing each other.

I didn't really feel like a Dad yet; I felt almost like a big brother. And Lorraine was still pretty stiff with me. But this was going well, really, really well.

After I dropped Patricia off, I was going to have dessert with the Lovas' at their restaurant. Ines and I had gone out a few times; we even went to a show with Carolyn and Steve. It wasn't anything serious yet, but, who knows?

I was clean and sober and happy.

It was going to be a great day. A true day of Thanksgiving.

CPSIA information can be obtained at www.ICGtesting.com
Printed in the USA
267977BV00005B/11/P